CURSE

⟊ OF THE ⟊

FORGOTTEN

ELIZABETH A. DRYSDALE

SWEETWATER BOOKS

AN IMPRINT OF CEDAR FORT, INC.
SPRINGVILLE, UTAH

ISBN 13: 978-1-4621-3842-5

Published by Sweetwater Books, an imprint of Cedar Fort, Inc.
2373 W. 700 S., Springville, UT 84663
Distributed by Cedar Fort, Inc., www.cedarfort.com

LIBRARY OF CONGRESS CONTROL NUMBER: 2020946360

Cover design by Wes Wheeler
Cover design © 2020 Cedar Fort, Inc.
Edited and typeset by Valene Wood

Printed in the United States of America

10 9 8 7 6 5 4 3 2 1

Printed on acid-free paper

To Danny.

You always encouraged me, and without your help, this never could have happened. Thank you for helping me fight to make my dreams come true.

Chapter One

Slipping *Frankenstein* into my back pocket, I grab my backpack from under the seat in front of me and follow the line of comatose passengers off the plane. The stale recycled air sits heavy in my lungs, my shoulder knocking into every other seat as I struggle through the narrow aisle.

I follow the trail of people to baggage claim, chewing on a black-painted fingernail. An older man decked out in a suit gives me a side glance and I stick my tongue out at him. Startled, his eyes go wide before his brows narrow and he turns away.

A chemically chipper voice announces an arrival from Houston as we march past an empty Mexican restaurant. We funnel down an escalator where our luggage waits on slowly rotating conveyor belts. My bag sticks out like a sore thumb, a faded grey that used to be black with layers of silver duct tape holding it together.

"Wren!"

Grinding my teeth, I pull my bag off the belt and look up at the woman rapidly moving toward me on stilettoed feet, her narrow figure swathed in white skinny jeans and a peach cardigan.

"Wren!" she shouts again, waving at me as she pushes through the growing crowd. "Don't move, I'm coming!"

As if I had any other choice.

She grabs my arm with a vice-like grip and pulls me into an involuntary hug. "I'm so glad you're finally here. Your dad and I have been so excited!"

"He's not my dad."

Linking her arm through mine, she gives me a red smeared pout. "It would devastate him if he heard you talking like that."

She steers me through the airport without waiting for a response. It's not like she doesn't know how I feel. I'll never think of Mom's internet boyfriend as my dad. Regardless of how "serious" they think it is. Or that I've had to move across the country to some western forgotten desert state just to be with them. She lost the right to call us a family when she left me with Aunt Cora after Grandma died.

Walking through the double doors, I stumble in blindingly bright light and a burst of dry heat. When my vision returns, I almost run back inside. It's like I've gone colorblind. The ground, the cars, the people, everything stretches out before me the color of dust.

My legs freeze and the person behind me rolls over my foot with their suitcase.

Mom babbles on next to me, not even pausing so that I have to stumble after her. "I was so upset to have to leave you behind in New York like that. I've thought of nothing but having our family reunited this last year."

"They're not my family."

"Don't say that!" she gasps. "Just give them a little time and you'll love them just like they love you."

At this rate I'll grind through my enamel in the first day.

Mom smiles, pert-pink lips tightening as we approach her shining silver Honda. "I need you on your best behavior, Wren. Don't ruin this for me."

Ignoring her, I pull the trunk open and shove my battered suitcase inside before slamming it closed. Climbing into the passenger seat, I sigh as the air conditioning blasts into my sweat damp face.

"I know this isn't New York, but honestly, sweetheart, it's so much better. You're not going to miss the city at all." Her words pound at my skull. "It's so refreshingly real here."

She pulls out of the parking lot, the clicking of the blinker filling the silence between us. The car surges forward as she merges onto the highway headed north.

"Have you thought about fixing this up at all?" she asks, gesturing to my messy black dyed ponytail.

"It's fine."

"I just want you to have the best start possible. People here aren't so rough around the edges."

I glance down at my baggy jeans, the toe of my converse poking out underneath the flare cut. "I like the way I look."

Her lips pucker but she doesn't argue with me.

I try not to look at her, but the click from her manicured fingers against the steering wheel makes me want to puke. No matter what she says, I know what's hiding beneath the plastic veneer she's put up. The same grungy nothing as me. New clothes and a new attitude doesn't actually make her any different. And I know what really lies beneath.

"I enrolled you in our local high school with your sister. She's so excited to show you around."

"She's not my sister."

Mom sighs, a crack showing through her fake front. "We're all family now. I wish you could learn to accept that."

"Just because you moved across the country for your internet boyfriend doesn't mean we're a big happy family." My fingernails dig into my palms, leaving crescent rings behind.

The miles pass in silence before she turns the blinker on again, getting off at the Greendale exit. The irony of the town's name isn't lost on me as more of the same dusty brown permeates the landscape.

We drive down a main street barely worth mentioning, just a few slumping stores covered in a layer of tan dust before she turns again and pulls up to a '70s brick split level.

"At least try to smile. It would do wonders to soften the edges of your face."

I contort my mouth into a grimace and she sighs again, turning off the car and getting out, her heels clicking against the cracked sidewalk. Grabbing my suitcase and slinging my bag over my shoulder, I follow her into the house.

The walls of the entry way are painted a cheery yellow, and at the top of the stairs a half bald man clutches the arm of his cheerleader-type daughter.

"Bill!" Mom yells, despite how close they're standing to us. "I'm so glad you're here to meet my Wren!"

She shoves me forward, my sneakers squeaking against the tile.

"Welcome to our home, Wren," Bill says, smoothing the nonexistent wrinkles out of his tan button up shirt. "We've been so excited for you to get here."

Their smiles look straight out of an orthodontist office.

Mom rushes up the stairs and into Bill's arms, leaving a lipstick kiss on his cheek. "Isn't it so great? Our whole family finally together?"

Bill opens his mouth to say something, but I cut him off. "Where's my room?"

"I thought we'd spend the evening together," Mom says with a pout.

"You want my suitcase to sit by the door all night?"

"It's this way," Bill's daughter, Ruby, says. She points down the stairs and I pick up my suitcase and follow her into the dark split-level basement.

Ruby flips a switch and the narrow hallway is flooded with yellow light. She turns to the left and gives me the rundown of the three closed doors. "Yours, the bathroom, and mine."

Out of sight of either of our parents, the fake smile slips off her lips. "Sweet."

I turn the knob and shutter myself in my new room, closing the door as quickly as I can. Leaning against the doorframe, I don't bother turning on the light. There's nothing here that light would improve.

The curtains covering the half window are two inches too short, letting in the last burst of orange light before the sun goes down. The walls are painted a pale lavender, the white wood frame of the twin bed is pushed under the window, illuminating the pattern of pansies sprawling across the comforter. The bed and the dresser are the only furniture, both carved in a whimsy more suited to a little girl, and definitely not fitting for anyone who actually knows me.

Throwing my bag down, I climb on the bed and pull my book out of my pocket. The words swim in front of me as I try to concentrate. Leaning against the headboard, I close my eyes.

I only have a year left, just one year before I can go back home and get on with my life.

A soft knock echoes through the nearly empty room. "Wren? Are you coming up for dinner?"

"Not hungry."

"Are you sure? It was a long flight, and the food they serve on planes is barely palatable if they feed you at all. Plus, you'll want to keep your strength up for school tomorrow. Bill grilled some hamburgers. Don't you think you could come up and say thank you?"

I roll over, giving her my back despite the fact that she can't see me.

"Wren?"

After a long pause she sighs, and I listen to Mom's heavy footsteps as she heads back upstairs. She may have made me come out here, but that doesn't mean I'm going to play nice.

The pounding on the door is anything but gentle as I roll over, the faint hints of morning sun peeking through the gap in the curtain.

"Get up, Wren. You have school today!"

Groaning, I turn over and press the pillow over my head.

"If I don't see you upstairs in ten minutes, I'm coming in."

I toss the pillow at the door with a thump and Mom's footsteps recede up the stairs. Stumbling toward my suitcase while pulling off my tank top, I unzip the front pocket and grab my deodorant and slather it on. Another dark tank top and a zip up hoodie lie on top of the unorganized mess inside my suitcase. Tugging them on without thinking much about it, I head into the pristine white tiled bathroom and give my eyes a thick outline of black eyeliner and brush my teeth. A jeweled barrette sits on the counter. I slip it into my pocket with a grin.

Ruby audibly gasps as I climb the stairs from where she sits with a half-eaten bowl of cereal at the island counter. "That's quite a look."

Shrugging, I sit next to her, waiting for Mom to see that I've surfaced.

"Wren! That can't be what you're wearing to school," Mom says, voice hushed as she turns around from the pantry cupboard holding a box of Captain Crunch.

"Is that for me?" I ask, pointing at the box.

Ruby slides me an empty bowl and I snatch the box and pour myself a bowl before Mom can start her tirade.

"I tried to tell you before, this isn't New York, people don't dress like that here, or scowl so much. Can't you just try to fit in a little? For me? This move is very important to me. We're going to be here a long time and I just want the best start for us." She looks near tears, but her mouth stays in a tight line. "Now, if you didn't bring anything acceptable, I'm sure Ruby wouldn't mind sharing something with you until we can get you more appropriate things."

Ruby gives me a half smile, her eyes still wide as she watches me shovel down the cereal. She's wearing a nondescript pair of skinny jeans and a floral blouse with a cream cardigan thrown over the top, a single silver ring winks on her finger, and her blonde hair is straight and shining down her back. No, thank you.

"It's just school. This is the same thing I wore last week to school. I'm sure it's fine," I say, dry crumbs scattering across the counter.

"Like I just said, you're somewhere new. You should try a little harder to make a good impression. Do you have any idea how hard it was to get you enrolled in the middle of the school year?"

I put the spoon down. "Then why didn't you just leave me with Aunt Cara? I didn't need to come out here, we were all pretty happy with the situation when you took off to live with your boyfriend and abandoned me." No one had to pretend anymore.

Mom's jaw twitches. "You're here now, with your family. It's time for you to get used to it. Now, if you won't borrow something from Ruby, then I'll have to take you shopping after school today. Be sure to come home promptly after last bell."

Mom marches from the room, heels clicking against the cream floor tile. Ruby grabs her pink backpack from where it slumped against the side of the white cabinets.

"Should we get going?" she asks.

"If we must."

I follow her down the stairs and through the front door. She gives me a sidelong glance as we walk along the cracked sidewalk.

"What?"

"Don't you want your backpack?" she asks.

I shrug. "What for? I don't plan on doing anything today."

Her mouth makes a small *o*. "But we're going to school. I'm sure they'll have tons of make-up work for you and new assignments to keep up with us."

I shrug again. Her shoulders tense but she doesn't push it. The corner of my lips quirk in a smile. I know not caring about school really plays into the "I don't care" persona I've got going on, but honestly, I finished everything I needed to for this year back home. I took all the required classes for junior year during fall semester and was going to use this one to get ahead of my senior year. There's only a couple classes I need before I graduate. I'm sure the high school already knows this, Mom made me send my transcripts two weeks ago to make sure everything would go "perfect" when I got here.

It's a short walk to the school, only a couple blocks before an old yellow tinged brick building labeled "high school" comes into view. It's like this town has been frozen in time, everything looking only a little bit sadder than it must have during construction.

Dew sticks to my shoes, bleeding through the black canvas tops as we jump across the grass. A few other students linger on the stone steps, laughing and talking as we push past them through the double doors.

I catch my reflection in the glass window of the door and smile at my black blur as it swings shut. Ruby points at the door to the left of the main hallway. "That's the main office. I'm sure they'll want to see you first thing."

"Sure."

She speeds up as she passes the office and goes down the locker lined hallway.

Whatever.

A heavy woman with a '50s coif sits behind the counter height front desk. She gives me a wide smile.

"Can I help you?"

"I need my schedule or whatever. It's my first day."

"Oh, you must be Bill Waterford's daughter," she says with a grin, going through the files on her desk.

"I'm not his daughter."

Her smile fades a little, but her hands don't stop moving.

"Well, Bill called last week to tell us you'd be coming and your school sent us your transcripts earlier this month." She pulls out my file and gives a low whistle as she thumbs through it. "You've certainly been busy, haven't you? Your counselor hasn't set up a schedule for you yet. I'm sure he wanted to know what your goals were here before he slapped you into any old class."

"How considerate of him."

"If you go down the hallway, his office is the first door on the left," she says with a smile.

I saunter down the hallway, feeling my low-rise pants shift against my hips. The door hangs open and I knock on the red-painted doorframe.

"Wren! I've been expecting you." A heavy-set man stands behind his desk, tucking his tie against his chest. "Come in."

Sitting in the generic office chair, I balance it on the back two legs. His smile falters as he sits back down.

"So, I thought it'd be best if we went over your transcript in person." He glances at my file and then over at me, his jaw twitching. "You weren't what I was expecting."

I raise an eyebrow at him and he looks down at my transcript. He pats down his hair, what little of it is left, and leans toward the computer.

I give him a tight-lipped smile and the printer behind him goes off. As he turns to grab the paper, I palm a small picture off his desk. He hands me the still warm paper with my schedule printed on it. There are only four blocks of classes, not the eight I'm used to. He's signed me up for two study halls, American Literature, and a gym class.

"If you can pass American Literature, then you'll be ready to apply for graduation this year."

"Apply?"

"Well, you're a junior and we want to make sure you're genuinely ready for college. Have you thought about where you'd like to go to college?"

Instantly the flyer for NYU flashes through my mind but I just give him a shrug.

"Why don't you make an appointment with me in the next few weeks so we can go over your options? Knowing what you want to do will make a big difference when applying for graduation." He gestures toward the door. "It was excellent meeting you, but you'd better run along before you're late for your first class."

Biting my cheek and shaking my head, I leave his office and the hallway the secretary's desk is in. The hallway that was empty when Ruby and I got here is flooded with students and the deafening roar of their noise. Glancing down at my schedule, I bite back a laugh as my first class is a study hall.

There's a map printed on the back of my schedule and I use it to lead me through the labyrinth of hallways to the library. It's the only room I pass that isn't full of people.

Grateful for the silence, I find a seat by the wall of windows and settle in for the next hour and a half. There's a small trash can next to me that I dump the counselor's picture that I took into. Pulling *Frankenstein* from where it's been folded in my back pocket, I concentrate on the words and ignore the hum of announcements coming through the speakers.

This day can't be over soon enough.

The day passes uneventfully, the American Lit class not posing anything close enough to a threat. Definitely nothing to warrant the counselor's worries.

When the final bell rings, I don't bother waiting for Ruby. I walk through the front doors, snapping the pile of bracelets on my wrist.

The chill in the air of spring should mean the world becoming a bit greener, at least it would at home. Here it's just a dull brown. Not even the beginnings of weeds sprout from the cracked sidewalk.

I take a deep breath to rid my lungs of the smell of chalk dust that feels like its seeped into my skin. Buses pass me, the sound of laughter coming from the open windows.

It feels like defeat to go home right after school. I don't want to give Mom the satisfaction of following orders. Back home I'd spend the majority of my free time on the streets with my friends. Sometimes we'd have enough spare change to hit up the Chinese place on the corner by our apartment complex.

I wonder what they're doing now. If they even miss me.

Whatever, if what the counselor was saying is true, I could be home by this summer. So worrying about what they're doing without me is pointless.

Instead of following the road back to Mom's, I cut through a dusty field. I straighten my shoulders, ignoring the nagging fear at the back of my mind that whispers of snakes hiding out here.

A pair of black handlebars stick up through the brown grass to my right and I skip over to it. Wrenching the bike out of the dirt, I'm surprised to find it in decent shape. Rust is the predominant decorative color, but the chain spins when I press on the pedals and the wheels are still pumped.

I'd prefer a skateboard, but any wheels are better than none.

Grinning, I climb on the bike and take off through the field, onto the street, and through the row of houses behind the school. Picking up the pace, dry air blows through my hair, lifting it off my neck. Town only extends two blocks past the school, and I pedal hard for the desert.

I get as far away as I can while still being able to see the outline of the last row of houses. Just in case.

Climbing off the bike, I clamber up a wide low rock. I peel the paper off a granola bar I find in my pants pocket and chomp down. The sun grows blood red as it crests the mountain range in the distance.

Why anyone would want to live here is beyond me. Why Mom would leave New York for this is even more baffling. She couldn't pay me to stay here after I graduate.

The desert to the left of me dips down. I walk along the crumbling edge of dirt of what was probably an old riverbed, listening to the small clumps of dirt hitting the rocky bottom. Ahead a particularly large dirt clod hits the bottom with a hollow thud, even though I'm not even close to it.

I stop walking, turning toward the riverbed with a tilted head. Something's not right. Drawn in like a spell, I make my way down the steep incline.

Rocks skitter suddenly under my feet and I grab the dirt wall to keep from falling. A jagged piece of stone catches my palm, ripping a red line through my palm. I rip my hand away and curse under my breath.

Moving my hand sends a hot flash of pain through my arm. It jolts me back to the present, and I shake my head. The top of the riverbed looks so much farther away than it did from above. Cursing again, I ball my fist and ignore the pain to protect it from the dirt floating through the air. I want to turn away and leave, but I can't. Something pulls me forward, farther into the riverbed.

The dirt clod that initially caught my attention shifts. I only have a second to look at it before the ground around it crumbles away and I scramble back against the earthen wall.

A two-foot section of the riverbed falls into the widening hole, rocks pinging as they bounce off whatever lies underneath.

My breath comes in short gasps, my hand clenched over my rapidly rising and falling chest. A metallic looking reflection sends a small glint of light out of the hole. I lean forward a little, to see where it's coming from, and another several feet of riverbed falls away, revealing a glittering pile of something in the late sunlight. Could it be gold? I heave a shaky laugh. That would be perfect. I lean over farther, pulse racing. The ground shifts under my feet and I back up. Okay. That's fine, I don't need to see what's down there. I can always come back later.

I turn toward the wall of the riverbed and using a few rocky handholds, I start climbing back the way I came. I make it a few feet off the ground when the rock I'm holding onto dislodges from the wall and I'm falling down. A strangled scream rips from my throat as I get closer to the hole. I grip the wall, digging my fingers in the earth until my nails are filled with dirt, but I stop short of the pit.

Taking a deep breath despite the quivering in my limbs, I try to climb out again. I take it much slower, testing each hand hold before using it. After a tense ten minutes, I pull myself onto ledge.

Laying there, I let out a breath of shaky laughter. Tears stream down my face as I roll onto all fours. I use the palm of my hand to wipe them away, ignoring the tingling in my ripped palm. The sun sinks below the jagged mountains, making it seem later than it actually is.

I stumble toward the bike and pedal it into town. The trip back feels much longer than coming out did. Maybe because of the line of red blood dripping down my wrist and splattering into the dry earth.

Dropping the bike into the fake green grass surrounding Mom's house, I let myself in the front door. The rich smell of baking bread fills the entryway as I climb the half flight of stairs into the main floor.

"I thought I told you to come right after school." Mom's disapproving voice drifts over me as I enter the small galley kitchen.

Her hair is pulled into a tight blonde ponytail as she mixes something in a large plastic bowl. The timer on the yellowed counter ticks down as I lean against the doorframe.

"Don't you have anything to say for yourself?" She glances up at me and stops moving with a gasp. "What happened to you now?"

I shrug. "Fell."

"You fell? You look like you've been rolling around in a gravel pit!"

Looking down at myself, I realize she's not that far off. A thick layer of grime covers my black pants and shoes, sticking to the skin on my arm.

Mom closes her eyes, mouths one, two, three, and opens her eyes with a dazzling smile. "Clean up and come back for dinner. The meatloaf will be ready in about twenty minutes."

Shaking my head, I jog downstairs and into the small bathroom. I leave my clothes in a pile, dirt falling off them to settle on the white tile. Turning on the shower, I wait until steam fills the air before climbing in.

The hot water cascades down my back, washing away the dirt and turning my skin red. I put my hand in the water, flinching as the water makes it burn. The dried blood refuses to budge, so I grab the bar of soap off the ledge and scrub it against my skin. The foam turns pink before I wash it off.

It smells like lavender which doesn't surprise me. Of course a vanilla like Ruby would like a smell like *lavender*.

When I'm sure every inch of my skin is dirt free and the bottom of the tub no longer has the flaked remnants of my adventure, I turn the shower off. My feet sink into the plush white bath mat and I grab an equally white towel from under sink and wrap it around my body while I dig around for something to wrap around my hand.

I actually laugh when I pull out the small first aid kit from the back of the cabinet. Of course.

Pulling out a few Band-Aids, I lay them out over my palm. It takes three of the regular size to completely cover the cut. The skin around the cut is puckered but not red yet. I should be fine.

When I get in my room, I grab my suitcase and flip it upside down, emptying it out onto the vacuum lined carpet. Digging around, I find some clean-enough clothes. Aunt Cara wasn't super worried about little things like laundry.

I brush my hair and leave it to air dry before heading upstairs. As much as I don't care about being with "the family," the rumbling in my stomach has me eager for dinner.

They're all sitting at the table off the kitchen when I get to the top of the stairs.

"Nice of you to join us," Mom says with a frown. "I thought I told you twenty minutes."

"Hard to keep track of time in the shower." I shrug and slide into the seat at the end of the table, a couple of chairs from Mom and Ruby.

Bill clears his throat. "Now that we're all together, let's bless this meal."

They reach out to hold hands, Mom and Ruby holding theirs out to me. This is a hard limit for me. Mom lifts her eyebrows at me, but I don't move to take their hands. I cross my arms over my chest and lean against the back of the chair.

Mom sighs and nods to Bill. He nods and bows his head, uttering a short prayer of thanks. They release hands and go right into eating, the only sound for a few minutes is the clinking of forks against plates.

"So," Mom says, her plate half empty. "Wren, how was your first day of school?"

I shrug, spinning peas around my half-eaten meatloaf. My appetite has vanished since I left home. "It was fine. I think I'll finish this year."

There's a thud as Mom's fist comes down on the table. She glances at it in surprise before looking back at me with a plastic smile. "What do you mean? Are you saying you'll be able to finish you junior year on time?"

I match her fake smile. "No, I mean I'll be able to graduate in May."

"I won't sign permission for that." She turns back to her food. "You'll finish your senior year just like everyone else. There's no reason to skip it."

"No reason at all, except for the fact that I'll be finished with all the classes I need."

"I'm sure there are some electives you haven't taken yet. It could be fun to have a year of elective classes."

I tilt my head at her, jaw dropping. "You can't be serious."

"I think it's a great idea," Bill adds.

"I don't think you're ready for real life yet. Life with us for another year will put you in a much better place when you go to college." Mom takes Bill's hand and squeezes it.

"You're insane! I'm not taking a year of empty classes so you can live out this Stepford dream you have going on!"

Mom narrows her eyes. "I think you should be excused. You're obviously exhausted from the day."

"But I am ready. I have plans. New York plans. If you'd just—"

"That's enough. You need to leave now." Mom's hands are white where she grips the table.

I slam my chair into the table so hard the glasses rattle and stomp down to my room.

Throwing the bedroom door closed behind me, I flop onto the bed with a sigh.

There can't be anything she can do to stop me from graduating. If I'm finished with classes then I'm finished, what more is there to do? I'm not going to hang around for her vanity, no matter how many dainty frowns she gives me.

I hate that now that she's gotten her life together, I'm supposed to just fall in line and change mine too. Then somehow she thinks that this will make up for everything. For leaving me over and over again and always choosing whatever man over me. I don't need her to pull my life together and one more year of high school isn't going to be enough to make her into a real mom.

Tossing the pillow over my head, I take some deep breaths to get our latest altercation out of my mind.

My palm twinges as I close my hand in a fist.

Sitting up, I pull the Band-Aids off and stare at the red streak running through my hand. This afternoon was definitely something that's never happened to me in New York. Safe in my room, my mind is free to wander over what happened.

I don't know why I felt like I had to go down there, but now that I've seen something, I can't just let it be. What was in that hole? Something was definitely reflecting sunlight out of it. If I were at home, I'd assume it was just water reflecting sunlight, but I'm not home anymore. Did I discover some old gold mine? This is the West after all. Isn't that how just about every town was started out here? By miners and cowboys?

Chewing on my top lip, I cover the scrape up. If I can find some rope, I'm going back tomorrow. There has to be something good about being stranded in this backwards town. If I discover gold here, I'll call it even.

Chapter Two

I'm up and ready before Mom can interfere with any of her picture-perfect intentions.

We sit across from each other at the kitchen island, her eyes lingering on the black smudges of my eyeliner, the pile of silver necklaces over another black tank top.

"I expect you home in a timely manner today. We really need to get you some new clothes for school."

Ruby rescues me before I can say anything nasty. "Ready to go?"

I grab my bag from off the floor and follow her down the stairs without saying a word to Mom. Ruby and I walk in the chill silence for half a block. Thoughts of the riverbed chase themselves around my mind and I can't hold it in anymore.

"So Ruby, do you know anything about the history of this town?"

Her brow furrows. "What do you mean?"

"Like how it was founded or something?" There's no way I'm going to ask Mom, she'd enjoy that too much, but if I can find out how the town started, it might give me an idea of what's waiting under that riverbed.

"I'm pretty sure we were started by cattle ranchers," she says, lips pursed in thought.

My heart sinks. "Oh."

"Were you hoping for something in particular?"

"I thought you might have been founded by miners or had something interesting happen in the past." She doesn't need to know exactly why.

"You'd want to go to California if you wanted mining towns. We're nothing as exciting as that," Ruby says with a laugh. "Although . . ."

I wait for her to continue, but a few minutes pass in silence, the school looming closer. Finally, I take the bait. "Although what?"

"Oh," she laughs. "Sorry, I didn't realize I'd trailed off. The most interesting thing that's happened in our town history is the flood."

"The flood?" I ask, voice tinged with skepticism.

She nods. "Yeah. Like a hundred and fifty years ago there was this huge flood, it completely buried our town in water and mud. When the water went down, the town that had been here was completely buried. Nothing left. No more houses or cattle or anything. It was almost the end of the town altogether."

"So what happened?"

"Some crazy guy showed up, started digging, saying the town couldn't end yet."

"Weird." I laugh.

"Yeah." She laughs with me. "But because he didn't give up, more people showed up and they built right on top of where the town had been before. If it hadn't been for him, this place wouldn't exist."

"What a tragedy that would have been."

Ruby sighs. "I know you didn't want to come here, but your mom really is happy you're here."

"She didn't give me any option not to or I wouldn't be here."

Ruby flinches at my candor. "She's really great, I'm sure you guys will work things out."

Shrugging, I follow Ruby into the school. I'm not ready to get into my and my mother's tattered past. If Ruby knew what my mom was really like, she might not feel so warmly about her. I just have to wait until the fake veneer she's put up falls off. There's no way she can keep this up forever.

But if I'm lucky, I'll be long gone before I have to deal with the shambles that will be left. My only hope is graduating early. I have to do it.

Without any challenging classes to push me, the school day trudges on and on. All I can think about is the promise of gold at the bottom of that hole. When the clock hits three, I almost don't believe it. The shrill ring reverberates in my ears as my new classmates pack up their backpacks.

I grab my bag, slinging it over a shoulder. The tide of teenagers floods the halls in a constant stream pooling toward the door.

Ruby sits on the stone ledge beside the stairs, cleaning dirt under her nails as she waits. Seeing me coming, she gives a small smile. "Hey."

We walk together, headed toward the house, at least for now. As soon as I can ditch her, I'm heading to the riverbed.

"So I was thinking about what you asked me during class today." She tucks strands of blonde hair behind her ear. "About how our town was founded. I checked it out during lunch and actually found something pretty interesting."

"Oh yeah?"

She nods. "Yeah, so I thought we were just another cattle town, but that's not the full story."

"So what is the full story?"

"We *were* founded by cattle ranchers for the most part, but the land actually belonged to someone else. He leased out large portions of his property for the ranchers to use. Some guy from a wealthy family back east. Anyway, he'd been leasing his land for ages when suddenly his whole family disappeared."

"Because of the flood?"

"No," she says in almost a whisper. "Just disappeared. The men would go to pay their rent and couldn't find the house anymore. Families got concerned when their relatives that worked in the house never came home, but no one found them or the house again. Eventually, the land was just absorbed by the men using it. I'm sure that was a pretty great day, no more landlord."

I twist my lips. "That is pretty weird."

"Right? I figured you'd want to know."

I can't imagine something like that happening nowadays. There's no way some mega rich family could disappear into thin air.

The dried up riverbed is too close to town for that to be where the house that no one could find was located, but perhaps the flood hit the house and pushed something down the river. Maybe something that could pay for me to get out on my own and get to college without Mom's help.

What could she say then? There would be no argument if I could afford my own way.

An idea blooms in my mind.

"Hey Ruby, does your dad have any rope or climbing gear?" I ask, keeping my voice light.

Ruby gives me a sidelong glance. "Why?"

"I thought about going for a walk in the desert and didn't want to be unprepared," I lie with a shrug.

"That's not really what you would want for desert exploring. There's not many places where you'd need climb. You'd want things like sunscreen, and water, and maybe a compass."

"A compass?"

Ruby nods. "You can get really turned around out there. You'll think you've turned around and are headed for home when really you're walking around in circles until you collapse."

"That's a nice image."

"It's happened." She rubs her shoulder with a tight hand. "At least once a year someone gets rescued out there near death while they babble nonsense from their desert hallucinations."

I've been so distracted that the house sneaks up on me before I realize it. Its overwatered green grass a stark difference to the pale browns on either side of it.

"You've made your point. Would it be okay to have those supplies plus the rope I asked for, just in case?"

She smiles. "I don't think it would hurt."

The smell of gas swamps me as Ruby leads me through the garage door.

A fluttery anxious feeling in my stomach as Ruby gets down a plastic tub labeled "camping" from a series of shelves set in the wall.

She peels off the lid and digs through the rustling layers of canvas inside. "Dad and I like to go hiking to look for the fire stone. There's some dumb legend that it will bring prosperity back to our town and we spent a lot of summers looking for it. This is where Dad kept everything, so if we have anything, it'll be here."

Finding a compass, she places it on the cement floor, going back for more. A small pile grows next to her as she gets out what she deems to be the essentials. When she grabs a second compass, I panic.

"Why would I need two compasses?" I ask with a strangled voice that I cough to get back under control. "Wouldn't one be enough?"

"First rule of exploring, never go alone." She grins, her perfect teeth blindingly white in the dim light.

My brows furrow. "You never said you wanted to come with me, and I never said it was okay."

"Well." She stands and wipes her hands off on her pants. "It really is safer to go with someone else, in case you do fall off that cliff you're expecting and it goes without saying that your mom probably won't like what you're up to. So I don't think you have any other option but to take me."

She gives me a slice of blackmail with a cover-girl smile. Her tenacity makes me grin.

"Why would you want to do this? It's not like we're really sisters or anything."

"You can't honestly believe this is all me. Consider me just as stuck as you but with fewer chances of getting out."

"Why don't you live with your mom?" The question pops out before it can be tested by my filter, and I cringe as Ruby flinches.

"Let's just say it isn't possible." Her voice has an edge to it that I haven't heard from her before.

I raise my hands in surrender.

Ruby ignores me as she pulls her backpack open and shoves all our supplies inside. She takes a deep breath before handing me the second compass.

An apology bubbles up my throat, but I squash it down. I'm not looking for a friend. I'll see if I can ditch her as soon as we get out there. I only have one plan right now, get enough cash, or maybe a pile of gold at the bottom of that hole, and get back to New York. I don't need to play nice with Ruby for that.

Using the rusty bicycle still laying in the yard and Ruby's ten speed, the trip to the riverbed takes half the time it did yesterday. I lean my bike against the big rock and crane my head to try and see anything before Ruby can.

We edge toward the riverbed. The hole from yesterday hasn't grown any further. Its jagged edges remain contained to the middle of the bed.

Standing on the edge of the bank, I try to get a look inside the darkness of the hole. The glint I saw yesterday is gone despite the sun being higher in the sky than before. I chew on my upper lip as I lean forward over the edge.

"Are you crazy?" Ruby asks as she yanks me back by the arm, the lip of the bank crumbling.

Small rocks skitter into the hole and I wait to hear if they hit anything before answering her. "I'm just curious."

"This isn't an exploratory ride, is it?"

"I mean, we did ride over here, and I do have plans to explore, so that kind of is what we're doing," I hedge.

She crosses her arms over her chest. "I didn't sign up to come out here and check out a hole in the ground."

"I didn't invite you to come with me."

Ruby sighs. "Well, I still can't let you do this alone."

"Very chivalrous of you."

"Ha, ha, ha." Ruby pulls the rope out of her backpack. "We should probably tie this around something up here. That whole thing looks about ready to give way."

We loop the rope around the big rock, the only thing remotely close enough to use. I tie it with a knot that looks pretty good to me, but Ruby laughs, unties it and does some complicated fisherman's knot.

"Haven't you ever been camping?"

"I've never seen a tent that needed a complicated knot to put it up."

I grab the rope and trail it over to the edge, holding it between my legs as I start walking down toward the hole. Ruby frowns at me and doesn't follow.

"You should've tied that around your waist or something. What if you lose your grip?" she asks, switching from one foot to another.

"Don't be such a worrywart, I'll be fine."

Famous last words. The phrase echoes through my mind and I tighten my grip on the rope.

The rocks skittering toward the hole is the only sound besides my heavy breathing when I get to the body of the riverbed. There's nothing but darkness at the bottom today. I can't even accurately tell how far down I'm going to need to go.

"Are you coming down?" I call to Ruby, one hand around the rope.

She stands with a hand on the big rock. "I'm not sure yet."

"It's not a big deal if you want to go home."

I edge closer to the hole, not bothering to look at Ruby when I'm finally so close to seeing what's down there.

The rope tugs in my hands and I glance up to see Ruby coming down toward me, her legs pale where they stick out under her shorts. My hands loosen their grip as the rope tugs in my hands, the braided material burning a little as it tries to jerk free.

When her feet touch the bottom of the riverbed and nothing happens, Ruby gives me a tentative smile.

"It's not too late to turn back." I tell her as I turn toward the hole again.

"What do you think is down there?" she asks, coming up behind me to peer over my shoulder.

"Whatever it is, I'm telling you right now I have no intention of sharing it."

"I'll try not to be too jealous of your new collection of rocks then." She laughs and gives my shoulder a little shove.

"I'm betting it's something cooler than that." My voice comes out in a whisper as the edge of my sneaker toes the ground by the hole.

Ruby doesn't follow me as I get closer. Her heavy breathing is loud behind me.

"Are you sure you don't want to just go—"

The ground gives way under me and I plunge through the earth as Ruby screams.

My hands burn as the rope rips through them. Too shocked to scream, I fall soundlessly into the dark.

Blinking awake, the only thing I can see is a small glimmer of bright light above me. My head pounds. I try to sit up and my leg twitches. A feeling like fire shoots up it, making me scream involuntarily.

"Wren?!"

The voice echoes down from the light and I hold my head in my hands in an attempt to block the pain.

"Wren?! Wren, can you hear me?!"

"Ruby?" My voice is hoarse, grating against my ears as I pitch it toward the ceiling, my mouth filled with the coppery taste of blood.

"Oh thank goodness." She says something too quiet for me to hear before speaking up again. "Should I go get Dad?"

I groan, making sure to keep my leg still as I twist toward her. "Don't get him yet. Let me see what's down here."

The hole was a lot deeper than I anticipated, the sliver of rope illuminated by the hole not even reaching halfway toward me. If I could get some light down here, maybe I could see that glittering thing I saw yesterday. Ripping me out now would just be a waste of time.

"If I can't make it out, just call 911."

"Don't you want your mom to know?"

I can just imagine her wringing her hands up there as she waits for me to answer.

"That's the last person I want to know I'm down here."

There's silence for a moment. "How long should I wait?"

"Give me half an hour."

Rolling onto all fours, I bite through my lip in an attempt to keep from screaming as my leg hits the ground.

"Are you hurt?" Ruby calls down. "I could go and get someone right now."

"I'm fine!" I yell through clenched teeth.

Crawling closer to the wall, each move making me see spots, I use the wall to brace myself into standing. I have to put my weight on my left leg, but I'm standing. That's all that matters.

"Do you see anything?"

It's nothing but different shades of black in the darkness. Good thing Ruby's backpack has all the supplies.

"I need a light."

Ruby's close enough to the hole that I hear the zipper as she pulls her backpack open.

"How will you get it?"

I sigh. "Just throw it and I'll try to dodge."

Never mind the fact that there's no way I could move fast enough to avoid it.

"Are you sure?"

"Just throw it, Ruby!"

I press my body as close to the wall as I can get.

"Here it goes!"

There's a black speck blocking the light as it hurdles toward the me and the sharp thud as it hits the ground and the light flickers off.

"You okay?"

"Fine."

I scramble for the flashlight, leg killing me. I need that light though. Hopefully the fall didn't kill it. My fingernails scratch at the dirt as I feel along the ground. My leg threatens to give out altogether when I feel the hard shell of the flashlight's plastic.

Sliding my hand across it, I search for the switch. There's a squishy button on the end of the flashlight, and I push it in and wait. The light doesn't turn back on. I shake the flashlight a few times and knock it against my good leg. It flickers on, the beam coming from it weak compared to where it probably was when Ruby threw it.

"I see you!"

"Just remember to wait the full half hour before getting help," I yell back as I sweep the light over the cave walls.

It's narrow down here, like a forgotten one-way road stretching on in either direction. I do a mental eenie-meenie-miney-mo before deciding to head in the direction opposite of town. The wealthy don't usually live among the rabble and if they rebuilt the new town on top of the old one, odds are pretty good it wasn't close to the building I'm looking for.

One hand braced against the wall and the other holding the flashlight, I limp into the darkness. The flashlight weighs at least five pounds, its solid weight quickly becoming too much, the beam shaking as I try to keep my arm steady.

Turning my head back, I can't make out the hole where I fell. I hope I'll be able to find my way home when this is over. Finding the money to get out of here won't matter much if I've discovered my tomb.

My leg throbs with every step and the tunnel looks as long and dark as it did when I started walking. Hesitantly, I point the flashlight at my leg, looking at it for the first time since I fell. Nothing looks out of place, no blood or bone protrusions. Hissing between my teeth, I bend over and roll up my pant leg. My ankle has swollen to twice its normal size. I poke at the purple skin, my fingerprints showing white for a moment before fading into the swollen mass.

Closing my eyes, I count to three and roll my pants back down. It's probably not broken. If it were broken, wouldn't I be completely unable to walk? I don't know much about medicine, but that sounds right to me.

I brace myself against the wall and keep moving. When my weight comes down on my ankle, I grimace and do my best to ignore it. Focusing on it won't help me right now.

I turn the flashlight off when the light flickers. There's nothing to see here anyway. The wall and floor are smooth, nothing to trip on, and it's just one straight line.

The darkness makes it hard to keep track of time. My half hour could have easily been up a while ago, but I wouldn't know. Good thing I left my cellphone in my backpack.

My body moves automatically, my mind wandering without much to linger on. Maybe I'm in an abandoned tunnel under the city. Some early subway plan or something. Why else would it be so straight and smooth? I doubt the evaporated river would have been this thorough. Or maybe a tunnel for utilities, some future plan for sewer or something.

I debate whether or not I could go blind if I stay down here in the darkness too long when a white pinprick of light dances across my vision like a firefly. Holding up my hand as though to catch it, my arm becomes backlit. It's not as close as I thought.

The light bounces, dancing from side to side, then zips farther way. "Wait!" I squeak out.

As though it could hear me, it hesitates for a moment before moving faster through the tunnel.

In a panicked frenzy, I take off after it. In a surge of adrenaline, I barely feel my ankle anymore. All I can feel is the pressure to get to that light before I'm lost in the dark forever.

My breath comes in ragged gulps as I run with uneven steps. Then the light vanishes into the ceiling, leaving a pale yellow halo behind. Breathing a sob, I run to where it vanished and stop. Without the constant movement, the pain in my ankle comes full force. Brushing black streaks of hair out of my face, I look up to the ceiling.

"What now?" I ask it. I glance around. There's nothing better to do unless I'm ready to go back.

The circle of light drifts close to me then disappears back into the wall.

"What the?"

Turning on the flashlight, I run my hand over the smooth wall, feeling in every slight indentation and irregularity in its surface. It feels just as solid as it looks. Sighing, I turn away, my fingertips trailing along the wall as I move. As my fingers leave its surface altogether, I feel a lip where the wall curves in a little.

Bringing the flashlight around, I press against the lip and discover the wall isn't completely flush. What looks like a solid wall at first glance is actually two overlapping pieces of wall.

There's only a foot of clearance between the two pieces, but this must be where the light went. Glancing back at the unwelcoming darkness, I turn to face the narrow passage with the light. Swallowing a childhood fear of tight spaces, I press myself between the wall. I'm not risking getting stuck in the dark down here, and I'm not going back empty-handed. I hold the flashlight out and turn my head to look forward as I sidle between the rock. The air fills with a faint layer of dust as my body scrapes against the wall.

I start counting my breaths as I climb all the way inside the wall. Panic threatens to swallow me whole.

1, 2, 3, 4
1, 2, 3, 4

I close my eyes and prepare to start again when there's a shift in the rock to my right. It pulls open a little bit further and my chest is able to fully expand. I open my eyes. My light is back. A knot loosens in my chest and my breath comes easier.

The firefly-like light bobs up and down, moving slowly toward me then flittering farther into the crevice. With its gentle encouragement, my steps become bolder, moving me quicker through the tight space. As my ankle becomes too much to bear, I use the wall as a brace to take my weight off it.

The mundane actions of walking and following takes away the sharp edge of fear that even my deodorant hasn't been able to hide as I've traveled through the dark. Funny how following a thing that doesn't make any logical sense makes me feel more safe than I did on my own with a perfectly normal flashlight.

The tunnel narrows again and I briefly think about how hard it will be for Ruby and any help she might bring to find me. Will they make it past that initial wall? Even with my little light help I might still die down here.

Whatever. I'll be fine.

Then the tunnel opens wider and I push the worries from my mind.

As I sidle forward, the walls turn, twisting from their initial straight path. My stomach rumbles and I swear I've been down here for hours.

I stumble as the walls on either side fall away and I'm exposed once more. Without the wall holding me up, I sway as the light bobs farther away.

Its narrow beam bounces along and stops. I narrow my eyes, trying to see what it's illuminating. There's something different there, something that doesn't look like more cave. Wincing, I walk closer and gasp.

Stone stairs.

There's a set of stairs jutting out from the rock wall. Flicking on the flashlight, it sends its weak beam across the floor and I realize I've been walking on a real stone floor, not just the cave. How long has it been like that?

Making it to the stairs, I slide the flashlight through my belt loop and crawl up the wide steps. Counting the stairs, this flight must be ten feet tall. I focus on the climb, coming to a stop only when I've knocked my head against a thick mahogany door.

The light bobs once then pushes through the door.

Climbing to standing, I feel around for the knob in the dark. I close my hand around its chill surface and turn it.

A blast of frozen air pushes through the open door, freezing me to the spot and sending goose bumps along my exposed arms. Standing on the threshold, I look for my little light friend, but I'm on my own this time.

Dim light illuminates the room from tall windows set in the far walls. Where is it coming from? Rows of counters hug every wall with a large island in the middle. The kitchen. Great. Just where any billionaire would hide his gold. At least I've found the house I was looking for. Knowing that should make me feel better than it does.

Walking into the room, I use the counter as a brace, my hand instantly becoming coated in a thick layer of dust.

The kitchen looks like something out of an old movie, with a fireplace so big half a dozen people could stand in it with room to spare. I wonder how many people used to work here. Did they die here? Am I about to stumble onto some decayed corpses? They'd just be skeletons by now right?

The hallway out of the kitchen is full of the same dim light, furniture shadowed and hulking against the wall. This would be a great time for my light to come back.

I click the flashlight on, its faint light doing nothing to press back the shadows.

My heart beats loud in my ears, my palms sweating the farther I limp into the house. I should be looking for something valuable, but I wouldn't even know where to start. Aren't safes usually in the basement? Did I already pass what I came looking for without even noticing?

The hallway is so wide a truck could drive through without coming close to hitting anything. Dark portraits line the walls, faces too steeped in shadows for me to see clearly. Still, the feeling of being watched makes the hair prick on the back of my neck.

Shaking my shoulders, I try to get rid of the feeling of the ghosts of the past watching as I attempt to loot their home. It doesn't work.

The feeling of being watched becomes too oppressive, and I turn and look behind me. But there's only my own shambling footprints through the dust. Popping the joints in my neck, I turn around and keep moving.

Several large rooms open off the hallway, the chairs pushed out and furniture in place like the owner left to run errands and never came back. I'm just glad they didn't cover everything in sheets. Nothing screams scary movie more than sheet-covered furniture.

The stress and fatigue of my climb through the cave makes my limbs so stiff that moving becomes difficult. It's so stupid. My overactive imagination and low-key fear of ghosts are making me have to stay longer in this spook fest than necessary. I need to find what I came here for and get out. Fast and easy.

But I can't get my knees to loosen.

The hallway turns, the left wall becoming a curved solid wood staircase. Sighing, I turn toward it. Maybe there's a safe upstairs. Or some women's jewelry, something small I can stuff in my pockets that could be turned into big money later.

I crawl on my hands and knees, giving my ankle a break as fear settles into my stomach. But taking all my weight off it just makes it throb more and I regret the decision. I don't waste time trying to stand back up. I've got too far to go up to climb a staircase to the next level when this one has easily twelve-foot ceilings.

My body cleans the stairs as I climb, revealing the rich wood stain underneath. This must have been a beautiful place in its day.

The same dull twilight peeks through the floor to ceiling windows across from the stairs. Is it that late already? But I should still be under ground. I peer through the crack in the curtains but there's only twisting fog out there. There's nowhere to run.

A chill that has nothing to do with the temperature creeps across my skin as I reach the landing. Whispers dance through the air and the feeling like I'm being watched only increases.

I let my fingers trail across the embossed fleur-de-lis emerald wallpaper above mahogany wainscoting as I reach the second floor. My brow puckers in a frown. The level of dust is much less here than it was downstairs and the openness of the floor and the heavy feeling in my chest has my pulse racing. I need to find cover to calm down.

Ducking into the first opening I come across, I can't stop myself from slamming the door shut behind me. Chest heaving, I press my open palms against the planes of the door. The rattling sound of my breathing echoes through the room.

Closing my eyes, I focus on calming my beating heart. Still the rattling fills the room.

I press my hand against my chest, prepared to still my breathing. But my body is quiet, only slightly shaking with the trembles of fear.

The floor behind me creaks.

Legs shaking, I turn with as much stillness as I can muster.

A king-size four poster bed fills the center of the room, its drapes almost connected to each other with the thick cobwebs hanging from them. From the center of the bed a creature shifts, sitting up with a clawed hand extended toward me.

My chest seizes tight, hand shaking as I reach for the doorknob behind me. The cool metal meets my fingers but I can't grasp it.

The creature lurches forward, back lit by the foggy light. It lands next to the bed, claws clicking on the hardwood floor. Turning its head, the deep-set eyes are illuminated yellow for a moment before it lifts its head and I hear it sniff toward me.

It takes a sluggish step forward and I'm released from my temporary paralysis. Grabbing the handle, I throw the door open and fling myself through it.

The creature roars, the deep tones reverberating through my ears and spiking my adrenaline as I run down the long hallway. My feet are silent as they hit the long runner.

Then the creature rips through the door.

Glancing back, I watch it stand on two feet as it picks up speed. Tunnel vision takes over as I panic. All I can see are the stairs in front of me. I just have to get to the stairs.

The runner ends and my feet slide along the wood floors. I grab the banister, my sweaty hand slipping down it as I take the stairs. Fabric rips in the hallway and the creature roars again. Fear tears through me like a living thing, taking away my ability to move fluidly. My heart presses against my chest in a very real threat of breaking free.

Looking behind me for the creature, I misjudge how far down the next step is. I'm weightless for a moment as my hand slips off the banister. The silenced scream that's been living in my throat since I climbed these stairs bursts free as I stare at the steps coming at my face. My hands cover my head in preparation of the hit I'm about to take as I screw my eyes tight.

Jolting, I'm jerked backwards instead of crushing into the floor. Opening my eyes, I'm suspended perpendicular to the ground. My heart pounds and I count to three, turning my head to look back.

I'm staring face to face with a monster.

Chapter Three

I can't stop screaming, my throat growing hoarse as the pitch rises higher. My body goes stiff as I hang over the stairs.

The creature jerks me closer. "Stop."

The deep voice is every bit as much of a growl as the roar had been, but it does the trick. My scream freezes back in my throat and my legs shake as it lowers me enough to stand on my own.

Coughing to clear my throat, I ignore the high-pitched whine in my voice. "Let me go please."

Honestly it seems like such an accomplishment that I can talk at all, let alone say something coherent and even polite as I stand jelly legged on the steps.

From my position below the beast, I can see more of it than I've been able to before. It's a giant hulking monster, standing like a man at least eight feet tall and entirely covered in layers of dark coarse hair. Its head turns toward me, showing curling horns that almost rest on its shoulders.

"I don't think so."

It yanks me off my feet and I bite my lip to swallow down my scream. Claws click against the wood as it finishes walking down the stairs. My feet hover in the air, my body suspended over the parquet floor.

"Where are you taking me?" I ask in a high-pitched shriek.

"It's been a long time since they deigned to send anything down to me."

"S-sent something to you?"

I'm honestly confused for a moment. Then I remember.

My ball of light.

The little friend that found me in the dark and led me to the house. I never would've made it here if not for its gentle coaxing and showing me the way.

And no one will ever find me here without its help.

"Sometimes she sends people to tempt me with the idea of what I cannot have."

It reaches the main floor and continues its slow gait through the dust laden hallways. Dirt floats in the air and clogs my throat as I gasp out my panic.

Turning through a door I don't remember seeing before, it takes us down another flight of stairs hidden behind the first. These are far less elegant. Simple wooden slabs take us into the depths, what little light reaching down here illuminating the smooth stone walls.

The creature's taking me to a basement.

Could it be the same one I came up out of? If the monster leaves me alone long enough, I could find a way to escape. I'll have to give up my dreams of gold. It's not like I could take this creature on for its treasure. Unless it thinks I've left. Then maybe I could still have both.

The beast sighs, hot breath cascading down my back. We reach the bottom of the stairs and the smell of mildew permeates the air. My eyes drink in every detail of the room I can see, halting on the iron bars the beast opens with a squeak. I jerk my head around just in time for it to fling me inside and swing the bars shut.

I'm in a cage.

Iron bars extend from the floor to the ceiling, leaving me a small two-foot-square space with a ceiling extending into the darkness. Grabbing the bars, I attempt to shake them. My fingers wrap around the cool metal and pull but they don't budge.

"I'm sorry it has to be this way. I won't fall prey to her tricks again," the monster says as it turns its back on me to walk up the stairs.

"Wait!" I yell as it closes the door, darkness filling every crack of my prison.

It hesitates on the threshold.

"Where am I? What are you going to do to me?"

It breathes deep, massive chest shifting.

"I will come back."

Then it closes the door.

The only sounds in my prison are my rapid breathing and the slow drip of water somewhere in the darkness. I repeat the monster's words over and over in my mind to keep from going into a full-blown panic attack.

It'll be back.

It'll be back.

It'll be back.

Darkness pushes in like an oppressive force, pinning me against the bars of my cage. I stay crouched against them for so long that my legs cramp up and force me to slide to the floor. The chill damp seeps into the knees of my pants, sending cold shocks through my legs. The pressure builds in my chest as panic pushes in despite my chanting.

Is Ruby looking for me? Will anyone ever find me here?

Hot tears trickle down my cheeks but I don't bother moving to brush them away. There's no one to see them anyway. They create burning lines down my face, puddling by my collarbones.

There's no way to track time in here. I'm not sure if I've been left for days or only hours. Either way, I've spent a good chunk of time frozen in self-pity. I bounce my shoulders to shake loose my emotions. It's time to move. Waiting for a monster to come back doesn't seem like such a good idea if I'd like to survive this.

Wiping away my tears, I scan the walls again even though the complete blackness makes it hard to actually see anything. Sighing, I go down on all fours and feel the edges of my prison with my hands. The walls are smooth under my fingers, not even a hint of the crumbling decay I was hoping for. Moving onto my knees I try again, feeling along the walls just a little higher, repeating this until I'm standing on tip toe fingers stretched toward the ceiling. There's no weakness there.

Turning toward the bars, I try again. My weak attempts to shake them or find one loose come up empty too. But there's a door, so there must be hinges. Hinges can be made weak, can't they? They could be my best bet at this point.

My hands search for where the beast threw me in here, but once again I come up empty. There's no way I could've missed the exit. What kind of trick is this? A prison with magic doors only a monster can find?

The door at the top of the stairs squeaks open, a crack of light illuminating the room. I fling myself against the wall as the creature pounds down the stairs. It seems much more pulled together this time, if I could call a monster "pulled together." It smells fresher, not as much dust, and it's put on clothes including a heavy navy cloak that slides across the floor.

"So you're real after all," it says in a rough grumble.

"I could say the same about you." My voice holds a boldness that belies the shaking of my hands behind my back.

It cocks its head at me. "I felt sure I would come down here and it would all have been a dream. I haven't seen anyone new in decades."

"That would explain why you haven't bothered to clean up down here."

It laughs, the sound like waves tumbling. "You have more spirit than many of the others I've been brought."

"Where are the others?" My voice turns to a whisper, and I wonder if I'll be this creature's next lunch.

"Long turned to dust and none of your concern. If I remove you from this cell, will you behave?"

"Yes."

I'll say anything to get out of this hole.

"You are my guest now, and I would expect you to behave as such. No wrecking the place."

The beast grabs the bars I've just looked at and pulls them open. They move seamlessly but even in the light I can't see any hinges or hints of an actual door. Where there once were bars there just aren't anymore.

Still, I scurry out of my prison before the beast can change its mind.

Without waiting for permission, I vault up the stairs. Standing on the main floor, I glance around, calculating my odds of making it into the tunnel. If I get away now, I could always come back later for the gold. I don't have to do everything all at once.

The thick layers of dust that had coated this hall are gone. Sconces set high in the wall are lit, their little fires flickering almost merrily as they brighten the dark woods and heavy fabrics of the hall. The portraits I noticed before feel much less menacing in the light, yet as I walk farther from the prison door their eyes still seem to follow me.

"If you would be so kind," the creature has come up the stairs behind me, much quieter than I would've thought possible and gestures toward a room on our right. "I'd imagine you're hungry."

My stomach growls, but I almost expect a trick that will put me in a new cell. Walking on hesitant feet, I peer through the doorway.

A table large enough for twenty fills the room, candelabras set at two-foot intervals. The table itself is covered in food. Platters and platters of steaming dishes sit so heavy that I half expect the table to collapse. Two chairs sit at either end and as I approach the table, the chair closest to me pulls out.

The monster passes by me, settling into the seat at the other end. "Will you not sit and dine with me?"

"You're not going to eat me?"

It laughs. "Why would I bother with the pretense of this meal if I'd intended to 'eat you'? Wouldn't it have been simpler to consume you downstairs?"

"I don't know how you work. Maybe you don't like to eat in the dark." It's easy to fall back into old habits. Act confident and no one will question you.

It laughs again and I sit with folded arms.

At some unknown signal, people fill the room, each one taking their place by a dish. They stand in black clothing cut in an 1800s style, the women with collars halfway up their necks, holding out serving spoons. The whole effect is so "haunted mansion" that I can't take seriously. This can't possibly be real. The beast nods his head and they dish our plates, piling them with food I've never seen before.

I reach for the woman closest to me, her brown hair pulled into a severe bun, but my hand passes through her. She gives me a sad smile and turns, her body rippling like a hologram.

"Wha-what the crap?" I gasp. "What are you?"

"They're very real," the monster answers. "This is just their part of our situation, cursed with a half-life much like myself."

"Cursed?"

Even seeing what I have, the word makes me want to laugh. This isn't real. It can't be real. There's some other explanation. Maybe I hit my head in the caves and this is all just a dream. It has to be a dream. At some point soon I'll wake up and tell Ruby about it and we'll have a good laugh and life will go back to my new normal.

"Oh yes, and now that you've discovered us, you've had the curse placed upon you as well."

"You've got to be kidding me."

My imagination is better than I thought.

The beast lifts a fork with surprising ease considering its long-clawed hand. "Unfortunately, I am quite serious. You've discovered a nightmare."

It spears a piece of glistening steak, and I wonder if it's already been cut because its paw can't handle a knife. Lifting the food to its short snout, I can't look away from it. It really is like I'm dreaming watching this well-dressed monster eat like a gentleman.

Picking up my own fork, I almost immediately put it back down again. Nothing on my plate is familiar enough to eat. I don't have whatever my monster host is eating that looks like steak and might be worth attempting.

"Is something wrong?"

It stares me down, eyes almost black under its thick brows.

"I'm not very hungry."

It leans against the back of its chair. "I find that hard to believe."

"Who are you?"

It tilts its head at me, considering for a moment. "Prometheus."

The answer startles a laugh out of me. "Are you serious?"

"Completely."

"Prometheus like the Greek—"

"Yes, the Greek titan who was punished by Zeus for stealing and forced to die again and again every day. Yes, that is where the name comes from."

"So you're not . . . ?"

"No, I'm not *the* Prometheus. That would be absurd."

My mouth twists to the side and I can't help myself from the joke he must have heard a million times. "Your parents must not have loved you very much."

"My father loved literature and my mother didn't know better." Its voice remains controlled.

"You have parents?"

"Do not all creatures, even those that creep along the earth on their bellies, have parents?"

I fold my arms across my chest. "I don't know why you expect me to believe something so basic as all creatures have parents when you're trying to convince me of the presence of a curse. That defies all logical sense."

"I was a man once." It looks down at its plate. "But that was a long time ago."

"What happened?"

His head jerks up. "That is a story for another day. Eat and I will show you to your room."

"My room?"

"Unless you'd prefer I brought you back to the prison?"

"No, a room is fine. But why?" I don't bother to pick up my fork again.

He meets my eyes then looks away. "You'll be here a long time. It would be best if you were comfortable."

"I can't stay here." I hate how my voice shakes. "My mom will look for me. I've already been gone too long."

He glances at me. "There will be no rescue for you."

It's like a door slamming closed on my heart. Tears prick at my eyes. "What are you talking about?"

"Eat."

He doesn't say anything else to me for the rest of the meal, our spectral servers flickering against the wall. My stomach puts up too much of a protest to keep ignoring food for long and I dig into something that looks like it could be mashed potatoes.

Only one bite in and I'm convinced it's not.

I clear the plate anyway, eating until my stomach becomes a round ball under my tank top. Ignoring the flavors, I focus on the sustenance. I'll need it more than ever if I'm going to get out of here. There's no way I'm believing Prometheus. Someone will find me. Mom will come looking for me. I know she will.

I put my fork down and Prometheus stands, the chair scraping across the floor behind him. I follow suit. If I pretend to play nice, I might be able to find out more.

"This way."

He leads me down the hallway and I can't keep myself from staring at him. Now that I know he was a man, so much makes more sense. His clothing and his gait are much better suited to a man than a monster. Why would a monster bother wearing riding pants? He's dressed like he stepped out of an old western. A monster wouldn't bother with that, right?

We ascend the stairs, the layers of dust my body scraped across vanished as though they had never been. My ankle sends flashes of pain up my leg with every step. Clenching my fists to keep from crying out, I do my best to hide this weakness. There's no way I'm letting him know I can't move fast.

Passing the room I first found him in, I glance inside and can't stop the gasp that comes out. The room is spotless. The cobwebs and dust gone, replaced by bright emerald curtains and thick maroon rugs.

Prometheus glances at me and sees my stare. "Part of the curse I suppose. It's been a long time since we've had a guest."

He leaves it at that and I'm too numb to pursue the issue further. This makes absolutely zero sense. It's like I'm Alice in Wonderland and I've just fallen down the rabbit hole. Everything is the opposite of what it should be.

We pass a few closed doors before Prometheus stops and opens one. He waves me inside with a giant paw.

My breath almost stops in my chest altogether. It's the biggest room I've ever seen, easily four times the size of my basement room in Mom's house, and covered from floor to ceiling with bookshelves. An enormous bed sits in the middle, done up like an English king with a canopy extending over it with layers of brocade cloth. A fire snaps merrily in a fireplace set between two large bookshelves at the end of the room, leaving the whole space feeling homey and warm. The last thing I would expect from a monster and his cursed home.

It takes a few tries before I can find my voice. "Thank you."

He nods. "I thought this would suit you best when I saw that." He gestures at the folded book still wedged in my back pocket.

"It's wonderful." Like a dream.

"I'm glad you like it."

He closes the door behind him, leaving me alone in the room of my dreams. I run my fingers down the spine of the closest books. Not surprisingly, whatever dust was in here has gone too. This room is a version of a dream I might have created for myself someday. I wrap my arms around my chest, trying to contain the levels of excitement and distrust warring within me. This shouldn't be how I react to my prison.

"May I turn down the bed for you?"

I shriek as the woman from downstairs appears next to the bed.

She stares at me with a patient smile. "Shall I lay out a nightgown for you?"

"But-but you're not real."

"If only that were true," she loses her composure, eyes growing sad before she shakes it off. "Are you ready for me to assist you for bed?"

"How would you do that?" I try to play along. "You know, since you're just . . ." I wave at her insubstantial form.

She looks down at herself, watching her fingers waiver as she holds them up with a frown. "This may not be ideal, miss, but I assure you it has never stopped me from fulfilling my tasks."

Biting my top lip, I watch her skeptically as she lays out an old-fashioned nightgown, the bottom extending to the floor and the top complete with a turtleneck collar, and folds back the sheets on the bed.

"Will you require anything else, miss?"

"Do you really expect me," I gesture down at my own decidedly dark outfit. "To wear that?"

I know it's stupid but there are some things I'm unwilling to budge on. If my Mom can't get me to change how I dress, there's no way I'm doing it for these freaky ghost holograms.

Her face stays carefully blank. "I wouldn't know. All the other guests have worn what has been provided."

"Other guests?"

She nods and drifts through the closed door.

I don't know what to focus on first, the spectral presences around here or that there have been others before me. How many people have found their way here? It's not exactly set on a hill with a flashing sign. And Prometheus made it sound like there hadn't been anyone here in a long time. How long have these people been stuck in this never-ending limbo?

Picking at the white lace frills lining the chest of the nightgown, I sigh in disgust and focus on the problems that make sense because I can't handle the rest of this weirdness. This whole thing is stupid. There shouldn't have been anyone here. I should've been able to explore, grab gold, escape my mother's fantasy world, and go back to New York.

I definitely shouldn't be stuck in a legitimate fantasy complete with monsters, ghosts, and curses.

It's not real and it's not possible. Yet here we are. It's like I've fallen into the pages of a book and can't find the way out again.

Prometheus hasn't even told me how I can get free of his curse or even what exactly it is. Maybe he doesn't know. That would explain why he's still here, trapped among the opulent luxury of his past.

Leaving my tank top on, I pull off my shoes and pants and climb into the bed, letting the nightgown fall to the floor. There's no way I'm wearing that nasty thing and living the daydream the rest of these people have been forced into.

My body sinks into the cool plush of the mattress, dust coating the sheets as it rubs off from my skin. The fire immediately burns lower as though someone is readying it for the night. I pick at my black nail polish. The chips fall like dark specks on the white sheets. Guilt pricks at my conscience. I should be trying to leave now, should be scouring the house for the way out immediately instead of lying in a bed that's probably bigger than a California king. But honestly, I'm tired. I don't know what else I could even do right now. And the pain in my ankle that resurfaces when my weight is taken off it is a clear indicator of just how unready I am for an escape attempt.

Is Mom worried about me? Or is she relieved? I was never going to fit into her world, and somewhere in the back of her mind she must have known that. Right? She couldn't have forgotten everything about me from our life together so completely, could she?

She's been living with Bill for a year now. That could be enough to forget about a problematic daughter from a previous relationship she'll never be able to shake. But that wasn't good enough. She had to remember and wrap me in her fantasy of what life should be. All in the name of making me a better person.

Rolling over, I bury my face in the pillow.

I'm going to have to take matters into my own hands. Prometheus is right, it's possible no one will ever find me. I refuse to stay here.

I wake to the sound of rushing water. Opening my eyes with the eager hope that yesterday was a dream, I'm sorely mistaken when the scene that awaits me is only a giant metal tub in the middle of the room being filled with water by the same woman from last night.

"The master thought you'd feel better with a bath," she says, seeing I'm awake.

"Don't you have a bathroom?"

She shakes her head. "If you have a need, I can fetch the chamber pot for you."

"I'm sorry, the what?!"

"The chamber pot," she repeats without any inflection.

I should've tried to leave yesterday after all.

As I swing my feet off bed and try to stand, all thoughts of chamber pots disappear in the rush of pain flowing up my leg. Gasping, I peek at my ankle, afraid of what I might see.

Its swollen and purple, my foot looking like a tiny nub on the end of it. I try to stand again, but it completely refuses to take my weight. Resting it all night has made everything freeze in place with the increased fluid.

"Is everything all right, miss?" my specter servant asks, feet not actually touching the ground as she approaches me. Catching sight of my ankle, she hisses through her teeth. "I'll have to get the master for this."

"Don't!" I shout, coloring with embarrassment. "Please don't get him. I'm sure I'll feel better."

She raises her brows. "He's ordered you a tub and you can't even get in it. I'll have to report this either way."

"Could you help me in?" If she can hold sheets and tubs and buckets of water, there's no reason why she can't hold me up too.

She tilts her head to the side, hand on her chin as she contemplates. "If you'll undress, I'll see what I can do to help you in."

Sighing in relief, I try not to think too much about this stranger seeing me naked. She's not real, so it shouldn't matter, right?

Pulling off my clothes, I wave her over, and she slings a surprisingly real arm around my shoulders. Leaning into her, she works as a crutch to help me take a few steps closer to the tub.

"If you're so real now, why couldn't I touch you yesterday?" I groan as my bad foot hits the ground.

"I am only able to serve in the capacity of my station. Being touched doesn't qualify as a need."

"That sounds terrible."

She eases me into the tub and I sink into the warm water with a sigh. The heat eases all the knots in my body from the last couple of days and I lean my head back against the lip of the tub. The throbbing in my ankle subsides enough that the pressure in my chest eases. This bath is like heaven.

"How long have you been like this?" I ask, eyes closed.

There's a pause and I imagine her face tightening as she considers her answer. "A long time."

"Have you ever tried to get away? Surely leaving the house would solve your problem." I peek an eye at her this time and catch the lines of tension running down her jaw.

"It's impossible to leave. We've all tried. We'll be here until the curse is broken."

Her statement leaves me speechless to the point that I don't even object when she begins washing my hair.

We. She said *we*.

I have to try and go home as soon as possible. I'll crawl the whole way if I have to, but I'm not staying here a minute longer than I have to.

Waves of jasmine cascade through the air and I try to focus on the scent instead of the building bundle of nervous fear in my chest. My servant's strong fingers knead through my hair, massaging my scalp, but even so the spell has been broken. I can't relax now, not when the threat is so real that I'll never be able to go home.

She rinses out the soap and the water begins to cool. Clearing her throat, I open my eyes to see her standing with a towel outstretched and waiting.

"If you wouldn't mind." She gives a small shake of the towel.

Grabbing the side of the tub, I inch my way to my feet. The pain is still there when I stand on my ankle, but the bath has done wonders and some of the swelling has gone down. Good.

She wraps me in a plush towel, moving my hair to the side before wrapping it in its own towel.

"The master would like you to join him for breakfast. Would you mind if I helped you dress?" She gestures to the bed where a new outfit has been laid out. All layers of satin and lace in a deep eggplant.

"Only if you're helping me dress in my own clothes. There's no way I'm wearing anything like that." I'll wear the same nasty rags forever before I try on their magic clothes.

She gives me a patient smile. "This would all go much smoother if you'd let me help you. I know this is a lot. I could—"

"What's your name?" I cut her off. I can't keep calling her a servant, especially not if she's trying to be my friend.

"Sarah. Let's get you dressed."

Chapter Four

Sarah refuses to let me back into my own clothes. I fight with her, but while I was in the bath, my clothes were removed from the room. I have no idea where to even look for them. I contemplate staying naked in my room in protest, but the grumbling of my stomach convinces me otherwise. The black silk we settle on has a high stiff collar that itches against my throat as she helps me down the hallway. At least she let me keep my shoes.

If I was going for Gothic Halloween, the dress would actually be kind of cool. It has a bustle and a train in back, the front more smoothed to my body. The back has a row of buttons going all the way down. If it wasn't for all the thick starched layers of lace down the front, I might actually enjoy the costume.

The heavy skirts shift with every clumsy movement as Sarah acts as my cane. Heady smells of bacon and eggs waft down the hallway and my mouth salivates. Finally, something I recognize.

Prometheus sits at the end of the table, and his hard to read face shifts as he watches us hobble in.

"Is everything all right?" His voice is a smooth rumble.

Before I can even begin to deny what he can see, Sarah interjects. "She's injured. She hasn't said how, but it's enough that she can't walk on her own."

"That didn't seem to be a problem for her yesterday." His lips curl in a smile.

And it won't be a problem later.

"Well, you should consider doing something about it now," Sarah insists.

He leans closer, resting his chin in his clasped hands, the tusks protruding from his mouth hanging over his bottom lip. "What would you have me do?"

"Let me go."

He sighs. "Sit and eat. I'll think of something to ease your pain."

Sarah fluffs out my dress behind me as I resume my chair from the night before, the bustle sticking out a good foot behind me. My plate has already been dished with none of the spectral show of last night. It sits temptingly piled high with scrambled eggs and bacon, a muffin sitting in a small dish next to my main plate.

I shovel it in without a second thought. They can poison me if they want to, I'll just be glad they're using food I recognize.

"Does this suit your palate better?" Prometheus asks, his tone filled with humor even as his face is still as stone.

I nod and grab the muffin, wrenching off its fancy wrapper and breaking off pieces to eat. Tart blueberries fill my mouth with each bite and I can't help but sigh.

"Good. I'd hate for you to think I was an unaccommodating host."

He eats slowly, movements filled with a grace I could never dream of accomplishing despite my advantage of being human. Plate empty, I watch him, my hands tapping against the side of my leg.

"What's your name?" he asks, head tilted as he watches me watch him.

"Wren."

"Like the bird?"

"Like me." I'm not some common fat little bird.

"I think I can see the resemblance."

My hands curl into fists. "What do you mean?"

"Beautiful, flighty, tell me, can you sing too?" He leans back in his chair, and I swear he's grinning.

"Whether I can sing or not is none of your business. It's just a name and I claim no relation to birds." I try to maintain my aloofness, but his compliment has me blushing, though I know it's stupid. Why should I care what a monster thinks I look like?

He picks up his glass. "We're going to be together for a long time. I hope if you can sing that you'll share it with me someday."

Fat chance.

"That dress is very becoming."

I bite the inside of my cheek as it heats up. "I can't say that it's really my style."

"Even so, it's beautiful."

I stand, the spectral man behind me sliding the chair out of the way. Prometheus watches me and I raise a brow.

He sighs and sets the glass down without drinking. "You may leave."

Ignoring the stiffness in my ankle, I sweep out of the room, the train of my dress following dramatically behind me.

The hallway is deserted, but I don't know how much I can trust that. I thought the dining room was empty earlier, but that proved to be a lie. So, despite the appearance of being alone, I do my best to creep along the shadows, sticking to the sides of the small tables set along the walls with their vases of spring flowers.

Each step is slow, even though my ankle actually does feel a lot better. I'll be sure to let the nurses at the ER know hot baths help the pain when I show up.

Pausing as I step into the kitchen, I can't believe the change from yesterday. The rest of the house just got cleaner, but this room got *busy*. Everywhere I look things are in halted motion. Pots line the top of stove, the main island is covered in half-finished pies, and flour sifts through the air.

Shaking off the feeling of invisible eyes watching me, I make a beeline for the solid wood door at the end of the room. I wrap my hands around the cool metal doorknob, and it doesn't feel real that I only came through it yesterday. A shiver runs down my spine as I turn the knob and swing the heavy door open.

My stomach sinks as two long rows of shelving filled with glass jars and canvas bags are revealed, the door swinging open on smooth hinges.

"What?" The word forms on my lips, but the rest of the question refuses to follow. I fall to my knees, not even feeling them hit the marble floor.

"I told you that you were part of this curse now." Prometheus comes up behind me and places a clawed hand on my shoulder. "There is no way out until the curse is broken."

"But it was right here. Right here. I came up these stairs, I traveled through the underground tunnel. Where is it?" My voice is small, mind struggling to comprehend what is happening.

He sighs, fingers digging into my shoulder. "There is no way out now. Not for the cursed."

"But I'm not cursed! I didn't do anything!"

My chest heaves up and down as my lungs work overtime on short breaths. Prometheus spins me to face him, careful not to hurt me with his claws.

"It doesn't matter if you did anything or not. People around me end up cursed. You're no different from the many that came before you."

My hands shake as I press them into my sides. "How many have been here before me?"

"After the last one, so much time passed that we did not expect to see anyone new again."

I take a deep breath and close my eyes. As I slowly open them, Prometheus releases his hold on my shoulders and offers me a hand up. The palm of his hand is leathery and cool to the touch, what I imagine a gorilla's hand would feel like.

"What am I supposed to do? I'm assuming there's something I have to do to release me from my part in the curse."

I refuse to believe I'll be stuck here forever with the rest of them. That just isn't an option.

Prometheus shrugs. "I cannot tell you what you must do. But once you have done it, you will be free to leave this place."

"Will the curse be broken when I do whatever it is you can't tell me?"

"Only for you."

"That seems screwed up." Even in my mixed-up state, I can tell when something's unfair.

"Be that as it may, there is nothing we can do to change it."

I lean on my good leg, bracing a hand against the wall. "What would have to happen for you and the people trapped here to be free?"

His eyes widen in surprise. "No one has ever asked me that before."

"That's not an answer."

"Well," he sighs. "The sorceress would need to be destroyed for me to be free."

"Have you never tried to do that?"

He chuckles. "I am not free to leave the castle. How would I do that when she doesn't visit?"

"The castle?" I can't focus on the curse now that I know this isn't just some big house. "This is a *castle*?"

"My father considered it to be such when he built it."

"Wait, wait, wait," I hold a hand up. "How did a castle get out in the middle of nowhere desert land?"

He leans toward me. "It's a desert up there?"

"How long have you been here?" I screw my eyes shut, trying to process.

Pushing off the wall to change positions, my ankle sends out a spasm of pain. I gasp, and Prometheus grabs me by the arm, holding me up.

"Let's not talk here any longer. You should be resting."

He practically holds me up, letting me glide across the floor as he takes me to a room complete with a couch, two chairs, and a roaring fire in the fireplace.

"Cozy."

"Its one of my favorite rooms here," he says as he lets me sit in a chair and collapses on the couch.

I take in the little details, the carved wood of my chair, the ornate swirls in the crown molding, the thick plush of an antique rug. This place must have cost a fortune to build.

"Have you always lived here?"

He looks at me with a tilted head. "For much of my life. I did go away for school as all young men do."

"Like college?"

His eyes narrow as he considers me. "Not quite."

"So why can't you tell me what I have to do to break the curse?" I ask as I pick lint off the front of my dress.

"It's part of the cruel irony of the curse. To be trapped with someone who is only here because of you, but to be unable to help them leave."

"I'm sure it's caused it's fair share of resentment," I comment, watching his face.

He looks away from me. "That is how it goes, but I wouldn't call it fair."

"Why not?"

He leans forward, watching me with imploring brown eyes. "I didn't ask for anyone else to be stuck here with me. This curse should be mine alone to bear. Yet people continue to find their way here to be trapped with me. I never asked for any of this and yet I bear the brunt of the punishment."

"I'd say the others trapped here are carrying some of that cross with you."

He flops back into the couch. "I'll spend the rest of eternity in this purgatory, remembering everything I could have done better with no way to change what happened and with the added bonus of other's punishments weighing on me. Forgive me, but I still think I have borne a lot and will continue to bear the brunt of the curse, as I was meant to."

I purse my lips, studying him. He kneads his forehead with his paw, one long leg crossed over the other. His foot is like a wolf's, elongated like a man's with long dark claws.

"Do you ever worry you'll scratch the floors?"

Prometheus smiles, showing elongated canines. "It's happened before."

"I just haven't seen anything that would suggest that a mon—" I stop myself, a hand over my horrified mouth.

"That a monster lives here," he finishes, brows slamming down over his eyes.

My attempt at levity has been completely thwarted and I have no one to blame but myself.

"My staff is very well equipped to handle whatever physical disturbance I create," he continues. "Don't worry, you'll never have to see any evidence of what happens when you let a monster in the house."

Standing, his body has the unnatural stillness of a stalking animal. He stalks from the room, claws clicking against the floor. Pausing in the doorway, he looks back at me with slumped shoulders. "I'll find something to help you with that ankle."

Alone, I slump further into the chair and pull my book out of a pocket I folded in my dress when Sarah wasn't looking. The words swim before my gaze and I can't bring them into focus.

I want to be able to read. I really do. But I can't stop thinking of the pain in Prometheus's eyes when I called him a monster. Which is even more annoying because instead of reading or daydreaming about Prometheus, I should be breaking the windows to get out of here.

And yet I can't stop. What I said shouldn't matter. I don't know him, and what I do know isn't super pleasant. He is the reason for my being here after all. The reason for the curse that trapped us all.

Why should it matter if what I said affected him?

I throw the book down in disgust. I'm not going to be able to enjoy it anyway. Why can't I keep my fat mouth closed?

"Miss?"

Blinking groggily, Sarah swims into my view. I don't even remember falling asleep.

"The master thought this might be helpful." She holds out a long ebony cane, the handle curling into a snake's head. "Would you like to try it?"

I don't see why it matters if I can get around or not. It's not like I'll be any more able to leave. Still, I sit up and take the cane when she offers it to me.

The wood is smooth under my hand. I turn it over, staring into the ruby eyes of the viper's face. "Where did he get this?"

She shrugs. "I'm only here to make sure it works."

As I stand, I stretch my back, leaning on the cane for strength. Sarah narrows her eyes but gives me a small smile. I take a few tentative steps forward, doing my best to stay off my ankle. It's gone stiff again, the bath of this morning feeling far too long ago.

"Will that do?"

I take five more steps, measuring each movement. "Yeah. This is better than walking on my own for sure."

Sarah smiles at me, face tight. "I'll let the master know."

She walks toward the doorway and I hobble after her, cane clicking against the floor. "Where are you going?"

"To let the master know," she says with a sidelong glance.

"Can I come with you?" Maybe if I apologize I can get him off my mind.

"It's not a place you're allowed to be."

"So I'm supposed to stay here forever in this castle and there are still places in it I'm not allowed to be?"

Sarah sighs. "The master likes to have his privacy."

"Am I entitled to any privacy?" My tone grows hard. "Or is this something special for the *master*?"

"Just the master."

She keeps walking, picking up the pace so that I can't keep up. It doesn't stop me from trying.

My cane clicks like a metronome across the floor, muted when I get to the rug running down the hallway. Sarah lifts her skirts, exposing black laced boots and takes the stairs two at a time. I grind my teeth together and follow after her, albeit at a much slower pace. I'm only a quarter of the way up the stairs by the time Sarah is so far down the second floor hallway that I can't see her anymore.

I get to the top, leaning against the banister while I catch my breath. The hallway looms before me, all closed doors and evenly spaced chandeliers, the candles flickering in the still air.

I check the door I found Prometheus behind first but the room is empty of everything but the four-poster bed. Every step I take gets me more and more angry. He can't treat me like a child. I wouldn't even be here if it wasn't for him!

The farther I go down the hallway, the more everything looks less . . . perfect. The shine on the floors is faded, the hems on the curtains ragged, and the chandeliers are missing candles. Floorboards creak under my feet. The whole thing has a very haunted mansion feel that makes me shiver.

"Sarah?" My voice is quiet, too quiet for anyone to have actually heard me. "Anyone there?"

A curtain flutters in the breeze coming in through a crack in one of the hallway windows. The air smells like wet earth, cold and clammy against my skin.

The hallway ends in another solid door, but this one is different. Five long gashes have been dug into the door, revealing the unstained wood underneath. The doorknob is ripped out and I bend over to look inside the jagged hole left behind.

It's another wing to the castle, complete with its own parlor. A table balances precariously in the middle of the ripped-up floor, one of its legs missing. Prometheus's servants must not be allowed to fix the evidence of the monster in this area of the castle. Is that why I'm not allowed in here?

A dark figure stalks past the window, blocking the light. I press closer to the door, my face touching it as I try to get a better look.

The figure roars and swipes at the table, sending it flying into the door. I jump back with a shriek. Silence comes from behind the door and all I hear is the quick beat of my heart.

Pressing a hand against my chest, I make up my mind to leave when the door is wrenched off its hinges.

"Come back to look at the monster?" Prometheus roars.

Falling back on my hands, I stare into his contorted face, eyes rich with pain. I open my mouth, but it refuses to make a sound. He stands over me while I gape on the floor like a fish.

"Well?" he practically screams, the heat of his breath cascading over my face.

"I-I-I . . ."

I hold a hand up in protection as he steps closer. Looks like I won't have to worry about an eternity here after all. He sees my position and hesitates, the rough pads of his feet scraping against the floor. He raises a hand then lowers it, my breath caught in my throat.

"I'm not going to hurt you," he says after a long pause. "I should have controlled myself in your presence."

Peeking at him from behind my arm, I slowly lower it, half expecting him to pounce.

"It's been a long time since I've had to deal with strangers not used to my appearance." If he had a human face, I almost would've thought he looked sheepish. "And I did not expect you to seek me out."

I swallow what little saliva has pooled in my dry mouth. "I was upset you had put limitations on my presence in the castle."

He rests a hand against the doorway. "I've not allowed others into my quarters to protect them."

Glancing past him, I take in the damage left from his presence in the room. Wallpaper hangs in shreds from clawed up walls, deep punctures mar the floor, and the light fixtures are missing altogether. He doesn't follow my gaze but his shoulders slump as I look over his domain.

"Why don't you get it fixed?"

Not the question Prometheus expected, he jerks, claws digging into the doorframe. "You see evidence of the monster living in the castle and you only wonder why it hasn't been fixed?"

"You've kept the rest of the castle so nice. Why destroy this part?"

"A monster shouldn't live in opulence."

Narrowing my eyes, I grab the cane and pull myself to standing. "It's your house."

"It's a man's house."

"Weren't you once a man? Aren't you still? Underneath all of this . . ." I gesture to his creature-like body.

He steps past me, leaving the door to his room removed to expose the evidence of the wound I keep pouring salt in. "Let's not stay here any longer. And please . . . don't come this way again."

⊷⊷⊷

Days pass and I hate how easy it's been to get comfortable here.

"So Wren." My name tumbles from his lips and I focus on him instead of my plate, cheeks heating. "I'm assuming you're a reader, but tell me more about yourself."

"That seems like a pretty big assumption based on one book." I scrape my fork against the nearly empty plate left from our lunch.

This is our new routine, meals together and avoidance with a book for the rest of the day. I finish *Frankenstein* and start it again. Prometheus has given me a whole library for a room but I can't seem to touch it. Touching anything here only makes this purgatory more real.

"Care to show me your 'one book'?" he gives me a sly smile.

It's still shoved in my makeshift pocket. Sarah hasn't been able to get me into anything new since my first wardrobe change. I pull it out, the spine of the book curling, the pages dog eared and worn.

"That looks like the mark of a reader to me."

I shrug and drain my glass of water.

"I'd like to know more about you," he presses.

I cross my arms over my chest. "Why don't you share something about you. All I know about you is that you're cursed and as riveting as that's been, it's not exactly a personality quirk."

He's wearing a blue button up shirt with brown riding pants and how he's managed to get these on is beyond me with his humped back and the lack of dexterity in his clawed hands. In an uncharacteristically human gesture, he smooths back the wild mane of dark fur.

"What would you like to know exactly?" he asks, teeth gleaming in the candlelight.

"What did you like to do before the curse?"

He raises a hand and servants appear to clear away the potato soup we had for lunch. "I liked to dance, and I liked the opera."

"You liked music then?"

"My question a few days ago about your ability to sing was probably more out of selfish desire than true curiosity," he admits with a small smile, brown eyes twinkling.

"I wish I could be more useful to you, but I really can't sing."

Unless you count my shower sonatas, which will never see the light of day, or darkness of this cave I guess.

Prometheus stands. "What about the dancing?"

"Definitely not."

"I don't know how they dance now, but I'd be more than willing to teach you some that I used to love." He approaches me.

I hold up my cane. "In case you haven't noticed, I'm not really up to dancing at the moment."

"I can help you." He holds out his hand. "Please, would you dance with me."

I hesitate. And yet . . . his hand hovers in the air, reaching for me, pleading with me.

"Okay."

I put my hand in his and he lifts me to my feet. Wincing as my weight lands on my ankle, he swoops me from the room. He doesn't wait for me to hobble, lifting me by the arm to keep up with him as he almost jogs through the highway, taking a left turn down an even longer hallway and pushing open heavy double doors.

Huge gold chandeliers suspended from the twenty-foot vaulted ceiling flare to life as we walk into the empty room. It's the size of a football field with only a grand piano and a few chairs to fill the space.

Prometheus sets me down like I'm a china doll and I can't stop looking at the curls of gold filigree on the ceiling, the walls completely covered by mirrors, the way the shadows dance along the floor.

"What is this place?" I ask, my voice in a whisper.

"The ballroom," he says with a smile that would've looked more like a grimace on my first day. "We used to have the most wonderful parties here."

"I feel like you could fit the entire town's population in here." Wide eyed, I don't notice at first when Prometheus takes my hand again.

"Shall we?" he asks, leading me further into the middle of the room.

I stumble, focusing on his eyes. "We don't have any music."

"I'm sure I can come up with something."

Prometheus places a hand on my back, almost covering it completely, and keeps his hand in mine. He hums, the sound reverberating through his chest where it's even with my head. My breath catches as he presses my torso into his, lifting my feet from the ground.

We sway through the room, moving to his nameless tune. The lights dim and his movements are so fluid that I can hardly tell he's moving at all. We're pressed together so tight that I can feel his chest rise and fall with his breaths.

"Are we waltzing?" I ask, trying to pick apart the beats he's humming.

"It seemed like the easiest dance when my partner needed so much help," he says and I'm sure he's smiling even though I can't see his face.

My cheeks burn. "You're the one who wanted to dance, knowing my ankle made it impossible."

"You mistake me." Prometheus loosens his grip enough that I can see into his dark eyes. "This is more than I could have hoped for."

I can't begin to imagine why. "Have none of your other guests danced with you before?"

"I've never asked."

He starts humming again. I watch his feet move, mine dangling a foot off the ground. Sighing, I rest my head against his chest. This should be impossible. I can't be here.

Prometheus squeezes my hand in his and my chest hitches. I wriggle in his grip, eyes wide. I can't be here.

"Let me go," my voice wavers but he complies, setting me on the ground and looking at me like I'm a spooked rabbit.

I stumble backward, my ankle sending waves of pain up my leg. I don't know where my cane is. My gaze darts around the room, landing on nothing. The chandelier lights flare up as I turn for the door.

"Wren?"

My feet keep moving, taking me out of the room and into the hallway I'd never been in before. It doesn't matter. I have to get out of here.

Ankle throbbing, I make it into the hallway. My toe catches on the rug and I sprawl onto my hands and knees.

"Wren? Let me help you." Prometheus comes behind me and I flip over on my back to see him extending a hand, brows wrinkled in concern.

"Stay away from me!" The words come on the wave of a scream ripping through my throat. "Just stay away."

His fingers curl into a fist. "You need help."

"I'll be fine."

Crawling forward, my legs tangle in the layers of tulle and silk.

"Did I do something?"

Screwing my eyes tight to keep myself from acknowledging the hurt in his voice, I clamber to standing. With a zombie-like gait, I make my way down the hall. The fork that led us to the ballroom earlier is much farther away than I thought. Every step sends fire up my leg.

"Wren, let me help you."

Prometheus keeps pace next to me even as I try to go faster. Sweat beads along my temples.

"Wren?"

When I don't answer again, I hear his jaw clamp shut. He stays with me through the slow procession without further comment. Getting to the kitchen takes every ounce of willpower.

I pound a fist on the pantry door and my leg gives out. My knees slam on the unforgiving floor and I knock my forehead against the door, hand gripping the handle. Tears stream down my face and I don't understand how I got here. We were having a nice time, weren't we?

"I wish you would tell me what I did," Prometheus whispers. "No matter how long you sit here, that door won't become what you want it to be."

A tear dribbles down my nose, following the curves of my face to my mouth. Its salt sits on my tongue.

"I can't stay here," the words are a whisper, a plea.

There's a thud as he hits the ground next to me. "I wish I could help you leave."

Staring at him through red puffy eyes, I believe him. His shoulders slump against the side of the counter, head bowed as he stares at his hands in his lap. He looks every bit as dejected as I feel.

"I'm sorry," he whispers.

I want to tell him it's not his fault, a response that's been trained in me since childhood, but we both would know it's a lie. It is his fault. Whatever happened that brought this curse down on everyone is his fault, and I suspect his fault alone.

"Why did it choose me? Why was I lured down here?"

The question is rhetorical in nature, but Prometheus shifts on the floor.

"What do you know?" My voice is sharp in the silence between us.

He runs a hand through his mane. "It might have something to do with me."

"Care to elaborate?"

"It's kind of a cruel joke really." He gives a weak laugh but my lips don't even twitch. "I'd given up. I wasn't going to attempt to break the curse anymore. I'd sworn off involving anyone else, then I climbed into bed, determined to let death take me.

"I'm sure you noticed the decay around here. Without my movements, without the presence of a potential curse breaker, there was no need for the others. They essentially ceased to exist. And so I waited. But the sorceress had different plans."

"So she's the reason I'm here?" At least I won't have to blame Prometheus for the curse selecting me.

He bites his lip and I wince as his canines dig deep enough to draw thin lines of blood. "There was another woman once. A long time ago. She's part of the reason for my punishment. She had black hair like yours."

"Are you kidding me?" Forgetting my pain, I jump to my feet. "I'm here because of my hair? It's not even real!"

"It's not real?"

A hysterical laugh bubbles in my throat. "No! It's a dye!"

Prometheus laughs, shoulders shaking as he hunches over. My hands clench and unclench in tight fists as I stand over him, the top of his head still taller than mine.

"I fail to see how this is funny."

"This has always been about guilt, making me really feel it, but you're not what she expected either I bet. Not even real, ha! What color is your hair then?" He's practically crying from his heavy laughter.

I don't share his sentiment.

Stomping from the room, his laughter haunts every footstep. I'm all the way to the end of the island before he can control himself.

"Wren! Come back! I'm not laughing at you, I promise."

I give him a withering glare. "Have you laughed at every woman brought down here because of your preferences?"

His jaw closes with a snap, all traces of mirth lost as I sweep from the room on my throbbing ankle.

Chapter Five

I don't leave my room for three days.

Sarah brings me meals on silver trays that she then takes away still full hours later. I wrap myself in the thick blankets lining my bed, as if hiding behind the lush walls could change anything.

On the first day, Prometheus comes to the door. His knuckles give a gentle rap but I don't answer. I don't answer when he calls my name either, pleading with me to come out. After an hour he pounds against the door and demands to know what he did wrong. He has the strength to break down the door if he wanted, but he never even tries to turn the handle. He simply waits with breathing that turns ragged for me to let him in.

The second day he doesn't come back.

Despite ignoring him the day before, I miss his presence and I hate myself for it. I don't need to expend any emotional energy on the man responsible for my imprisonment. But I can't help it. Staring into the gold brocade lining the canopy above my bed, I count elaborate stitches and wish for someone to save me.

On the third day, I decide to save myself.

Despite the curse and the fact that Prometheus can't, or won't, talk to me about it, I will find a way out myself.

In one of the desks lining the walls, I find thick, textured paper and a few charcoal pencils. They have a propensity for drawing, but I'm no lady locked in a tower. Instead, I map out what I know, both about my location and about the curse.

Based on my injury, I can't imagine that I'm more than five miles from where I fell, no more than five miles from town. That puts me in a perfect radius to be found if I can get out of this house. There's no way Ruby hasn't told anyone yet. I can't imagine she even waited the thirty minutes I asked her to, that goody-goody.

As far as the curse goes, I know even less, but I refuse to let that stop me. I know that it affects everyone brought to the castle and I'm assuming it's affected everyone in the castle at the time of the cursing, hence the host of servants. I've tried to talk to the servants before, but so far only Sarah has responded. Prometheus can't tell me specifically about the curse and his talk of "potential curse breakers," so I can infer that breaking it might have something to do with me and the others lured here to die.

Sarah interrupts me with dinner. Sitting sprawled in the middle of the floor, my tentative plans spread about me, she only raises an eyebrow before setting my tray down on a round table.

"Sarah?" I don't look up from the sketch of the castle I'm working on. "Yes, miss?"

"I need my clothes back." There's no way I'm taking on this curse in some old-fashioned frippery because of Prometheus's preferences.

She hesitates. "We don't have them anymore."

"I don't believe that for a second," I glance up at her with narrowed eyes. "If you want me to leave this room again, you'll retrieve my clothes for me. I'm through with these little games."

She wrings her hands, gaze sweeping the room before landing on me. "I could be your friend if you wanted . . . if you need someone to talk to about all this."

"Get me my clothes and we'll see."

"Yes, miss." Her shoulders cave in as she leaves the room.

Good. I have work to do and I refuse to do it in a bustle.

Only twenty minutes later, Sarah returns with my confiscated clothing. She lays them out on the bed and I approach my dinner tray. Starving myself isn't going to help me get out of here.

The plate is crowded with a slab of steak, fluffy mashed potatoes, and an assortment of summer vegetables. My mouth waters just looking at it. I didn't realize how hungry I was until I decided to give in.

Sarah waits in a corner of the room until I've scraped the plate clean. She takes the tray, her mouth twitching.

"Should the master expect you for breakfast?"

I tilt my head, considering the question before giving her an answer. "Why not."

She gives me a curt nod and moves to leave the room before hesitating.

"I've got this."

"Can I ask you something?"

"Of course." Sarah's never asked me anything before.

"Why are you fighting this so hard?"

I sigh. "I don't even know if this is real. Why should I go along with everything you guys say?"

"Unfortunately, miss, this is very real."

I don't know why, but having her say it makes everything come into clearer focus. I want to crumple up and cry. I'm really stuck here.

Sarah sits on the side of the bed and puts an arm around my shoulder, saying nothing as I shake in her arms. She hums, resting her head on mine until I'm able to calm myself.

"I'm not going to die here," I huff through a stuffy nose.

"Of course not. I'll help you." Sarah brushes down my hair and rises from the bed. "Can I help you with that?" She points to my clothes and I nod.

Together we struggle to get me out of the antiquated dress. Rows of buttons undone, the dress slips off and I fling it on the floor and sit in the paper circle. Sarah looks at what I've collected with a furrowed brow.

I'm going to need to comb over the castle, there's no way around that. I need answers and if Prometheus won't give them to me, I'll have to find the evidence of them around the castle.

Will I find the evidence of the people who were here before me? Or do their belongings and the changes made in the castle disappear when they die? If I die down here will someone come through and erase me too?

I shake off the chill that runs down my spine. It doesn't matter what happened to the others. I'm not going to die here.

The fire burns low as I work and when its nothing but embers, Sarah leaves and I crawl into bed. I don't bother cleaning up my plans. This is my space, as Prometheus proved.

⋆❈❀❈⋆

Anticipation for the day has me out of bed before Sarah can wake me. I pull on my jeans and tank top. They smell like lavender. Did someone wash them after they were taken from me?

It feels like I'm pulling on armor as I lace up my sneakers. Playing along has been dangerous. I can't get too comfortable here. With my own things I can at least remember this isn't my home. I'll have a constant reminder of what I'm working towards. Prometheus can't distract me.

The three days off my ankle have done it some good. The swelling is gone and I can walk on it without assistance. I still limp a bit, but I can move on my own and that's all that matters.

Taking the stairs down for breakfast, I let my gaze trail along the ground floor, counting the open doors lining the hallway. Searching this place could take a week at least if I'm going to do it thoroughly.

Sinking into my place at the table, Prometheus gives me his version of a smile. I place the napkin on my lap and wonder if maybe he'd be willing to help me. Or at least point me in the right direction of where to look.

"I'm so glad you came down. I've been worried about you." His voice is soft. Maybe I'll ask him later. Give myself a day or so first.

"You shouldn't have been worried, you know I can't leave."

He sighs. "Other things can happen."

"Well, I'm fine." I don't know what he's so worried about. The only thing that can happen in this place is dying of boredom.

I pluck a muffin from a silver tray on the table, peeling back the paper and digging in. The smells of sugar and chocolate chase each other through the air. Prometheus's plate is heaped full. I don't have time to wait for him today.

Finishing off my breakfast with three big bites, I don't wait for permission before rising from my chair.

"You've changed." There's an odd note to Prometheus's voice as he considers me.

"Dresses aren't really my thing."

"It's not that," he says, tilting his head. "Are you going to share your plans with me?"

"Not today."

I limp from the room before he can ask any more questions. I don't know why I feel like keeping a secret from him. By all accounts, he should be happy I'm looking for a way out. Isn't that what we both want?

Making for the end of the hallway the ballroom was in, I only count five doors. I pass by the set I know belong to the ballroom. There are no answers for me there.

I go for the doors across from it. They swing in to reveal a library much grander than the one in my room. Mouth forming an *o*, I step reverently into the three-story room. Twirling staircases line each corner, the shelving continuing in an unbroken line straight up. This is the kind of room I could stay in forever. But I have work to do.

Grabbing a small book from the shelf, I shove it into my pocket and force my gaze back to what I'm here for. I look over the scattered tables, hoping to find some sort of clue. The table in the far back of the room has a few papers on it and I march over on quick feet.

I'm not sure what I was hoping for, but it definitely wasn't this. The few sheets someone left behind look like inventory pages. Long lists of belongings run in columns down the papers. Pretty routine stuff, although I would have expected them to be in an office.

The rest of the room is clear, only empty tables and old books. With a sigh, I leave the room, marking it to memory so I can find it later.

Heading for the next room, I see Prometheus at the end of the hallway watching me. I give him a small wave and walk through the door.

It's pitch black in here, and I walk with hands outstretched to keep from falling. That'd be the last thing my ankle needs when it's finally getting better.

My fingers slide across a smooth surface at hip length and I balk with a shriek, pulling my hands back. I just need to make it to a light.

I take a few more steps forward and reach my hands out again. Feeling fabric, I wrap my fingers in it and pull. The tightness in my chest eases when pale light floods the room. Curtains. I've found curtains.

Turning to face the room, a half laugh bubbles out of my chest. It's a music room. The smooth surface is only a piano. The elegant, dark wood grand piano sits in the center of the room, light gleaming off its veneer. The wall is lined with instruments, violins, flutes, a few trumpets, all sitting silently.

Prometheus stands in the doorway, no doubt alerted by my overreaction.

"I'm just exploring." I cross my hands over my chest.

He ignores my posturing and steps into the room. "Do you play?" he asks, gesturing to the piano.

I bite my lip. "A little."

"Would—" he hesitates before trying again. "Would you play for me?"

His question is so soft and it plays on the walls I've been building around my heart. He clenches and unclenches his fists as I consider his question, his unease clear. His vulnerability decides it for me.

"You don't have—"

"Okay."

His eyes widen before he can mask them. With a smile, he gestures for me to sit at the piano while he takes a spot in a leather chair facing the instrument.

I settle on the hard bench, running my fingers over the smooth keys. Probably ivory. Despite telling him I'd play, I can't get my fingers to press any of the keys. It's been years since I played. About five years since Mom discontinued my lessons. That was probably the moment I should've realized she'd been rethinking our relationship.

Prometheus sits quietly. I take a deep breath, closing my eyes to blot out the memories.

When I start to play, I try not to think about it. My fingers glide against the keys, music coming without my overthinking mind to stop it.

Prometheus chuckles, breaking the spell I've created within myself. Opening my eyes, I see him leaning toward me with a grin. "The Moonlight Sonata is rather appropriate, don't you think?"

So that's what I'm playing. I laugh with him then throw myself into the music.

It is an appropriate choice even if I didn't consciously make it. This castle is constantly in a state of half-light that could be described as moonlight by someone more poetic than I.

I come to the end of the piece, my fingers stilling as the last chords waver into nothingness.

Prometheus stands. "That was beautiful."

"Mom thought music lessons were necessary if I was going to be a lady."

He purses his lips as if holding in a smile. "And was she successful?"

I gesture to my outfit. "What do you think?"

"I think there is more to being a lady than whether or not she can play or what she wears."

I pick at a chip in my nail polish, ignoring the prick at the corner of my eyes that comes with his words.

"What were you doing down here anyways? If you'd wanted another dance lesson you could have said so." He says it teasingly, but panic spreads through my limbs and I jump up from the piano.

"I told you, I was exploring," the words drip from my numb tongue. "You can't expect me to stay here forever without even knowing what this castle has to offer."

He takes a step toward me. "Could I accompany you?"

"I . . ." I'm not ready to tell him the truth, and his presence would force it from me.

He curls back the hand he'd been in the process of extending. "That's fine."

But it isn't. We both know it isn't.

"It's okay, you can come along." The words come before I can think better of them. I want to take the sad tilt of his eyes away.

He smiles. "Where should we start?"

Prometheus leads me from room to room, almost smiling as he shows me priceless paintings and knickknacks I wouldn't have spared a second glance. Drawing rooms and receiving rooms and rooms just for art await me on the first floor. He talks almost nonstop as we go, describing everything in minute detail.

"I've never had anyone want me to show them around before," he says as we pause beside the stairs.

"No one's ever wanted a better look at their prison?" My tone implies teasing and he gives me a grin. It's a good question though, why wouldn't anyone else look for answers?

"I think it's more like no one else wanted to spend any amount of time with me."

It's not like I asked to spend more time with him either. Maybe others did snoop around, they were just more careful about it. Should I have waited until he'd gone to bed or something?

"Would you like to see upstairs?"

"Are you sure it wouldn't encroach on your private quarters?" Now I really am teasing. After the respect he gave me the last few days, I'll let him have his own space. At least until I go over everywhere else for clues.

"I'm sorry my desire for privacy has offended you so," he says, shoulders drooping as he mounts the first step.

I grab his arm. "It's okay. I'm not upset about it anymore."

I'm not even sure he heard what I said. Instead he continues staring at where my hand rests on his arm. I pull my hand away.

"I'm sorry, I—"

"No," he interrupts me, rubbing the place on his arm where I touched him. "You did nothing wrong."

He leads me up the stairs and I follow him in silence. I'm not a really touchy person, but that doesn't mean I spend all my time without being touched. Playful shoves, high fives, all the little marks of friendship are a common part of my life in New York. I can't imagine what it would feel like to have no one willing to touch me at all.

It's not like he's that hideous. Sure he was scary to look at originally, but now his animal features don't give me pause. He's just Prometheus, and he happens to look like a beast.

"So, is this room not yours then?" I ask as we crest the stairs. The room I first found him in sits empty, the door swung open.

He sighs and gives me a side smile. "No, this isn't my room."

"Are you going to explain what you were doing here buried under a mound of dust or what?"

"This was someone else's room," he says, leaning against the door-frame. "Someone I loved very much."

For whatever reason, his declaration makes my heart sink in my chest. "Oh yeah?"

He runs a hand along the intricately carved door. I never noticed all the little vines and buds on it. This door definitely doesn't match the others.

"My sister's room," he says in a near whisper.

"Your sister?"

"Let's continue. Shall we?"

He moves without waiting for me to follow. His sister? He's never mentioned siblings before. I peer into the room one more time before sprinting to catch up with him, noticing a large painting on the side wall of a girl with golden curls and rosy cheeks.

"This is your room," he says with an absent wave. "As I'm sure you already know."

"Was my room anyone in particular's?"

Beneath the layer of fur covering his face, I swear Prometheus blushes. "Actually, yes."

"It's a pretty great room, I'd be surprised if it had always been empty. So who's was it? Anyone good?"

He clears his throat. "Um, ah, mine actually."

"No freaking way." I bark out a laugh. "Why put me there? Why not keep it for yourself?"

"After my father died, it made sense that I take his larger apartment of rooms. Keeping this room as well felt frivolous."

"Has anyone else stayed in your room before?"

He doesn't meet my eyes, fingering a frayed hem on his shirt. "No. I've never allowed anyone to stay there before. This time just felt . . . different."

I don't have anything to say to that. Silence grips the space between us and I bite my cheek so hard my mouth fills with the coppery taste of blood.

"Is it okay if we continue the tour later?" Prometheus asks, gazing over my head.

"Of course."

He sweeps past me toward his rooms, leaving me with a million unasked questions.

I debate looking through the second-floor rooms on my own, but something about doing that feels inappropriate without Prometheus now. He's shared something personal and continuing to snoop alone feels like a betrayal of his trust. Not that I've really given him any reason to trust me.

Even being in my given room feels too personal. Like I'm looking into a hidden part of him.

The books lining the bookshelf have a new meaning for me. Did he pick these out? Were they put here by a father hoping to encourage his son to be well educated? The covers are too worn for them to have been picked by anyone else. Why did he put me here? Why me above all other "guests"? What made him decide I was worthy of inhabiting part of his personal space?

As I look over his books, I notice a small picture frame nestled in one of the shelves. Fingers shaking, I pull it out and hold it closer to my eyes so I can see the small figures in the portrait.

Its two men, one looking far younger than the other, in knee high work boots, riding pants, and button up shirts. The older man wears a cowboy hat and a stern expression, the younger's head is thrown back like he's laughing. Is one of these men Prometheus?

I slip it into my back pocket to go over later. Maybe I'll compare it to the portrait in his sister's room and get an answer as to who these men are. If only I'd done more research on Ruby's story of the town founding. Maybe I would've known who Prometheus was by name alone.

If there's one thing Mom has always been on me about, it's definitely my lack of planning. I get an idea and go for it, just like coming down the hole after some gold without really thinking it through. Sometimes that works and I get on track to graduate early. Other times I end up in the bottom of a hole. If I'd done things her way, we would have researched the area, made sure the ground was stable, thought about it for another month, then maybe gone down the hole.

Maybe I should've been more like her.

The thought settles on me like a blanket of nettles. Literally itching in my skin, I rub at my arms, leaving red streaks behind. It doesn't matter what Prometheus will think of me, I have to do something now.

After nearly wrenching the door off its hinges in my need to get out, I take a breath and carefully close it behind me. The hallway is empty and I'll have to accept that it really is as it appears.

I still have the majority of this floor to comb through, each room putting me closer to Prometheus's wing. It's not against the rules to be by myself though, so why won't my hands stop shaking?

Not surprisingly, every door I open is a bedroom. Bedrooms of all different styles depicting the taste of their previous occupants sit waiting. I find it hard to believe all of these rooms ever could've been filled. Especially with how out in the middle of nowhere as this place must have been before modern technology and cars. Being forced to live here then would've killed me.

Five bedrooms in, I come across one that makes me stop. It has none of the elaborate trimmings of the others, just a metal framed bed and the heavy smell of mildew. Has Prometheus's staff not been in here yet?

But as I step into the room, there's no dust or anything to say it hasn't been cleaned. Still I can't shake the feeling of being in a prison. Wallpaper's been ripped from the wall, laying in tangled sheets on the scuffed-up floor. There aren't even any sheets on the mattress. The floorboards creak under my feet as I walk further into the room.

The source of the smell becomes apparent as I get closer to the window. Streaks of water damage spread like a root system from the ceiling, trailing off a foot before it can reach the floor. A breeze blows through the room, rippling the curtain to reveal a crack in the window. I shiver, but it isn't from the cold.

A desk with a broken leg leans against the wall, a notebook ruffling open as the wind picks up. Shaking off my goose bumps, I grab the book. It's fat from use, the pages refusing to lie flat anymore.

I flip through the pages, watching the writing change from the beginning to the end. It starts with immaculate cursive and ends with writing only a doctor would recognize. Odd. My first thought is that it's the same person as they gradually decline in the conditions of this room, but then I wonder, did Prometheus keep all of his other "guests" here? Did they all contribute to this book?

Footsteps pass by the open doorway, and I jump, slamming the book shut. This isn't the safest place to be going over potential clues.

Notebook clenched in my white knuckled fist, I close the door and slink down the hall to my room. Safe in my guaranteed privacy, I climb onto the bed and lay the notebook open in my lap.

The first few entries are nothing to get excited over. They talk about the town, the mountains, the desert climate. It's almost enough to make me toss the book away. I'm not interested in someone's geographical thoughts on the area. But then things change.

While exploring today, I came across the most beautiful specimen. I had never seen anything like it before, it had a purple stalk with tiny white blossoms and it grew right out of the rocks themselves. I decided to follow the blossoms as they climbed through the rocky crags. As I climbed the rocks, my hand slipped and I clenched my body tight as I expected to fall the twenty feet I had climbed. When I landed after only a short fall, I opened my eyes to find myself dangling from the branches of a giant oak.

You can imagine my amazement at this point because there had been no oak growing here only moments before. Now as I looked around, all I could see was trees. The mountain I fell from had completely disappeared, as well as all the floral plants I had been following. I've been wandering through the forest for at least three hours now and as I sit here commemorating the day and watching the sunset, I can see the outline of what appears to be a castle. I'll have to look into it tomorrow as right now I'm far too exhausted to walk another step.

The book falls from my hands, the cover attempting to close. A magical forest? A mysterious castle that only showed up as night was falling? Is that where I am now? It must be or else the journal wouldn't have been in that room. I wonder if the forest is how the castle was hidden before the all too convenient flood.

I flip to the last entry.

Today was monumental. Despite him being unwilling to share what I need to do, I'm pretty sure I've figured it out for myself. When I asked Sarah if I'd finally cracked the code she just smiled at me. I feel certain she meant yes.

But I can't do that. There's no way for me to do what the curse is asking of me. And so, we shall rot down here. The monster in his room, and I in mine. I doubt he'll ever find someone willing to do what is needed. The sorceress has asked the impossible.

"But what did she ask?" The question roars out of my throat, reminding me of Prometheus for a moment.

Of all things to write down, why wouldn't she just say what she'd discovered? How hard would it have been to say, "I have to do this___, but I know I can't."

I flip through the journal again, but find no names. For whatever reason, this makes my heart break. Even if I get out of here, there's no way for me to bring any of their families closure, because I don't know who they are.

There's a light knock on the door and I shove the journal under my pillow. "Yes?"

The knob turns slowly, the door creaking on its hinges as it opens. Prometheus's face peeks around the door, his body filling the frame.

"I'm sorry for what happened earlier."

I shrug. "It's not a big deal."

"If you'd like, we could resume our tour."

I think about the room and wonder if he'd show it to me or gloss over it. There would be no way for him to explain it away now that I know who stayed there.

"That's okay."

If the last girl could figure out how to break the curse, I can too. And I won't need his help to do it.

Chapter Six

The next morning, I flip through the rest of the notebook. Nothing really jumps out as helpful, just a lot of rambling thoughts. Almost none of them talk much about Prometheus. Did they really avoid him like he said?

There is a section where several pages have been ripped out, but I try not to think too much about those. Regardless of what they might have contained, they're not here now.

"Wren?" Prometheus taps at the door. "Were you coming down?"

"Sure."

I shove the journal back under my pillow and slip my shoes on. Opening the door, Prometheus waits in the hallway, wringing his clawed hands. Ignoring his nerves, I start for the stairs. He follows at a slower pace, clawed feet making soft thumps in the runner.

"There's something I want to show you," he says as I reach the stairs.

I slide my hand across the banister. "Another part of the house tour?"

"Not exactly."

He brushes past me, turning into the dining room to grab a pastry before turning around. "Can you eat on the run?"

I pick up a croissant with a smile, following him from the room. He heads for the foyer, striding to the double doors where weak light is filtering through. He turns the knob.

"Showing me more of the cave are you?" I ask with a snide smile.

"Not exactly," he repeats and swings the door open, waving me through.

Well, I'll at least get a view of possible exterior escape despite losing my initial entrance. But as I step through the doorway and onto a wide stone walkway, my breath catches in my throat.

I'm surrounded by trees. Tall oaks with wide trunks, thick pines heavy with pinecones, and so much color. All the color missing from the town is out here. Vibrant greens and rich browns spread out in a never-ending forest.

"What is this?" The question almost doesn't make it past my lips, too overwhelmed for coherent thought.

"A gift of the curse," he murmurs. "When I was hidden from the world, I was given this."

"So the trees weren't always here?"

"Not before the curse."

I step off the path, leaves crunching under my feet. "This isn't anything like what's in town."

"Do you like it?"

"I love it." Being away from the desert and out of the cave is like a dream come true. At least as much as it can be without being free.

He follows me silently as I walk through the woods, running my hands down the trunk of the closest tree. We didn't have a lot of trees in the city, but I loved walking through central park.

"Do you come out here a lot?"

He shakes his head. "I did for a while, but then it became . . . painful."

"Painful?"

"There's no way out," he sighs, gesturing toward the forest. "You can wander for days and you'll never break free of the trees. It's just another part of my curse. To have a taste of freedom with no way to obtain it."

"You don't come out here to think or anything?" I try to hide any disappointment from him. I've only been out here a few minutes, yet I couldn't help but wonder if being out of the actual castle was closer to my ticket out of here.

"I've had far too many years of just thinking."

His eyes turn sad as he watches me. There's no way for me to fix this, and I know I shouldn't care, but the more I'm with him, the more I want to fix this. Ever since my Mom left, I've been closed off, unwilling to let anyone but the bare minimum in. But being here has forced me to get to know him, and despite my efforts, he's breaking down more of my walls than I care to admit. I glance away, rolling a pinecone between my hands.

"Is there anything you can tell me about the curse?"

He jolts back. "I've told you before that I can't talk to you about it."

I drop the pinecone. "Have you ever tried?"

"It's a great way to lose my ability to speak for a few days."

I turn toward him, my gaze pinned to my shoes. "Have any of the others ever figured it out?"

He hesitates. "There was one, once. She discovered how to free herself, but decided that the price for breaking the curse was too high."

"Did she say why?"

"She just couldn't do it."

He sounds like the last journal entry I read. "It doesn't make any sense. If you would tell me what I had to do, I'd do it in a second. I wouldn't even think twice about it."

I know I would. I'd do anything to get out of here.

"You would," he says, voice quiet as he clenches a fist. "And you'd feel exactly the same way."

"Was she like me then?" I finally meet his gaze.

"Not at all." Prometheus smiles. "None of them have been like you."

He reaches out a hand, running a claw gently down the side of my face. I close my eyes, shivering under his touch with what isn't entirely revulsion.

When he pulls away, I feel colder. "So why did you show me this?"

"I couldn't show you until I knew you wouldn't go crazy with it. Some of the others . . . some of the others literally wandered through these woods until they . . .until the end. You seemed stable enough."

"Stable?" The word pricks against me.

"I didn't want it to hurt you."

I clench my jaw. "I'm sure I would've figured it out for myself."

Marching past him, I head into the castle in a cloud of fury. It's just another case of him treating me like a child. How stupid does he think I am? That I'd wander around in some enchanted forest until it killed me. If he knew I was nothing like the others, why does he treat me the same way? Why do all the same rules have to apply to me?

It's true that there have been some differences. He didn't put me in that creepy dungeon room. He gave me a real room. *His* room.

I head for the music room, no sound of Prometheus behind me. Good. I don't need him to be a silent specter to my misery.

Sitting down at the piano, I let my pain flow through me into the music. I've lost everything being taken here, but I'd lost everything before that anyway. I'd lost my mother years ago, way before she ever abandoned me for Bill. Leaving was just the last physical separation in a long list of them.

Bringing me out was a sadistic move on her part. She knew I'd never fit her perfect mold. Never be the daughter she wanted. I'm suited to the slums, not her fake version of a perfect life.

Notes tumble from my fingers, twisting in my perfect agony. Trust was never my strong suit.

Despite Prometheus's warning, I can't keep myself from wandering through the enchanted woods surrounding his castle. Knowing it isn't real, I can see the inconsistencies I know I wouldn't find in a real forest. A few of the trees are exactly the same, right down to the roots lifted out of the ground, and if I listen long enough, the bird song repeats itself. The longer I'm here, the more I can see the flaws in the magic.

It's eerie, like being in a video game, and not a high budget one at that.

Still, being out here somehow feels better than staying trapped in the castle. At least out here I can tell it isn't real. Inside the castle the lines begin to blur too much. It all looks too real and the servants aren't around enough to remind me of how messed up this all is.

On the third morning of being outside, there's a difference. A low mountain pops out of the tree line, a brown mound hovering above the trees. It has to mean something. Before I've even taken the time to think it through, my feet are moving deeper into the woods.

Small thoughts in the back of my mind whisper of the girls who wandered until they died. I should care more about that possibility. But all I want is to get out of here. Maybe from the top of the mountain I'll be able to see the way out. That possibility propels me forward, step after step as my legs begin to ache.

It doesn't seem like I've walked far, my legs don't even hurt, but when I glance behind me, I can't see the castle or the few paths I've walked before. I'm surrounded by the same tree formations.

The bird songs repeat faster too, just a few lines before they start over, like I'm trapped in a music box. My heart beats quicker, hair standing on end as a slick line of cool sweat forms down my back.

This isn't right.

Ahead I can see the barest hint of the mountain. Without the castle to go back to, I push harder for my initial destination.

I walk for thirty minutes, the pounding of my feet against the ground keeping time for me. Looking ahead, I can't see the mountain anymore. The trees have grown too close together, the way ahead and behind blocked by thick trunks and low hanging branches. My stomach sinks like a rock, my steps growing jerky as I feel my panic rising.

This is how it must have happened. Prometheus thought the girls left to get away from him, preferring a death by the elements compared to the relative luxury the castle offered. And while he waited for them to come back, the forest played tricks on them, trapping them regardless of their desires.

And I'm next.

Stopping, I wrap my arms around myself, tucking my hands into my armpits while I think. The mountain probably doesn't exist. That much seems obvious. It's just a mirage created by a curse and facilitated by a freedom-seeking mind. I should've been smarter than to fall for something like that.

But I still have options. Or at least I feel like I should. I can keep heading toward a mountain that probably isn't real for a view that wouldn't help me much anyway, I mean in theory we're still in a cave aren't we? Or I can try to get back to the castle. Prometheus says I'm different, doesn't that mean he'll react differently to my disappearance? Or will he just think about all the different times I've pushed him away as he started becoming close to me? Our moment in the ballroom flits across my mind before I can push it back down.

It's a risk I'll have to take.

Taking a deep breath, I steel myself for the fight to get back. Turning, I catch the trees changing out of the corner of my eye. They move like a creature, with lethal smoothness as they grow thicker, the trunks and branches sprouting inch long thorns that ooze sap.

Why would the trees care so much if I try to go back? Why should it matter if I die out here or in the castle?

I don't get to linger on my thoughts for long. Brambles shoot from the ground, growing at record breaking speed. My feet dance in circles to avoid the growing shoots. But all this does is make up my mind. There's a reason why the curse doesn't want me back in the castle, and I'm going to find out why.

Pushing against the branches, hands contorted to avoid the thorns, I jump over the brambles and start my way home. I smile, this won't be so bad after all. But as though my thoughts trigger them, the thorns grow another inch. One growing by my hand pierces my skin, beads of crimson blood blossoming from the wound. Yanking my hand back, the thorn slides free and I release a ragged breath.

I want to look at the cut. I want to make sure it's not that bad. But the longer I stay here, the worse it becomes. Stopping to inventory my injuries could lead to more if I'm not careful.

Cursing myself for not at least wearing something I could wrap my hands in, I press carefully against the branches. Gaining the next few feet takes twice as long as the first few did as I avoid the longer thorns and the growing brambles.

Sweat drips down my temples, blurring my vision as I take careful steps. As I lower my foot, a scream rips unbidden from my throat. I've stepped on a less than submerged root, a thorn piercing through my shoe and into the soft flesh of my foot. Biting my lip so hard I can taste blood, I lift my foot up and keep going. I can't stop now unless I want to be twisted up in a thorny python of branches.

"Wren?"

My heart jumps up my throat, cool relief flooding my tight body. "Prometheus?"

I knew things were different. I knew he would come for me.

"Where are you?"

"Trapped!" Hysteria makes a bubble of laughter burst out of me as I plod forward, hands turning into red ribbons of blood.

"I can't see you."

His voice sounds far away. Far too far away to have been able to hear my scream or my answering call. I brush the sweat off my forehead with the back of my hand, coating my face with dribbles of blood.

"How did you get here?" There's no way he could have traveled through this mess if he didn't know I was out here. I'm too far out.

"I'm . . ." he hesitates. "I'm not actually in the woods."

"You're not—"

As I pause to consider his words, the thorns grow longer. They pin me into the trees, points pushing through tender flesh.

He sighs, the sound reverberating around me. "I couldn't find you in the castle and when I looked on the grounds and didn't find you there . . . I used the glass."

If I wait any longer, any hole through the thorns will be long gone. "If you're not here, you can't help me, you're just a distraction."

I push forward, groaning as a thorn grips my biceps and leaves a line of blood down the length of my arm. I'm a human pincushion, but I'd rather that than simple impalement. Prometheus goes quiet and I don't know if he's still listening to me or not.

Getting through a tight spot between two trees feels almost like forcing myself through a shredder. Making it through, I start a sigh of relief that catches in my throat and almost chokes me. The trees have been replaced with a solid wall of brambles reaching at least ten feet in the air. The thorns coming from it are as thick as my arm and the inside is so tight it's turned black from lack of light.

"I-I," the words sputter out without meaning, hot tears spilling down my cheeks. There's no way out. There's nothing more I can do.

My knees hit the ground, hands open in my lap. Thin lines of blood trickle down my body, pooling into the plush of pine needles lining the ground. This is how it ends then. I can't get through those brambles without killing myself in the process.

I rest my head in my hands, hoping for a quick death instead of something painfully lingering when the ground begins to shake. Curling in tighter to myself, I clench my eyes shut and hope this is the end.

A roaring fills my ears, fills the entirety of the space around me, sending me trembling against the ground. The sound builds, pressing against my ears until I have to clamp my hands over them as the pressure threatens to split my head in two.

The ground continues to shake and there's a wrenching noise. Dirt flies through the air. I peek from the shelter of my body as I'm pelted with clumps of earth, and the brambles shake. They shake, twisting from side to side before ripping up through the air and landing on a pile of other dislodged plants.

Prometheus stands in the hole left behind, chest heaving, drips of blood mingling with his sweat. I scramble to my feet, swaying on unsteady muscles. Seeing me standing on the edge of the bramble forest, Prometheus gives me a smile of relief, long canines winking in the afternoon light.

"How on earth did you . . ." I gesture at the path of destruction behind him where I can see the castle looking like a doll house at the end.

Prometheus glances back for a second before locking eyes with me again. "I'm not afraid of the curse's devices anymore."

He starts to sway. With the smile still painted on, he falls forward onto his face.

Jumping over the discarded thorns, legs trembling as I hit the ground, I fall into Prometheus's side. I roll him onto his back with a grunt. His chest moves in shallow breaths, but he is breathing. We're going to be okay.

The cleared stretch behind him takes my breath away. Holes and broken earth crisscross over the space between us and the castle. It doesn't even make sense. It's like he's come through with a bulldozer, though I know he didn't have one. I look over his sleeping form, eyes closed and muscles relaxed in peace.

He really is a beast.

I don't bother trying to move him. There's no way I can lift him. He has to weigh at least 300 pounds. Night falls as he lays sleeping on the ground, just a brown carpet of fur. I lean against his side to gather warmth as the last of the sunlight disappears. The temperature dips, goose bumps prickling along my skin where the blood has long since dried.

Shivering, I tuck in closer. Pulling his arm around me like a blanket, it keeps getting colder until I can't feel my toes.

Far away howls pick up. We might not be alone.

"Wake up," I whisper, pushing against his chest.

Branches snap in the untouched woods next to us.

"Wake up, wake up!" My whispers get louder, my tugging a little harsher.

In the pale light of the moon, two yellow orbs flash in the darkness. My pulse spikes and I yank out tufts of his fur. The orbs come closer, flashing like an animal's in the dark, almost like—

"Watch out!"

I yank on Prometheus as a wolf steps out of the shadows.

Sleek black fur ripples down his side as he paces the tree line, watching us. He pulls his lips back, revealing sharp curving teeth.

Prometheus doesn't budge, his wakefulness completely unchanged by my prodding. He's not going to help me. The faint light of the castle blinks through Prometheus's path. If I left him here, I might just make it.

The wolf takes a step closer. Reaching with a blind hand, I grab hold of something and whip it out in front of me. I almost cry in relief when I see its a thorn ridden branch.

I hold it out farther, wishing it wasn't shaking in my hand. Backing up over Prometheus's arm, he jerks the tiniest bit in his sleep.

I can't leave him.

Flexing my grip and pretending I'm welding a sword instead of a stick, I step in front of his prone body, placing myself between him and the animal. Maybe a thorny death wouldn't have been that bad after all.

The wolf growls low in his throat as he approaches me on near-silent feet. I raise the branch higher in retaliation, ready to swing the second he gets within reach. He prowls in the same perpendicular line to us, parallel with the trees, slowly getting closer. My pulse pounds in my temples, matching the wolf's footsteps.

He snaps his jaws and I swing, a thorn cutting into the meat of my thumb. The wolf jumps back, eyeing my weapon as it continues to move. The branch shakes harder in my hand.

"Stay back," my voice shakes but I square my shoulders.

I won't go down without a fight.

The wolf growls, lunging at me in a fluid motion that I attempt to block. He misses me, but only because he hadn't been trying. He's playing with me, waiting for me to tire out. It's a good strategy, if I represented any threat at all. Fortunately for him, I'm most likely not making it past the next ten minutes.

Howls ripple through the trees and I can't stop the flinch that breaks my concentration. The wolf strikes again, this time letting his teeth graze against my arm. I swing the branch, but it's too late and he's leapt back for the trees.

Fresh blood courses down my arm, mixing with the rusty remnants left behind from my tangle with the trees. No wonder the wolves found us, I'm sure I smell like a walking buffet.

Amber eyes reflect light in flat discs from the darkness of the woods. Forget my ten minutes bluff. This fight is going to be over in the next ten seconds.

Four black wolves exit the trees, prowling with the male who has my blood dripping from his jaw. Numbed panic seeps into my limbs and the branch goes slack. I can't take them on. I couldn't even present a real threat to one, let alone five. A chill wind sends leaves fluttering down like rain as we face each other.

Prometheus groans, claws digging into the ripped-up earth as he shifts. "Where are we?"

"Wolves."

He springs to his feet, the traces of grogginess gone. "How long have we been out here?"

"Since you passed out."

The wolves prowl closer, sniffing toward Prometheus as he clambers to his feet.

"You stayed with me?" There are traces of awe in his voice even as his face shifts into a snarl meant for the wolves.

"Yes."

At my confession he leaps past me, tangling into the prowling wolves. Snarls and the weak sound of animals in pain shatter the cold night air. I hold out my branch with more confidence as all the wolves attention focuses on Prometheus. My breath curls in misty vapors in front of me as I shift from foot to foot.

Prometheus snarls, the sound just as animal as anything coming from the wolves. What would've made me stumble back just a few weeks ago now sends me strength.

He throws a wolf to the side, its back hitting a tree trunk with a sickening snap. It falls to the ground and doesn't move again. One down.

The remaining four back up, eyes shifting as they try to formulate a new strategy. Prometheus is not what they were expecting. He lunges into their pack while one breaks free and jogs around him.

"Prom—" the wolf lunges before I can warn him, and I jump forward, branch swinging.

The wolf's teeth sink deep in my arm, and instead of fighting back I scream. A high-pitched wail. Prometheus spins to face me, knocking back wolves with an arm. Roaring, he charges toward where I stand frozen with a wolf clamped onto me. He grabs the wolf's head, one hand wrapping around the top of the snout while the other grabs its lower jaw.

Instantly I'm freed from the wolf's grip. I stumble back against the ground while Prometheus continues to pull. The wolf's jaw extends past what's natural and I glance away as I hear a snap.

One of the remaining wolves yips and they flee into the woods, leaving me alone with Prometheus.

He leans forward, brow crinkled in concern. I wipe the blood from my face with a shaking hand, and realize I'm crying. My cheeks flame in embarrassment.

Prometheus grabs my injured arm, hands gentle on my broken skin. Hissing as he touches one of the deeper wounds, he pulls back with a low growl.

"We never should have been out here this late. I told you there were other things to worry about here than just me."

"Obviously." I wrench my arm back. "But I wouldn't have been out here so late if you hadn't passed out."

"I would have been fine."

"Sure." The embarrassment for my tears pushes me into anger but he ignores it.

"Do you need help getting back?"

"I can walk just fine."

"I know you can," he says, tone infinitely patient. "I want to help you."

Rising unsteadily to my feet I shake my head and he raises a brow dubiously at me. With a sniff, I wipe away the rest of my tears and make for the castle at the end of the choppy path he cleared. Prometheus keeps step beside me.

I stumble in a hole left by the torn-up brambles and he catches my arm to keep me from falling. I pull out of his grip, but with much less animosity than before as we walk through the chaos he created to save me.

"How did you do this?"

An uprooted tree lays across the top of the thick layer of brambles to our left, roots thicker than my torso.

He shrugs. "You were in trouble."

Glancing at him sidelong, I watch the muscles of his arm ripple as it moves. If he could do that to the trees and rip the jaw off a wolf, what could he do to me?

Prometheus clears his throat. "So, you stayed with me after . . . that must have been a long time."

"Yes."

"You must have been a little scared."

I'm grateful he doesn't phrase it as a question. I was a little scared, not that I'll ever say it out loud. Especially not to him.

"Thank you."

His concession stops me short and I stare at him with wide eyes. "What?"

"Thank you." He steps closer to me, facing me so that I have to jerk my head up to see his face. "Thank you for staying with me. Thank you for being willing to fight for me."

A warm flush travels down my body. "I couldn't just leave you there."

"I think you could have. I think it would have been easy to leave a monster to the mercy of the woods."

"You're not a monster." The words come out quickly, without thinking. But it's true. He may look like a monster but he doesn't act like it, at least not with me.

Prometheus smiles. "I haven't heard someone say that in a long time."

We're so close my shoulder nearly brushes his arm as we walk. I cradle my injured arm to my chest as blood continues to ooze out. Black dots splash across my vision, my head feeling lighter with each step.

"I'm not asking anymore."

I turn to acknowledge his words, but before I can, his thick arm swoops me up. He braces his other arm against my back, cradling me against his chest.

Wiggling from side to side, I attempt to get out of his grip, but each movement builds the feeling of nausea in my chest. I settle in, too physically weak to struggle.

"I'll get you for this later."

"I'm counting on it."

Chapter Seven

Repetitive bird songs tap against my brain over and over. My pulse pounds in my head as I sit up. My left arm twinges and pain sends me back into bed.

Taking a deep breath, I slowly peak my eyes open. The same dull light beats against the tall windows and I'm buried in a pile of plush blankets. I struggle into sitting again, hissing through my teeth as I move my arm. Pulling it out from under the blankets, all I see is a mass of gauze-wrapped skin. I poke at the wrappings, the attack from yesterday coming back with sudden clarity. Someone took care of my wolf bite.

A grunt comes from the corner of the room and my head whips over. Prometheus is sprawled out in a chair by the fireplace, eyes closed in sleep. Did he stay here all night?

The chair obviously wasn't made for someone of his size, and I can't imagine he was comfortable. He looks like a stuffed animal pushed into a Barbie chair.

Biting my lip to keep quiet, I peel away the bandaging from my arm. Cuts and scrapes from the thorns mar my arm, along with eight deep punctures from the wolf's teeth. Each spot has been carefully cleaned and stitched closed with tiny black thread. Despite the mess I was in, there's no signs of the hot, pink early stages of infection surrounding any of the marks.

Prometheus groans again, this time stretching his arms over his head and meeting my gaze when I glance over.

"You should still be sleeping."

I shrug. "I've never been a late sleeper."

"You went through a lot yesterday," his deep voice rumbles as he leans forward onto his knees.

"Did you do this?" I gesture at the discarded bandages.

He glances away. "I had some help."

I peer down at the tiny stitches. It seems impossible that he could have managed them with his large hands, let alone his claws.

"Thank you."

"I thought you might be up." Sarah breezes through the door carrying a silver tray. She lays it down on the bed, handing me a steaming cup. "Thought you could use something sweet after your ordeal yesterday."

She gives Prometheus a dirty look and I reach out to grab her arm to thank her without thinking. My hand lands on the long sleeve of her black dress and doesn't pass through it. We stare wide eyed at my hand resting on her arm, her body real and tangible. But how could she feel real when she's not doing anything to serve? I thought she was only solid in the capacity of her service, like when she helped me into the tub. But I don't need her now. Not like that.

Sarah glances at me and I pull my hand back, her body becoming like a hologram once more.

"Try it again," Prometheus whispers from where he's standing at the end of my bed.

I reach out for her and her body ripples until I touch her and she becomes real again.

"What's happening?" My voice is tinged with awe as I do the impossible.

"Could it be?" Sarah asks Prometheus. They stare at each other, ignoring my question.

"I thought it was impossible." He glances at me, chest rising and lowering in heavy breaths. His hand reaches for me before curling back at his side. "It should be impossible."

Sarah smiles at me. "Thank you."

"For what? I don't understand!"

She pats my hand, her skin warm on mine, then heads out through the door. As soon as its closed I can hear her whistling in the hallway.

"What's going on?"

Prometheus leans against the footboard of the bed, jaw slack as he watches me. "This has never happened before."

"That should be good then, right?"

Am I breaking the curse? I still haven't even been able to figure out what it was, let alone how to break it.

He doesn't answer, and my headache sends a stab through my thoughts.

"Is anyone going to tell me anything?"

Prometheus smiles. "I've already told you I can't say anything, but you're on the right track."

Prometheus leaves soon after his revelation and I'm left on my own to stew. I try not to bristle at the fact that Prometheus doesn't have to rest despite passing out for hours after using unexplainable strength. He should have to spend the day in bed too.

I take short sips from the cup Sarah brought, refusing to enjoy the warm chocolate despite how richly it rests on my tongue. Any other day I could love it, but I'm too worked up for simple pleasures.

What am I doing that's changing things? Why can't they at least tell me that? Why couldn't the last girl that came here have spelled things out? Stupid vagueness.

I grab a piece of toast off the tray, cinnamon and sugar crystallizing on top of the melted butter. Chomping down, I wonder if I should just ignore the curse. Working at it is next to impossible when no one will say anything. And apparently I'm doing something about it anyway, so active work might not matter.

My book lays open on the side table and I grab it, scanning over the open page.

He seems to feel his own worth, and the greatness of his fall.

The words blur as my eyes fill with tears. All I can think about is Prometheus. He wasn't like this before. What happened to him? Is he living every day with the greatness of his fall?

I drop the book and slide out of bed. A bathrobe hangs against the back of the closet door and I wrap myself in it before stepping out the bedroom door.

The hallway is full of people. Women with feather dusters stand on stools to reach the chandeliers, men walk briskly from room to room carrying buckets of tools, and everywhere there's the feeling of movement. I halt in my steps and as though I've signaled them, every person within eyeshot stops and turns to face me.

Pulling my bathrobe tighter, my nose tickles with the smells of lemon and bleach as I take the stairs two at a time. The main floor is just as chaotic, and a man polishing the hardwood floor gives me a nod as I pass by.

There's no sign of Prometheus or Sarah. I'm in a sea of strangers and my heart beats fast in my chest as I keep looking for a familiar face. These aren't even the same people from the dining room.

"Have you seen Prometheus?" I ask a woman halfway up a ladder dusting frames.

She stops mid-movement, her hand flying to her chest. "You can see me?"

A fluttery feeling grows in my stomach. "Of course. Why wouldn't I?"

"You've never seen us before."

I shake my head, pushing past what she's said to get the answer I came for. "Have you seen Prometheus?"

"He's in his office."

I don't remember him ever saying anything about an office. Without bothering to thank her, I take off for the ballroom hallway. It seems the most likely place, and I don't know if I can handle any more surprises.

My bare feet leave condensation impressions on the floor as I rush down the hall. The scrapes along my legs pull with each desperate movement, but I can't stop.

Passing the ballroom, the movement around me ebbs away. The rush of servants must not have been needed here, because it's quiet and still. The feeling of normality seeps into my skin, calming my erratic breathing. I pause, leaning against one of the tables lining the wall and steady myself. I don't want to run into Prometheus looking like I've seen a ghost. Even if I sort of have.

The door of the room two doors down from me is cracked open and in the silence I can hear a pen scratching against paper. Legs shaking, I work my way forward, almost crashing into the doorframe. Prometheus jumps as I slump into the room, hands wrapped in the fabric of my bathrobe.

"I thought you were getting some rest," he says, putting the papers on the desk in neat piles.

"There are people out there." Strangers. I should have said *there's more people and they're all strangers.*

He leans forward. "What do you mean?"

"The whole castle is full of people!"

He regards me slowly, folding his hands together. "Are you sure?"

"What do you mean 'am I sure'? You think I don't know what people look like?"

"No one's ever seen them before," he says, moving around the desk so that we stand facing each other. He stares into my eyes, and the tingling I felt before grows. "I can't believe this is happening."

"What's happening? Is anyone going to ever tell me anything?"

He reaches for my hand, watching himself do it as if not quite believing his own movements. He holds my hand loosely in his, daring to glance up at my face for only a moment before staring at where we're touching again. He steps closer, our breath mingling as I watch him, his eyes a mixture of sorrow and joy.

"What is happening to us?"

It's like I've finally asked the right question. He meets my gaze, lowering his face so that it's an inch from mine. "You're breaking the curse."

"Are you going to tell me how I'm doing that?"

"I might if I could, but I worry that it would ruin the magic that's already happening."

I bite my bottom lip, warring with myself about the logic of his argument. "Will I be able to go home soon?"

The joy fades completely from his eyes. "If that is your wish. The door should appear soon and then you'll be free to leave."

"What will happen to you?"

He gives me a half smile. "I'll remain here, unchanged in my prison."

"Shouldn't the curse over you break too? Won't you become a man again and all that?"

"There are things I haven't told you—"

"Obviously."

He shifts. "There is more at work here than what you can see on the surface. Your presence here is only the beginning. There would be much to do if I ever wanted to walk as a man again."

"Could you tell me about that, or is it against the rules?" My teasing has real bite to it. I can't stand everyone telling me they can't say anything anymore.

Prometheus considers me, running the pad of his thumb over my hand. "No one's ever asked about it before. I don't think it would be a bad thing for you to know. To make some decisions on your own." He paused, taking a breath before continuing. "This curse has two pieces, the one involving you and the one involving me. When you've broken your portion, you'll be free to go, but only if you stay will the curse on me break."

"What do you mean? If I leave, you'll never have the chance of being a man again?"

He runs his tongue of his enlarged canines. "I must find someone to fight the sorceress for me in order to be free."

"Why can't you fight the sorceress?"

"If only it were that easy," he laughs. "If I could fight her myself, I would've done it over a hundred years ago."

"Huh?"

"I can't leave the castle or the enchantment she's created. I'm just another one of her magical creations doomed to repeat its motions until the end of time. To fight her, she'd have to come here and face me, which she hasn't done since the first time I attacked her." His lips twist ruefully. "So you see, someone must first break the curse keeping them here, and then decide to leave this place to fight the sorceress instead of going home."

"She must really have hated you." I try to smile, but there's too much truth in the statement for it to make anywhere close to a good joke.

Prometheus smiles for me. "Yes, she did."

"So if I break my portion, all the people trapped here are free?" I ask, trying to find the parameters of the curse.

"I'm not sure. This has never happened before." He lets go of my hand. "No one's ever been able to do what was needed before."

I shouldn't be surprised. I *have* read portions of that journal after all, but for some reason, all I can think of is the curse being the cause of a personal slight to Prometheus. He crosses his arms over his chest as I stare at him, my heart breaking.

"Why are you crying?" he asks, brushing a tear from my cheek.

Starting, I raise a hand to my face, clearing away the flood of warm tears. "I'm so sorry."

He tilts his head at me, pondering my statement. "You of all people have nothing to be sorry for."

Cupping my face, he raises my head to his. We breathe together, lips close enough to kiss. I lean in, forgetting everything. Forgetting my imprisonment, his curse, the fact that for all intents and purposes he is a monster, just seeing the man who was willing to fight for me. He moves closer then jerks back. Removing his hand from my face, he stumbles backwards into the hallway, clawed feet clicking against the floor.

"I—"

"I apologize for being so forward," he says, cutting me off as he walks farther away from me. "If you'll forgive me."

He turns and picks up speed until he turns the corner and I can't see him anymore. I press my fingers to my lips, feeling the phantom press of the kiss that almost happened.

After adjusting the robe to more fully cover my many bandages, I take a deep breath and step into the hallway. Prometheus is long gone, but I follow him. If the curse on me is close to breaking, I owe it to myself to investigate further.

Flinching at all the movement in the main part of the house, I make for the kitchen. People sweep from room to room, none of them figures I've seen before. The kitchen isn't much better. A large woman in a stained apron stands at the island, pounding out a dough against the counter. She glances at me as I walk in, gives me a half smile and goes back to work. A slight woman works at the sink, banging pots around in an attempt to wash them. I slip through a cloud of flour to the door of the pantry.

I hesitate, hand extended toward it without crossing the final distance. I haven't tried to open it since the night Prometheus found me crying. If I turn the knob, will I see the same row of food storage?

The handle is cold as my fingers wrap around it. Knuckles white, I turn the knob, not sure what I'm expecting. The breath I've been holding whooshes from my lungs in a gush.

Leaning on my knees, I stare into the dark depths of the cave. The blinking light that led me here is nowhere to be seen, but I didn't expect it to be. Why would it linger after doing its dirty job?

Without thinking, I stumble down the steps, the scuffle of my feet echoing off the uneven walls. My hand cements to the handrail, my only grip on reality.

Halfway down the stairs, I glance up at the kitchen door. The light coming down the stairs is warm and bright. What am I doing? This is real. The cave is real. Was any of the rest of it real then? Did I wander around down here after knocking my head and it was all part of some weird concussion dream? Even as I think it, I know it's not true. What I've experienced down here with Prometheus and Sarah is real. They're real people.

Pressing the door to my past closed, I take a deep breath. I've done it. I broke this part of the curse. I can leave any time I want to. Choosing not to leave now doesn't mean anything. I can change my mind any time.

I don't know why I'm hesitating. I should be gone, halfway to home by now. But what for? So Mom can dictate my life without ever trying to get to know me? So I can continue pushing for a way out when I have one right here? No matter the logical reasons for leaving, or staying, that I try to convince myself with, I know what the biggest issue is.

I can't leave Prometheus.

I can't leave him to his fate. And I can't leave him alone.

Ignoring the temptation to flee, I force my feet up the stairs and into the kitchen. The slap of dough against the counter keeps time with the pulse pounding in my temple. The dank cave sends a chill down my spine, the complete opposite of what the castle offers.

With wobbly steps, I march from the kitchen. The cook doesn't look up at me, but a side smile grows across her face as I pass.

The farther I get into the hallway, the more confident I feel. My death grip on the bathrobe loosens and the edges flap in my wake as I leap up the stairs. Flinging my bedroom door open, I startle Sarah and she throws the garnish she was adding to my tray.

"I did it!" I proclaim, unable to keep the breaking of the curse a secret for a moment longer. "I broke the curse! I can leave!"

She presses a hand against her chest, shuddering with each of my exclamations. "Are you sure?"

"Definitely! I checked, and the way is clear for my escape."

"I see." She sets the toast down and brushes crumbs from her fingers, her gaze trained on the floor by my feet. "Thank you for taking a minute to say goodbye."

I laugh and she looks up with wide eyes. "I'm not going anywhere."

"What do you mean? You just said you broke the curse on you . . ."

Grabbing a piece of toast, I shrug out of the bathrobe and throw it on the bed. "I said I broke the curse. I never said I was leaving."

"I don't understand."

"Did you really think I would leave you all here? Learn about what you're going through and then take off as soon as I got the chance?"

"It's happened before," she whispers.

"But Prometheus said—"

"He doesn't know everything. No matter the curse's transformation, he's still a man isn't he? There was one once, a long time ago now. She broke the curse and left."

Sarah folds her hands, mouth drawn into a thin line. "Breaking the curse doesn't obligate you to help the rest of us."

I grab Sarah's hand, feeling her solidity and becoming even more resolved. "I'm not sure how I broke the curse, but I can't just leave now. You've helped me through everything since I've been here. I wouldn't leave you behind like that. I have to finish what I started."

"You don't know what you're saying." She gives me a pitying smile. "Setting us free is no easy task, and not one I would expect you to survive long enough to accomplish."

"What do you mean?"

She sighs. "Didn't Prometheus tell you? We'll only be freed when the sorceress is defeated. That's not something any of us could take on, let alone someone who knows nothing about how to go about it."

My mouth pulls into a frown, all the excitement I had leaching into the cold stone walls. "You know nothing about me, let alone whether or not I can take on a sorceress."

"Are you aware that Prometheus has already attempted to fight her?"

A chill runs down my spine, but I hold my chin up. "He mentioned something like that."

She smiles but it's cold. "When she first put the curse on him, she came to see the effects of it only once. The master was still half wild from his transformation, a condition he remained in for many years. When she appeared in the castle, he was like a rabid beast. He attacked her with all the brute strength the curse had gifted him but only managed to draw blood once before she vanished. Gloating had not gone how she'd thought it would."

"Does it ever?" I shrug. "So what do we do now?"

Sarah's jaw twitches. "You should go home."

"I already said I wasn't going to leave. Consider me warned and tell me what to do."

"He won't tell you where she is."

Sighing, I grab my clothes from where I discarded them on the back of the chair and shrug them on. "Do you want to be trapped here forever? Do you care that your life is over and you've been forced to serve this castle for the rest of time?"

"Of course I don't want to stay here forever," she snaps. "But I don't think anyone should die for my freedom."

"That's not your choice to make."

Her jaw tightens, lips thinning as she crosses her pale hands over her chest. I mimic her pose, foot tapping against the floor. The veins peeking out from under her bonnet along her temple pulse as she watches me. It won't change my mind.

"I can't make you do anything, but I'll tell you again that I don't think it's a good idea. I think the best thing for you would be to turn around and head back to where you came from. Going down this path will bring nothing but pain for anyone."

I give her a nod and run through the door, throwing it closed behind me while my breath turns shaky. Why couldn't she just be happy? Why couldn't she accept my sacrifice? And why does it have to sound like such a big sacrifice when she's talking about it?

Wandering through the hall, my mind on anything but my surroundings, I don't realize I've stumbled into Prometheus's quarters until I trip over the ripped-up rug. The damp smell from the prison room those girls were kept in permeates the space, chilling me in a single footstep. I should turn around. On a normal day I would turn around. But today doesn't feel so normal anymore.

Everywhere I look is a mess of ruin and decay. It's like staring at the photos of the abandoned homes in Chernobyl. The air hangs heavy as if waiting for a similar disaster.

Picking my way through a scattered mess of broken wood, I leave the foyer to his suite and enter more personal quarters. An enormous bed sits in the center wall of the room. The remains of thick four poster posts stand jagged at the corners of the bed, as though a giant wrenched them free and left the wicked splinters behind. Feathers lay discarded on the floor from a huge rip through the mattress.

The floor creaks under my feet. Startled I jump back into something very solid.

Heart beating fast in my chest, I turn on feet that feel like cement and look into a wide, thick chest. Arching my neck, I meet Prometheus' dark gaze. He expels a heavy breath, the air brushing over my face.

"What are you doing in here?"

Words freeze in my throat and I gape at him like a fish.

"Wren?"

"I-I'm sorry. I know you don't want me in here."

He runs a hand through his mane. We're almost close enough to touch, a thought that makes my pulse beat even faster.

"Wren," he starts then shakes his head and begins again. "I don't want anyone to see me like this. But that's not what I asked. What are you doing here?"

"I don't know. I was wandering . . . Sarah said some things . . . it doesn't matter. I should've left."

Prometheus grabs my chin, gently tilting it toward him. "What did Sarah say?"

"Well . . ." He doesn't know I've broken the curse and my tongue sticks to the roof of my mouth as I try to tell him. "I-I broke the curse."

His eyes widen, breath coming quicker. "What do you mean?"

"I went to check the door, to see if I could go home, and it opened. I mean it opened to the cave," the words spill out of my mouth now. "I can go home."

Releasing me, he steps back. "Oh."

"So I ran to tell Sarah and—"

"Are you leaving then?" He cuts me off. "Come to say goodbye?"

"What? I—"

"You figured out how to break it and that was enough? I wasn't enough?"

I can't read his dark eyes. His shoulders tense, hands curled into fists. "That's not what I said."

"You didn't have too." He turns away, spine straight with his back to me.

I want to lash out. His response feels like something my mom would do, but I hold myself back. Biting my tongue, I reach for him, cupping my hand around his giant fist. "I'm not leaving. That's the problem."

He jerks in surprise. "What do you mean?"

"Sarah's upset because I told her I planned to go after the sorceress."

His eyes widen.

"I wasn't going to leave you to the mercy of her curse."

"I'm going to have to agree with Sarah," Prometheus says, shoulders slumping.

He pauses and I pull my hand away, crossing my arms over my chest as I feel the burn of the promise of tears.

"I would never ask you to go after her—"

"But I—"

He holds up a hand to stop me. "I appreciate that you're willing, but Sarah was right. Going after her would be akin to suicide, and I'm sorry but I'm not going to part with you that way. I want to live down here forever, knowing that you are safe and living and growing old in the real world."

My bottom lip wobbles, vision blurring as tears push through.

"I'm so sorry, Wren," he whispers.

In an embarrassed huff, I push past him. Running from his rooms and through the empty hallway, I make for the safety of my room and slam the door closed. Breathing heavy, I jerkily brush aside the flow of tears making their way down my cheeks.

He can't do that to me. Anger and a sadness I don't understand battle for predominance in my emotions. My hands shake and I lean against the door.

It wasn't supposed to be like this.

Finding the way out wasn't supposed to leave me in a soggy heap in my room. What happened? Why didn't I just leave when I opened that door? Why couldn't I leave everyone here behind to the fate Prometheus might deserve?

I know what the problem is. Maybe I've always known a little what the problem is. I care about him.

Against all the odds. I've come to think of him, worry about him. Wish more for him. And maybe for me.

It doesn't matter now.

Shoving off the floor, I wrench open the door. Fine. If I'm not wanted here, then I'm not staying. Not for a second longer.

I run through the hallway and downstairs, following a path I could take in my sleep. The people on the main floor don't say anything as I pass but I feel their gaze on me. I'm taking their only hope of salvation with me as I go. Just like they wanted.

The kitchen is empty, and I'm grateful not to have any witnesses as I march through the cave door and down the stone steps.

The damp of the cave pushes into my bones and I welcome the discomfort. It's a relief to have the outside of me match the inside.

Darkness descends as the pantry door swings closed. I forgot how terrifying it was to come here and there's no ball of light to guide me this time. With a last glance toward the glowing outline of the door, I step into the pitch black.

Chapter Eight

I stumble through the dark, tripping on rocks and the uneven elevation. Walking like I'm blind, I hold my hands out in front of me, fingers twitching as I wait for the inevitable collision.

Leaving this way was rash, but I don't think I could find my way back to the stairs if I tried. I should've tried to find a torch or something first though. I'm nothing if not chronically underprepared.

Legs aching and knees burning from a few of my falls, I continue into the blackness. Despite not having even a hint of light, I can't stop myself from blinking and blinking, trying to see. I repeat the same process over and over, step step blink, step step blink. But nothing becomes any clearer. My fears from the first trip through this cave come back with a force. Will I die down here in my attempt to get home?

Home? Is that even where I'm going? Living with Mom and Bill isn't much better than any of my other options. The inhabitants of the castle didn't want me. What else could I do?

The wet lines from my tears chill my cheeks, but after what has to be hours of walking, the tears haven't stopped. It's stupid. I know it's stupid. But Prometheus' rejection hurts worse than the pain of leaving my home, of being with a mother who refuses to actually know me. She took off and forgot I was a real person. I didn't think Prometheus was like that. I thought he actually saw me. Actually cared about me. I opened up to him and I don't understand.

What did I do wrong?

Was there something I missed? Was he laughing at me this whole time? Laughing at the stupid girl who followed him around like a puppy from room to room. But there must have been something. I felt it. Didn't he?

The darkness around me matches the black layers of ink splashing through my mind, tainting my memories. Prometheus must have had a good laugh at me. No wonder he didn't want me to stay or help him. A joke loses funniness the more it has to be explained.

The toe of my sneaker catches onto a jagged edge of rock, and I tumble forward. My fingers slam against the solid wall of cave. In shock, my arms give out and my head slams into the wall. Head throbbing, I kneel with my cheek pressed against the cold stone of the cave. The tears I thought would never dry up have left wet stains against my face but in the face of real pain refuse to appear.

With a groan, I pull myself to my feet. Wary fingers trace the cave wall as I switch direction. If I'm lucky this is the narrow wall pass that I edged through on my way here. If not then I'm probably hopelessly lost in the absolute darkness of the cave.

Dry sobs wrack my chest, body shaking. Taking a deep breath, I will myself to move forward, force myself to keep walking. If I survived Prometheus and his curse, I will survive this.

The cave wall dips away from my fingers, and I take a step back to follow the change of direction. My chest loosens in relief as my hands trace a narrow passage between the cave walls. The narrow space is just as panic inducing as before, but I breathe easier this time knowing I'm in the right place. Without an injured ankle my progress should be a lot faster than before.

Wriggling through a particularly narrow space, sweat drips from my temple and splashes against an unwrapped cut. The salty burn is a welcome reminder of the real pain I've experienced instead of all the fake emotions I've subjected myself to.

I can't believe I ever thought he might care for me. I can't believe I let myself care about him. How could I want to be with a monster?

Breathing heavy, I pick up the pace. I'm ready to get out of here. I'll even do the extra school Mom wants if I need to. I just need to put all of this behind me.

Time loses meaning in the darkness as my body wearies. The cave opens up, my reaching fingers finding nothing but empty space to cling to. Good. I'm almost there.

Reckless in my readiness, I start running. My feet slap against the hard cave floor, the sound echoing through the empty space. The air gets drier, becoming much more like the desert above me.

Pausing to take a breath, a stitch growing in my side, I hear something ahead of me. At first I fear it's Prometheus somehow. That he got out of the castle and came after me. But the longer I listen, the less it sounds like him.

Lights flash ahead, searing my eyes after so long in the dark.

"Do you see that?"

I jerk forward, eyes narrowed as I do my best to see the men appearing in front of me.

"Yeah, that must be her."

"Wren, is that you? Wren?"

"It's," I clear my throat as the words are swallowed up in my parched mouth. "It's me."

The flashlights point toward the ground, allowing me a clear view of my rescuers. Two men in what appears to be full firefighter gear march across the cave floor to me. My knees give out in relief, head hanging heavy as they reach me.

"We're going to get you out of here. Just relax."

And I do.

I wake up in the hospital, fluorescent lights reflecting off sterile white walls. The smell of antiseptic washes over me as I shift in bed. The tubes stuck in my arm rustle against the paper sheets. Sitting up, I notice layers upon layers of bandages heaped upon my almost every inch of my skin. Flexing my arm, I notice the biggest wrapping around the area where Prometheus's stitches were. If I had any doubts that any of this was real, my wounds are telling another story.

"Glad to see you're awake." A nurse blusters into the room in light blue scrubs, a cheery smile painted on her round face. A cop follows closely behind her with a frown. "Would you mind if I took your vitals?"

"N-no," I manage before she yanks my arm out and slaps a blood pressure cuff on it, carefully avoiding the majority of my injuries. This must not be the first time she's worked with me.

"How long have I been sleeping?"

She glances up at me, stethoscope hanging from her ears. "Three days. You've obviously been through a lot." She makes a note on the file hanging from the end of my bed and stands straight. "I'll let your mother know you're up. Your family's been very worried about you."

"They're not my family." But the words are much less sullen than they would've been a few weeks ago.

"Before you do that, I have a few questions for her," the cop interjects, coming to stand at the end of my bed.

The nurse gives me a sad smile, brushing a few errant brown hairs behind her ear as she marches from the room.

"You've been missing a long time." He rests a hand on the plastic foot of the bed. "Care to explain where you've been?"

My mind whirls with a million different answers but none of them seem right. I shake my head.

"There's been a lot of worried people looking for you. We have to know where you've been so we can protect anyone else from doing the same thing."

Like it would even be possible. Without my magical firefly light, I wouldn't have even been able to find Prometheus.

"I was in the caves."

"We searched a lot of that area."

"I guess not all of it. I'm really sorry, I don't know what to tell you." The lies form and I can't keep them back. If I don't give this guy something, I'll never get him to leave. Normal people want normal answers. "I hit my head when I fell and I got disoriented and wandered around those caves until I found the way out again."

"How did you survive for so long down there by yourself?"

I wasn't by myself.

"There's some underground water down there. It provided everything I needed."

That seems to fit the bill. He nods and writes down what I said and gives me a sad smile. "I'm so sorry you had to go through that. We'll seal off that hole you fell in and make sure something like this doesn't happen again. Thank you for your cooperation. Now, let's get your family in here. They've been worried sick."

I lean against the bed, body nestled between tall plastic barriers on either side. Someone makes an announcement on the loudspeaker in the hall, but the words don't permeate the heavy wooden door cutting me off from the real world.

Three days. I've been sleeping for three days? I don't know what everyone thinks I went through, but I don't think it was three days in the hospital worth. Although, I can imagine the panic those men must have felt when they lifted me out of the that cave. Passing out probably didn't help.

The door creaks open and I tense, expecting Mom. But it's just the nurse again. She carries a plastic tray, silverware clattering on it as she sets it on a low table next to the bed.

"Thought you might be hungry." She slides the table over my lap and lifts the plastic cover off.

She's brought me some sort of meatloaf I think. At least that's what it closest resembles. I slide the plate away and grab the bowl of green jello from the side. Using a spoon, I scoop off the dollop of whip cream and pop it in my mouth. The fluffy sweetness makes me feel better than whatever they've been giving me through the IV. I close my eyes, a happy sound pressing against my chest.

"That's what I thought," the nurse says on her way out.

I dive into the rest of the jello and even manage most of the mashed potatoes before the door opens again. Keeping my gaze on my food, I listen to the patter of several different feet against the tile floor.

"Wren?"

It's Mom.

Glancing up, I try not to let my heart twist at the tears pooling in her eyes. I push the table away, giving her the room she wants to get closer.

She gives me a tight hug, pulling on the half a dozen tubes running from my arms. She squeezes me close to her chest and I can feel the shaking of her uneven breathing. Half expecting her to climb into bed with me, I'm pleasantly surprised when she lets me go and stays by my feet, her hand resting by my leg. Bill and Ruby stand next to her, Ruby looking much paler than I remember. She wrings her hands, everyone watching me in creepy silence.

"The policeman said you survived down there because you found an underground river. I can't imagine what would have happened if you hadn't. We were so worried. There were searches every day. I just knew you couldn't be dead," Mom starts, her mouth pulling into a crazed smile.

Ruby shifts on her feet, face pained. "I'm so sorry about what happened. I never should've let you go."

"It's not like I was asking your permission," I remind her with a smile.

"It doesn't matter. I knew it was dangerous and I could have said something. I could've prevented all of this."

Mom's face is tight as she turns toward Bill. "Want to give us a few minutes alone?"

"Of course."

Bill and Ruby shuffle from the room, Ruby giving me a last frantic glance before the door closes behind them. Mom turns to me, jaw so tight I can see the pulse points in her neck.

"Do you have any idea what you put us through?"

Of course. Of course this is how things would start. No profession of love or how much she missed me.

I clench my hands into fists as she crosses her arms.

"Nothing? Do you have any idea how your disappearance made me look?"

"Maybe next time I'll choose not to come back."

We stare at each other, her foot tapping against the floor as the veins in her temple grow. This was a mistake. If I couldn't stay with Prometheus, then I should have found another way. Coming here never should have been an option.

"I need you to rethink your tone."

I shake my head. "I told you before. I'm not living in your daydream with you. I wish I *had* run away. I wish leaving *had* been my decision. Instead it was all a beautiful accident."

"A beautiful accident?" Mom scoffs. "That's what you call being missing for months?" She stops as her breath catches. "I thought you were dead. Where is the beauty in that?"

"Let's face it, Mom. If I'd died, the only thing that would've mattered was your reputation as my mother, which I think we can both agree is not a title that you've earned. You don't get to abandon me for years and then decide you want to be my mother."

She pulls her chin up. "You have no idea what you're talking about."

I sit up further, cords tangling and paper sheets crinkling. "You have no idea what a nightmare it's been to try and survive your kind of mothering."

Mom steps back, hands clasped to her chest. Her face softens, mouth rounding into an *o*. I clamp my jaw shut. I won't take it back.

A long silence passes between us then Mom shakes her head. "I'll be here when they're ready to release you. You obviously need more time to heal."

Her heels click against the tile floor as she lets herself out without a single glance back.

The drugs they have me on drag me into an endless cycle of sleep and groggy wakefulness. In the days that pass, Mom doesn't come back. In the moments of lucidity, I have the wherewithal to be embarrassed by my behavior. Mom is selfish and flighty, but there's always been a part of her that's caring. Maybe it hasn't been in the way that I wanted. Maybe it would have been better if she'd ever listened to me, but this really was her final attempt at trying and I threw it away.

It doesn't take long for the fourth day of this cycle to come around, as I lay staring at the ceiling. The nurse blusters in, whistling to herself as she removes my almost full tray from breakfast.

She writes something down on my chart. "I think you're going to be released today."

"That's nice." I stare out the overcast window.

She follows my gaze. "I think it's going to rain, won't that be nice? We don't get a lot of storms out here."

I've got too much on my mind. I couldn't care less about the rain.

The nurse sets my tray down and reaches for my hand where it lies open on the bed. "I'm sure you've been through a lot. We have some great therapists in town if you wanted to talk about it. I'm sure it could help."

I don't respond and she picks my tray up and leaves the room, her cheerful tune left to die in here with me. I know I should've been nicer but I'm not here mentally. I'm wandering through those caves, wondering if there was something I could have done better.

The hair on the back of my neck prickles. A sensation passes over my skin like I'm being watched. I smooth down my neck but the sensation continues. Glancing around the room the feeling grows. Are there cameras in here?

Climbing out of bed, my legs go wobbly and I grab onto the IV stand. With its support to steady me, I wheel it around the room. Everything looks normal. White paint, white floors, a wall full of medical equipment. Nothing to say I'm being watched. But I can't shake the feeling.

The door opens and I almost shriek when the nurse comes back in. A small squeak gets out before I can stop it, and she stumbles back.

"I didn't expect you to be out of bed."

I step back as she comes in, stethoscope in hand. She leads me to the bed and I sit as she takes my vitals again.

"The doctor said you're free to go home today, but I told him you might want another night."

"Today works fine." Staying here longer won't change anything.

She nods but her mouth puckers into a worried frown. "If you ever need any help, you can come back to the hospital and ask for Janet. I'd be more than happy to assist you through this."

I shrug and she hands me a plastic bag. I pull out my clothes, the clean smell of detergent wafting through the room. The clothing is in tatters, more rips than clothes after my time in the woods. But it doesn't matter. Putting them on, my chest hurts as memories of Prometheus wash over me.

He came for me. He fought thorns and trees and wolves for me. What made him change his mind when we got back? Was it really because I broke the curse keeping me there?

Was I the only one who could help him break the curse? Or was he trying to protect me?

Now that I'm here in the real world, that seems like more of a possibility than before. I don't want to delude myself into thinking he cares about me, but I can't push past the thought that he does. That the idea of me facing the sorceress terrified him in a way thorns and wolves never could.

My tank top hangs off me, rips revealing the wrappings around my stomach. I'll need to take some time. I can't go after a curse-wielding sorceress with only a half functioning body. This gives me time to research. I'm not going in uneducated this time.

This time.

So I'm going then. I didn't consciously plan it, but it fits right in my chest. It doesn't matter if Prometheus gives up on me. I won't give up on him. The curse has connected us regardless of its hold on me now. I'm the only one who can end this.

I won't let them down.

True to her word, Mom waits for me outside the hospital. She doesn't get out of the car or even look at me as I get in, but I have bigger problems than her pouting.

Bleached roads and brown houses stretch out on either side. We pass a library a few blocks before we pass the high school. My gaze searches past the houses, past the field to where the entrance to Prometheus waits. Squinting, I can make out the faint orange of a few cones and what looks like caution tape. Like those weak measures would be enough to keep any curious kids out.

At least I know I can go back if I want to.

Pulling up to the house, it seems to sag in the desert heat. Everything looks sadder than it did when I left. Next to the opulence of Prometheus' castle I guess anything would seem tarnished. Mom gets out and even the shiny gleam on her black pumps does nothing to elevate our surroundings.

Mom turns to me, a worried frown pulling at the edges of her mouth, but I push past her into the house. A chill wave of air-conditioning blasts over me as I walk through the door. I peel off downstairs to my room, not waiting to give Mom the chance to corner me again.

Door closed safely behind me, I lean against the wall and take a deep breath.

Patience. I have to have patience this time.

No more foolhardy missions into the desert. It's lucky for me that Prometheus was down there. I'm sure a much worse fate than his curse would have found me if I'd continued roaming through the dark desert caves. Like snakes. Did I really not once think of snakes?

Footsteps plod down the stairs and past my room. Ruby?

I crack the door open to check, the blonde tail of Ruby's pony passing through the door to her room. On silent feet I follow after her, rapping my knuckles against her bedroom door.

There's a thunk against the floor before she opens the door just wide enough to see me through.

"Oh." She pulls the door open. "I didn't expect it to be you."

"Want to talk?"

A plan is only barely forming as she ushers me in. Her room is the exact match to mine, except for the cheerful posters and framed pictures of friends lining the walls. Ruby plops on the bed and motions for me to sit next to her. She wrings her hands together, unable to meet my eyes.

"I'm really sorry about what happened. I never should've waited to get you help. You can't imagine all the guilt I've had, thinking you were dead all this time." The words jumble into each other, fighting to get out as the beginnings of tears build in her eyes.

"Hey." I hold my hand up to stop her. "It's not your fault, and that's not why I'm here. I don't blame you at all. I wanted to go down there and nothing you said would've changed that."

"But I waited a whole day before I got help."

My eyes widen and I want to clap her on the back. I can't believe she was able to hold out that long. I've had her pegged for being in her dad's back pocket, but I've been wrong.

"That's the most incredible thing I've ever heard you say." I don't know whether to be mad or amazed. If she'd gotten help right away maybe I wouldn't be stuck with the responsibility of breaking Prometheus's curse. But she listened to me, which I didn't expect her to do and now I can really help him.

I decide to push back the annoyance that she could have helped me avoid all of this. It's worked out for the best. I wouldn't change it.

Ruby meets my gaze, her eyes red rimmed. "What do you mean?"

"I thought you'd have run for help the minute you couldn't see me anymore."

"It crossed my mind." She grins, her hands slowing in her lap. "But I didn't want you to think I was a loser."

"You actually care what I think?"

"Of course. We're going to be sisters. I've never had one before so I didn't know what to do, but then your mom talked so much about you—"

"How truthful was she?"

Ruby gives me a wry smile. "Not very, but you were better than what I was hoping for."

"Are you serious? I'm so. . ." I gesture at my layers of black. "And you're kinda not."

"You think I want to stay like this in this town forever?" Her eyes shine as she stares past me. "As soon as I graduate, I'm getting out of here. I might even try New York. If you didn't mind of course."

I snap the bracelets on my wrist. "This is not how I thought things would go."

"Why *are* you here?"

Sighing, I lean against the wall. "I was hoping to get some help actually."

"More help? The last time I helped you, you went missing for months. I'm not doing that again. Why don't you relax and keep recovering before you get any more crazy ideas."

"It's not like that this time."

"Oh yeah?"

I try to ignore the skepticism on her face. "Yeah. I had a few questions about what happened during that flood you said buried the town."

"Oh, that?" She climbs off the bed. "I've got a book around her somewhere. Dad got it for me for Christmas one year, wanted to encourage my town pride or something stupid like that."

Pulling a box out of the bed, she rumbles through piles of books and other odds and ends. At one point a stuffed Barney is unearthed before she shoves it under the bed again.

Cheeks pink, she holds out a hardcover book. "This should help."

I thumb through the table of contents. The only chapter that jumps out at me is ominously labeled "The Flood." Slamming the book closed, I try to ignore the rapid beating of my heart.

"Thanks."

Ruby watches, chin resting on her fist as I stumble out the door and back into my room.

It's stupid. I know it's stupid, but when I flip open the chapter and stare at the house featured on the page, my chest fills with a million butterflies. It's his house. Well, castle. The caption under the black and white photo simply says: Calderon Castle, one of the many lost gems of Greendale.

Calderon. The name isn't familiar, but there's no mistaking the castle. Even if it didn't look familiar, I'd assume it was his. How many castles could they possibly have out here? I feel safe betting this is the only one.

Scanning the page, his name jumps out at me. It's in another caption, this one under a picture of two men. Richard Calderon and his son, Prometheus. Peering at the glossy photo, I don't know why I didn't notice it first. It's so similar to the one I saw at the castle. Only in this one he's smiling. His hat is off, revealing loose brown curls. My fingers itch to touch them, run through them and . . .

I stop myself.

This isn't what I should be focusing on. It shouldn't matter to me what he looked like before. I shouldn't care about his strong jaw, the slight curve to his lips.

I'm going to break the curse on them. That's it. There's nothing else. There's no other reason for me to do this but to help the others.

The flood, the flood. I glance over the chapter, looking for anything that could give me a clue what to do. But there's a paragraph on Prometheus and I can't help reading it.

Richard Calderon, once a titan of the town, had been missing for several years before the flood took place. His son, Prometheus, had been seen a few times, but even the house itself became hard to find in the years before the flood. Prometheus had been a fixture of the town's limited nightlife, often joining the ranch hands in games and dancing at the end of the day. With a future that should have been as bright as his father's, with acceptance to a college in England the fall after the flood, it was a tragic loss to lose this influential family.

So, Ruby was right. Although their disappearance was being blamed on the flood, the castle disappeared long before that.

Looking back at the picture, I pause over what he was like before the curse. How did he end up like the beast I know now? How did he end up cursed?

I linger over the mention of his future. He was going to college, he had everything going for him before he was banished to live beneath the earth as a monster, a beast. He had everything going for him.

Setting the book aside, I chew my bottom lip. Should I take the opportunity he's given me? Should I continue on in my life and forget about him? He's been down there for so long, maybe the idea of being free isn't something he even thinks about anymore.

I push the thought away as soon as it enters my mind. No matter how much time passed, he'd never get used to living that way. He put up a good front, but his room revealed so much of his pain.

He'd never forget his curse. Never forget what he once was.

So I can't either.

It's crazy. Insane. I shouldn't be willing to risk my life for him. I just got out of there. I shouldn't be trying to figure anything out. I shouldn't be trying to find the sorceress. The Wren of a few months ago definitely wouldn't. But something changed down in those caves,

I let him in, and I can't forget that. I let myself care about him. I haven't done that in so long. I stopped pretending to be tough and let him see me.

I can't leave him there. I can't abandon him to his fate.

Resisting the temptation to rip his picture from the book, I flip through the rest of the chapter. Nothing particularly important is highlighted. There's no mention of what may have caused the flood. Not even a freak storm or heavy rain during the dry season. Quotes taken from historical journals said it came all at once, a wall of water and mud and debris that buried the town without warning.

I turn to the next chapter, skimming over the town's history of cattle ranching, when I stop short. A massive flood that came out of nowhere and removed Prometheus from history. Could that be the clue I'm looking for? How often does a big flood rip through the desert? I thought the whole point of the desert was that it was dry.

Moving with purpose, I pound on Ruby's door. She opens it without the earlier timidity, but her eyes still go wide.

"Did you finish the book already?"

"No, I need to look at the town's weather history." Pushing into her room, I don't wait for her to get up.

A small laptop sits on her nightstand and I scoop it up. Sitting on her bed, I pull up Google and start searching.

"Next time you could just ask." Her mouth pulls into a scowl as she sits next to me.

"Sorry. I think I figured something out."

I type in "Greendale climate history." Only a few pages come up but that's okay. I'll only need one.

The first link shows almost nothing, just the last few years of temperature. Average highs and lows in each season. Not what I'm looking for.

"So you wanted to know about the flood and now you're looking at the history of the weather. Do you not expect me to see something weird in that? You know in terms of your disappearance and everything?"

"Would it matter if I said they weren't related?"

"I wouldn't believe you for a second."

"How about half a second?" I wheedle.

She braces a hand on her hip. "Spit it out."

"I'm trying to find out more about what happened to Calderon Castle."

"The book I gave you said exactly what happened," she sighs.

I close the laptop, counting to three to let my patience catch up with my excitement. "It said a flood covered it. Don't you think there's something weird about the flood?"

"Floods happen in the desert when we get rain. That's just a fact of life."

"But had it been raining? Because the book said it hadn't been."

Ruby opens her mouth to respond then closes it. Thinking over what I said. "I've never heard anyone talk about what the weather was like that year."

"Isn't that weird? Shouldn't they say it rained so much it flooded. But it wasn't raining."

She wrinkles her nose. "Why's it so important to you?"

I don't know what to tell her. Why is it important? How will figuring this out break the curse on Prometheus?

"I want to find out what happened."

Ruby sighs again, running her fingers through the end of her ponytail. "You'd probably have better luck at the library."

My shoulders sag in relief. I don't think I could have handled too much prodding. There's too much I don't understand myself.

Slipping off the bed, I leave the laptop behind. "I'd better get going then."

"Like I'm letting you out of my sight," she laughs. "Plus, the library's closed now. You'll have to wait until the morning."

"Can I borrow this then?" I gesture to the laptop.

Ruby tilts her head to the side. "I was going to work on some homework, but I guess that'd be okay."

"Thanks."

I grab the laptop and head back to my room.

"Just wait for me, okay?" Ruby hangs out the door to her room.

"Sure."

Losing her when the time comes will be harder than I expected. I'm not letting her get pulled into the curse with me.

Chapter Nine

※◆◯◆※

Waiting for Ruby tests my patience when it's 11 and she's not up yet. If she hadn't made me promise to wait, I would've been long gone.

Eating a Pop-Tart, I wander through the yard, looking for the bike I stole. Maybe when all this is over I can try and return it.

"It's not here," Ruby says as she comes out the front door, slinging on a backpack. "You left it at the hole and I never thought about bringing it back. I don't think your mom would've let it sit in her yard for so long anyway."

"You're probably right."

Heaven forbid a rusty bike ruin her pristine lawn.

"So, we're on foot then?"

Ruby nods, adjusting her backpack straps.

Silence stretches out between us as we start walking. The desert sun beats down, burning the parts of my neck exposed by my ponytail.

I've been gone long enough that my pale brown roots peak out from the black hair dye. Maybe I can pick up more while we're out. I wouldn't want the sorceress to be disappointed in my true color. I wonder what Prometheus would think of it.

"So . . . where were you all this time?" Ruby asks as we pass the school.

I shrug.

"You'll have to tell someone eventually. They've been talking about filling in the caves. They're worried the whole town will collapse

114

in if there's a network down there big enough for you to be lost for months."

I stop short. "Who's saying that?"

"The mayor, the police. I don't know, people in charge."

My blood runs cold. I don't want anyone else discovering Prometheus.

"I already talked to the cop at the hospital."

"Did he assume the caves are the issue?"

I chew my bottom lip.

"The caves *are* why you were stuck down there, right?"

I shove my hands into my jean pockets, releasing a sigh. "I wouldn't say the caves are the reason I was down there for so long."

"What *is* then?"

Ruby scrutinizes me as I keep my gaze on the sidewalk in front of us. I'm not ready to talk about it. I don't want to talk about it. Prometheus is my secret to keep.

"This isn't going to go away. Decisions will be made regardless of what you do."

"How can I keep them out of the caves?" The question escapes, leaving me breathless. Maybe I shouldn't have said anything about the caves to that cop. Now things will only get worse.

Ruby shrugs. "I don't know that you can. You got lost in the caves, you were found in the caves. It's pretty much a closed case."

"Then why does it matter if I say anything more?"

"I don't think it would hurt."

She thinks that because she knows nothing about it. I'm not subjecting myself to the world's ridicule. If police get down there and find him . . . but if I try to tell them what's down there . . . no one will believe me. He doesn't need to be laughed at and neither do I. It's bad enough that women were drawn to him like I was, just for them to avoid him and proclaim him a monster. No matter how he looks, he'll never be a monster.

The library looms to the left of us, and our shoes clap against the cement steps as we go in. The musty smell of books permeates the semi-lighted room. The librarian looks over her glasses at us as we walk in, then returns to reading the book spread open on the table.

Ruby leads me through the tall shelves toward the back of the room. My sense of claustrophobia grows as the shelves grow bigger and the light gets dimmer.

"Shouldn't they invest in some more lights?" I ask Ruby as I rub away the goose bumps growing on my arms.

"This isn't a well-used section. I doubt they've gotten many complaints."

The back wall has a half table pushed up against it and Ruby throws her backpack down before heading back into the shelves. I follow after her, trying to focus on the words on the spines of the books we pass.

"Someone wrote a book about the weather patterns in Greendale?"

"It's more of a local interest piece than a book. There it is."

Ruby groans as she pulls on the drawer of a filing cabinet pressed against the shelves. It pops open with the shriek of metal grating against itself and reveals a jumble of loose papers.

She hums to herself as she flips through the mess of paper. The papers pass through her hands so quickly, I don't know how she manages to read anything. Especially considering they all look to be handwritten in looping cursive.

"Have you and Bill always lived here?" I need some sort of conversation to distract me from what we're doing. What I'm doing.

"Yeah, my family's basically always lived here, almost since it was founded."

"You have a lot of extended family around here then?"

"Nope." She pulls out a long sheet from the drawer. "We're the last ones left."

I'm distracted from further questioning when she holds up her find.

"I think this may answer some of your questions."

It's an extra-long sheet of paper that looks like it came from an old fax machine with its hole punched edges. The top of the sheet says "A Study of Greendale: Weather." I take it from her gently, resisting the urge to rip it from her hands like I want to.

"You're right though, this probably was a waste of time. You might be the first person to ever come looking for information like this on our little town."

We take it over to the table, laying it out to see the full length of information. Ruby scans it faster than I can, her forehead wrinkling.

"I don't think this will help us figure out why there was a flood that year. The whole thing basically says we're a pretty temperate desert. Nothing crazy or usual ever happens."

"Except the year of the flood."

"Except that."

We comb through the shelves until the ends of my fingers are covered in paper cuts. There's nothing in here saying anything that would explain the flood. These reports don't even mention the flood. Aside from Ruby's book, it's like the flood never happened. Which is weird.

Why wouldn't any of these scientists be interested in the year something went wrong? Isn't that usually what gets them going?

Ruby plops down on one of the two chairs at our covered table. "I don't think we're going to find anything in here."

"How can there be so much garbage here about average years and nothing on that?"

Ruby shrugs. "I don't know what to tell you. If there's anything on the flood, it's just not here."

I sigh, falling into the chair next to her. "I really wanted to find something."

"I wanted you to too. But I can't make books appear out of nowhere."

"Of course. Thanks for your help today."

Ruby leans forward. "Does that mean we can go home and eat then?"

"Sure." I laugh. "Hanging around here any longer might just drive me crazy."

I gather up the books we've pulled out in a stack, moving to put them away.

"Don't worry about it." Ruby puts out an arm to stop me. "Putting these away will finally give that old woman something to do."

We leave the shelves and pass the librarian who eyes us with a frown. Bursting into uncontrollable giggles, we stumble out of the library and into the glaring afternoon sun. Ruby links an arm through mine as she tries to get her breath back and I glance at where we touch, resisting the desire to rip my arm away.

Ruby catches me looking and pulls her arm out of mine. "Sorry. We were just—it seemed like we were friends for a minute."

"Yeah. It did." I sigh. "I'm not a very touchy person."

She crosses her arms over her chest, a finger pointing at me. "You're actively trying to push people away."

I try to ignore the ache her words bring to my chest. "At least I don't look like I'm running for class president every moment of my life."

"I know you don't really mean that," Ruby says with a frown.

"I don't know what you want from me."

She runs her hands through the blonde tresses falling from her ponytail. "I'm trying to be your friend. Why won't you let me?"

"I don't need any friends."

Ruby's face crumbles and I pick up my pace, leaving her behind me as I speed toward the house.

I don't need her. Why would I? I have friends back home. And I thought I had a friend in Prometheus and Sarah. I don't need any more surprises like that.

Throwing open the door and tromping down the stairs, I make a break for my room. The house is still around me; Mom must not be home.

It's only after I'm safe behind the door that I realize there's nothing left for me to do. I have no idea what to do next or how to find the sorceress. I've hit a complete dead end. I never even got her name. If I at least had that I could do a Google search or something. As it stands now I have literally nothing to go on. It was foolish to think researching a freak flood would lead me toward action.

My heart aches as I stare at my empty room, the wide-open suitcase and Ruby's book the only hint of personality. I want to go home.

Hot tears build in my eyes, leaving burning tracks down my cheeks. I wrap my arms around myself, trying to contain the expanding emotions in my chest. The late afternoon light falls in a pale arc around me. Wiping away the tears with my palm, I attempt to regain control.

This can't be it. It can't end this way. I made a promise to myself. I have to keep it somehow. Somehow.

That's the thing isn't it? I have literally nothing to go on. I have no information and I'm trying to defeat a sorceress that took down Prometheus when he was a beast. Am I insane? I'd have to be to even try it.

But I have nothing to go on. Absolutely nothing.

I slip to the floor and wrap my arms around my legs, curling into a fetal position as I try to think. But the more I think about it, the more I feel like I only have one option. If I'm going to figure anything out, I'm going to need to go back. Prometheus is the only one who would know anything about the sorceress. The history books here can't help me with mythical beings.

But how will I leave without making everyone panic again?

Could I leave a note saying I was running away? The town couldn't blame the caves at that point, right? I don't want anyone down there looking for me. That's the last thing Prometheus needs.

Grabbing the canvas messenger bag from my suitcase, I load it with another set of clothes. As I head for the door, my gaze lands on Ruby's book and I grab that too, just in case. Sneaking upstairs, I dig through the kitchen cabinets. I'm not wandering around down there without any supplies this time.

There's an emergency flashlight under the sink that I throw into my bag along with a few bottles of water from the fridge and some granola bars. I head for the garage, hoping to raid Bill's camping gear again. The tub Ruby pulled the rope from last time is gone. I wonder how much trouble she got into with all of that.

Body taut as I half expect Mom to get home and find me raiding their things, I read the labels on the plastic containers lining the wall. Nothing screams "rope" but one on the end does say "emergency ladder." Well, this feels like an emergency to me. And there's no way I'll be able to get anywhere with the wraps the hospital left me in without Bill's stuff.

I pull the tub down and crack it open. A long length of chain with metal bars sits in the bottom. Grabbing a piece, I pull it out. Sighing in relief, I find hooks on the end. I'm sure they're supposed to go on a windowsill, but they're going into the ground by my hole today.

The rope is too big to fit in my bag. Really it's too big to bring, but I'm not going to free fall to the cave floor.

There's a notepad magnetized to the stand-up freezer in the garage. Heaving the container back to the floor. I grab the pen lying on top of the notepad and start on my runaway note.

Words don't come easy. I know my leaving again will hurt someone, probably Ruby more than anyone else. But I can't stay and not try to save Prometheus. It doesn't matter what he wanted, it's my life to gamble with and I know this is the right choice for me. I have to save them.

It's this determination that brings the words out. They're lies, but I have to lie for this to work. I tell Mom I couldn't handle it here. I tell her that I need to go home to deal with my injuries. That I needed my Aunt to get through the trauma of being lost in the caves. Let them look for me in New York. Don't look in the caves this time. Please don't look in the caves.

Ripping the paper off the notepad, I shrug off my bag, leave it with the ladder, and take the note upstairs. I place it on the kitchen island. It seems a pretty safe bet that she'll find it there.

Glancing around the home my mother has made, my gaze lingering on a family picture on the fridge, I almost feel bad about leaving. I may not agree with her, but she's made a life for herself here. A fake life as I'm sure Bill knows nothing about her real past, but that's what she wanted. She's gotten everything she wanted.

I grab a cookie out of the jar and munch on it as I sling my backpack on and grab the ladder again. Getting it all the way to the hole may kill me, but it's all I have.

I'm not even halfway down the street when I feel a bruise forming on my hip under the lip of the tub. I move it to the other side but I know it won't matter. I'm going to be a mess by the time I find Prometheus.

Will he be excited to see me? Or will he hate that I've come back.

I hate this. I hate that I think about him so much. I hate that I care what he thinks. He's the last person I should care about. Yet here I am, lugging what has to be a fifty-pound metal ladder through the desert to lower myself into a "dangerous" hole to wander through the dark in the hopes that I *might* find his castle. But I need more information to find the sorceress. I can't do this alone.

But what if I can't find it? With the note I left, I'm sure to die down there.

I guess it's a risk I have to take. I can't move forward until the curse is broken. I want to get back to arguing about college or high school. And I want Prometheus to be with me.

Sweat drips down my back, puddling where my shoulder strap rests. My breathing rasps in my dry throat as I lug the heavy tote the rest of the way to the dry riverbed. I glance back once to the main road and see Ruby walking home, feet shuffling in slow steps. She looks up and we make eye contact before she turns and faces the road in front of her.

Did she really see me? Did she see someone and not know who it was from so far away? I can only hope. I don't need Ruby tagging along again.

The sun is already sinking behind the dry brown mountains when I get to the hole. A bag of cement leans against the caution cone. Looks like they're really going to fill this in. That's one way to protect the town's teenagers.

Pulling the ladder out of the plastic container, a few stray rocks bounce along the ground and down into the hole. It's a long pause before I hear the distant clink of them hitting the ground. I swallow a shaky breath. The ladder isn't going to reach to the bottom. It's going to be just like the rope again. Only this time the injury could be so much worse.

Gruesome images flit through my mind of lying at the bottom of the cave floor with shards of bone sticking through the skin of my legs.

Good thing I do everything without thinking it through.

I let out a long breath and hook the ends of the emergency ladder into the dense earth outside the riverbed's immediate vicinity. Several feet of rungs lay useless against the ground, but I'd rather come up short in the name of safety than fall to my death because the ground gave way.

The rest of the ladder clatters through the hole.

I rest my feet on the first rung, grabbing the ladder with sweating hands as I lower myself into the darkness of the cave. I should've bought one of those helmets with the lights in them before I left. At least that way I would've known what I was lowering myself into. For all I know, the cave could've changed drastically since I left it five days ago.

I count the rungs as I climb down. It's the only way to keep myself from thinking about the distance I'm crossing and the man who probably won't be happy to see me.

The ladder ends when I count fifty. Without a flashlight I have no way of knowing how far down I still have to go. I try to dig the flashlight out of my bag, but it makes the unsecured ladder swing back and forth in a way that leaves me too sick to do any productive searching. With the smallest breath of a prayer, I climb down until I'm hanging suspended, hands clinging to the last rung as my legs dangle beneath me.

I almost can't breathe at all as I hang there. I try counting again but the panic in my chest keeps it from being productive. There's nothing left to do but fall.

Blackness surrounds me as I come to. I must have fainted when I let go of the rung. Running my hands over my body, I'm relieved to find everything in its place. At least nothing is sticking out where it shouldn't. That's something.

My bag stayed around my shoulders during the fall, so before I move, I take the time to dig out the flashlight I packed. My hand finds the cool metal handle and I flick it on while it's still in the bag to get my eyes used to the change in the light. The bag glows orange in the darkness. I grab one of the water bottles and take a swig, my mouth too dry to even think of screaming for help if something goes wrong.

I swap the water bottle for the flashlight, swinging its beam over the all too familiar cave walls. Flashing it upwards, I let out a relieved laugh when I see the ladder hanging just a few feet higher than me. It must have been just enough of a fall for me to fear hitting the bottom before I actually did. That explains the lack of injuries this time.

Clambering to my feet, I rest my hand against the cool wall of the cave. Like last time, I run my hands along the wall as I walk. The feel of the wall helps to calm my erratic nerves.

Without an ankle injury, the trip seems to go much faster, although my side pulls with every breath. At least it doesn't keep me from walking. Maybe I'm so focused on my destination this time that I'm able to move so much faster. Before, I had nothing to move towards. Today, I have him.

My legs move faster and faster, breath becoming unsteady as I go. I have to get there. I have to find out more. And this time I won't take no for an answer.

The ball of light that lead me before never shows up and I'm grateful for the flashlight. Without it I'd never be able to pick my way through the wall illusion that held me up before. Now that I know it's here, when I get to the solid wall, I run my light up and down it, looking for the irregularities that could hint at where I can pass through. Even so, it takes me five minutes and several muttered curses before I find the narrow pass.

Pointing the flashlight ahead of me, I sidle between the cave walls. I close my eyes to avoid looking at the long expense of narrow cave. Counting my breaths does a little better this time as I attempt to keep my claustrophobia at bay. Every expanded breath causes my chest to push against the unforgiving wall and I have to start counting all over again.

But I have to do it. There's no way around this trip. Without Prometheus's help, I'll never find the sorceress. I have nowhere to even start looking. I have to do this.

And that's what I repeat to myself, over and over again. I have to do this. I have to do this. I have to do this.

My mantra carries me through the long dark tunnel. I turn off the flashlight and keep my eyes closed to avoid dirt falling in them. Plus, now I can't see how tight the space is. If I can't see it then I can ignore it pressing in on me.

As the space grows larger and my back isn't pinned by cave wall anymore, I dare peeking an eye open. The flashlight's beam falls into empty space. I'm almost there. Brushing the cool sweat off my forehead, I adjust my messenger bag and keep walking.

I know I'm really going to make it now. There's none of the fear of falling or getting lost in the caves, but fear finds a way in anyway. What will Prometheus think of my return? I'm so close to him now but I wish I had further to go.

The ache in my legs grows. I'm sure I've been walking for hours. Prometheus's castle wasn't built a convenient distance from town.

I throw light around the cave, revealing the stone steps leading to the pantry door in my final sweep with the flashlight. This is it then. Reaching the first step, my courage fails. I sink onto it, letting my knees hit the floor as I twist to sit on the step. I can't go in there and face Prometheus' rejection again. What if I walk through the door and he tells me to go home?

Maybe I should've listened to him and stayed home, forgotten about the curse and the subterranean castle.

A soft knock echoes through the cave from the pantry door. Whipping around to see the haloed outline of the door, two shadows blur at the bottom. Someone is standing on the other side.

"Wren? Is that you?"

My legs shake as I clamber to my feet. "Prometheus?"

"You came back." The relief is clear in his voice, and my doubts flitter away. "You actually came back."

Stumbling up the rest of the steps, I throw the door open. He kneels on the other side and I fling myself at him, wrapping my arms around his warm neck. His body stiffens for a moment before he embraces me.

"I didn't think I'd ever see you again," he whispers into my hair.

"And whose fault is that?"

He jerks far enough away from me to see my face. "I was trying to protect you."

"I don't need protecting."

"Just because you don't need it doesn't mean I don't want to give it to you."

I rest my palm against his cheek. "I want to help you this time."

"Are you giving me a choice?"

"Of course not."

He smiles. Releasing me, he stands, placing his hand at the small of my back as he leads me into the kitchen. A mug of steaming cocoa sits on the counter by a plate of pastries. I need no further coaxing. I grab a croissant from the plate, tearing it open and munching through its delicious layers.

"I thought you might be hungry when you got here."

"You knew I was coming?" I put down the mug.

He shuffles and doesn't meet my eye. "I might have been watching you."

"Watching me? How could you possibly do that?"

He glances up, mouth thinned in guilt. "I have ways of seeing things. Like I saw you were in trouble in the woods, I knew you were coming here."

"That doesn't make any sense." I shake my head. "What are you trying to say?"

"I have a . . . mirror."

"A mirror?"

"It lets me look in on people."

I brace my hand against my hip. "What kind of people?"

"Anyone." He shrugs. "If I know their name, I can search for them."

"Do you use it often?"

"I hadn't used it in over fifty years before you came."

My eyes narrow. "How long have you been watching me?"

"That day you were in trouble and every day since you left."

I step backwards, my back hitting the counter. "You've watched me every day?"

"I wanted to make sure you were safe."

I peer at him but he still doesn't meet my gaze. "You're the one that sent me away."

"And I had to make sure you didn't go after her like you said you wanted."

I pick the mug back up and take a long sip. "I'm still going to go after her. I'm not letting you live this way for another however many years. This ends now."

"I know you feel that way now—"

"Nothing you can say will change my mind."

He sighs. "I know. Remember how I said I was watching you? I know."

"Will you help me then?"

Prometheus reaches for me but stops himself before he can actually touch me. "I wish you would change your mind. I wish you would stay safe. But I won't let you face her unprepared."

"I'm glad to hear it." I beam at him. "I didn't know how I would do it without you."

He grimaces. "I don't think I'll be much help honestly."

I grab a cream cheese Danish, talking through a big bite. "You know more about what to do than I do. I don't even know her name."

"Maybe I don't either. I've never been able to find her in the mirror."

"Did she give you the mirror?"

He nods.

"Then it probably wouldn't work on her. I doubt she'd give you something you could use to spy on her with."

He leans against the island and I finish off the hot chocolate.

"Why *would* she give you something like that? I didn't think people mad enough to curse someone would be willing to give them a gift."

His hand forms a fist where it rests against the counter. "It's not a gift. Not like you're thinking. How much joy can an object bring you that lets you see others live without being able to live yourself?"

"Is that what it was like when you were watching me?"

"Worse." He loosens his fist and lets his arm fall to his side. "I shouldn't have asked you to leave."

"I understand why you did." It's a half truth, the lie concealing my insecurities.

Prometheus shakes his head, staring at me with his molten chocolate eyes. "It was selfish of me to ask you to leave, but it would have been more selfish to ask you to stay."

I lean closer to him. "I want you to be selfish with me."

We're close enough to touch and my lips part in anticipation.

"Master?"

Sarah sweeps into the room and we spring apart.

"What?" Prometheus barks, his voice like gravel.

Her body stiffens at his tone. Glancing up, she sees me for the first time. "Wren?"

"In the flesh."

Sarah's eyes widen. "What are you doing here?"

"Sarah," his tone is stern enough that even I jump back.

"I thought she left." She wrings her hands together. "I never expected to see you again."

"That's no reason to be rude."

"It's all right." I place a hand on his arm and his body softens. "I couldn't stay away it seems."

Sarah's face is a war of emotions. There's some relief mixing with sadness and anger. We stare at each other and I do my best to keep a pleasant smile on my face despite how sad her reaction makes me.

"What did you need, Sarah?"

She jerks as she turns from me to Prometheus. "I-I don't remember."

"Next time remember the message."

"Of course, master."

"You may leave now."

Sarah bobs a small curtsey and leaves the kitchen shaking her head.

I turn to Prometheus with a frown. "She's not happy to see me."

He sighs. "If you're looking for an explanation of her emotions, I'm not going to be able to help you with that. I don't know why she does what she does."

"I didn't think she'd be upset with me." Tears threaten to bubble to the surface. I hate feeling this way, but her rejection is part of what I had been so afraid of.

"I don't want you to think about her if it's going to make you upset. I'm more than happy you're here."

"Really?"

"Of course."

My hand is still pressed against his arm, warming from the touch. He's right, I don't need to think about Sarah. The person I care about the most is happy I'm here.

Prometheus stands straight and links my arm through his. "Would you like to rest?"

"That could be good."

He gives me a smile and his elongated teeth should make it less charming, but they don't. At some point I stopped seeing him as a monster. He's Prometheus, my friend.

As we leave the kitchen everything around us looks the same as it did when we left. I don't know what I was expecting, but it's shocking to see how my absence changed nothing. There's still a flurry of servants working in the myriad of rooms and the floor shines as much as it did the second day I got here.

"It seemed so empty without you," Prometheus says, his eyes seeing something much different than mine as he glances around the corridor.

"Are you sure? I've never seen it so full," I tease.

He shakes his head. "They could never compare to being with you."

My cheeks warm and I turn my face away.

I expect more people to take notice of me like Sarah did, but no one even looks up from their tasks. It's like I've become invisible. The sensation prickles against my skin.

Prometheus leads me up the stairs and to my room. Everything here looks the same as before too. The comforter on the bed is maybe a little smoother than before, but that's probably because no one's laid on it for a while.

"Everything should be as you left it."

"I can see that."

He gives me a side smile. "I wanted it to feel like home here if you ever decided to come back."

"You've succeeded," my voice is breathless, butterflies bubbling through my stomach.

"I'll see you for breakfast?"

"Of course."

He closes the door behind him and I flop onto the immaculate bed. It doesn't seem possible that all this is true. That I'm really here. And Prometheus was happy to see me. I can't keep from smiling and I pull my shirt over my mouth.

With the stress of what might have happened draining out of my body, I sink further into the mattress. It's been a long day, one that I can't believe started at my mother's house. Did I really do that? Pack a runaway bag and head into the mystery of the caves?

What is my mother thinking right now? Is she worried about me? Or just annoyed that I've tarnished her reputation even more with my latest runaway episode? I miss how things used to be.

It was never like this when I was little. Mom was home more. Sometimes when I came home from school, she'd have warm cookies waiting. We'd sit at the kitchen table and talk about our days. When Grandma died it was like a switch flipped. She'd be gone for days at a time with no note or anything to tell me where she might have gone. I started spending less and less time at home, preferring to be at Aunt

Cora's. But if Mom came home and I wasn't there, crap would really hit the fan.

Leaving to be with Bill felt like the best possible thing for her to do. When she told me I could live at Aunt Cora's, I had a physical release of pressure. Finally, things could be normal, stable.

Too bad she changed her mind when she got settled in and wanted to bring me with her.

I don't know what she told Bill about me, about our life together. I can't imagine it was the truth. What man would want a deadbeat mother? Whatever.

Without bothering to get undressed, I slip under the covers. The warmth makes my muscles feel like melting. Protected by the safety of Prometheus, I can finally relax.

Chapter Ten

Sarah bustles into the room without knocking, stoking up the fire in the grate. She gives me a look down her nose as she waits for me to surface from the layer of blankets I've cocooned myself in.

"Good morning, miss."

I blink blearily at her.

"Breakfast will be served promptly. A robe has been provided for your use while you're here."

"Sarah? What happened?"

She gives a small curtsey and leaves the room.

I sit up, rubbing my eyes as I try to figure out what just happened. Sarah's never talked to me like that before. What did I do to cause such a separation between us?

Slipping the robe on despite the fact that I'm fully clothed, I stumble out of bed. My muscles feel stretched out from all the work I put them through yesterday and everything moves a little differently than I expect it to. Still, I move much faster down to breakfast than I did my first morning here.

Prometheus has taken up his customary spot at the head of the table, a book open next to his plate. He looks up as the floor squeaks under me, a smile growing across his face.

"Did you sleep well last night?"

"Like a baby." I smile back, taking the seat to the right of him and piling it high with scrambled eggs and hash browns.

"Glad to see your appetite hasn't been affected by your journey."

"If anything, it's grown," I say through a mouthful of eggs. "But the food has definitely gotten better since that first day."

"I'm glad we were able to find something that satisfies your tastes."

He smiles at me as I lay my fork down. "All I ask for is something recognizable. I'm not that picky."

I take a big swig from my water glass and catch him staring at me. I raise my brow at him, but he just continues smiling.

"What?"

"It's good to have you back. You have no idea how much you coming back has meant to me."

"Oh yeah?"

His dark eyes smolder as he watches my face. "You are incredible."

I wrinkle my nose and he chuckles.

"I mean it. I know of no one else who would trade freedom for my imprisonment."

"But I'm not going to be imprisoned, remember? I'm here to free you."

The softness in his face vanishes. "I'd hoped you'd changed your mind."

I shrug my shoulders. "No such luck I guess."

"I guess not."

He reaches toward me across the table, hesitating when our hands almost touch. Leaving his hand there, the palm up as though waiting for me to take it, he meets my gaze again. "I will help you in this quest but know that it is against my will and my wishes."

"Really? I hadn't noticed." Giving him a big grin, I reach my hand out and lay it on his. Our hands rest there as a physical reminder of the emotional distances we've crossed.

"So, how do we take on a centuries-old sorceress?"

Prometheus's shoulders slump. "What method would you prefer? The best way to fight her would be using magic, something you don't have on your own—"

"How perceptive of you."

"—but I can teach you some swordsmanship, maybe even some basic shooting. I don't think we'd ever have enough time to make you truly proficient."

"Do we have the time to at least make me a threat?"

He blinks out of his musings with a sly grin. "I'll see what I can do."

Fat drops of warm sweat drip into my eyes and I blink away the burning as I wipe them away. Already I'm a worn-out puddle, a shapeless mass leaning against the packed earth floor.

"Again?"

Prometheus braces his hands on his hips, grinning wide.

"I don't think I have another one in me."

"Sure you do." He reaches out a hand for me. "But first you need to stand."

Easy for him to say. He's not the one who's been forced into running laps before dawn, lifting a wooden sword until his arms ache, and then doing some "light" grappling. It's a wonder I've lasted the week at all.

He waves his hand, waiting for me to take it and I shove it away. "I can't do it."

"If you want to be able to take on the sorceress, you're going to have to get up." He keeps his words as soft as possible, but I can hear the steel underneath them.

My going against the sorceress terrifies him. My inability to keep up during his drills isn't helping.

"Can I sit for a minute more?"

Prometheus sighs. "Fine."

He slumps next to me, the ground shuddering beneath his weight. His usual button up shirt lays discarded in the dirt and his bare chest heaves in a deep breath. Since we started training, he's been less and less formal and after the first few days I've been able to keep from staring at his fur and scar rippled chest. His torso resembles a man in its structure but with a thick pelt of fur. Patches are missing in odd places that could be slashes from swords or worse. I haven't asked though.

"I know I've been pushing you hard."

I glance up in surprise but he looks at a spot on the other side of the training field.

"But I'm doing my best to make you the most prepared you can be. You have no idea what she's capable of."

"I have an idea." I wave at his body and his mouth twists wryly.

"I'm petrified of what could happen to you."

"Afraid I'll make a better beast than you?" I tease, knocking into his shoulder with mine.

"I'm afraid she'll grow tired of prolonged punishment and favor something much quicker."

The idea that she could kill me has crossed my mind before. It would be impossible for it not to with how tense Prometheus has been. Still, for whatever reason, I feel confident that isn't the fate waiting for me. And anything else I can deal with. I have to.

"You worry too much. It's all just a curse. Curses are made to be broken, that's why they tell you in them how to break them. If she never expected any retaliation, she wouldn't have kept you alive for so long."

He nods but remains stone faced. He's been more and more serious the longer we've trained. I wonder if at some point he'll stop smiling altogether.

"I hope you're right," he sighs. "Now, let's get back to work."

I take his extended hand this time, letting him do the work of getting me to my feet. The muscles in my legs groan but after a couple wobbles I'm able to stand steady.

"Hand to hand?" He's not really asking though. That's part of the deal, he won't argue with me about going if I finish his insane training schedule.

I raise my hands in front of me, curling my fingers into fists like he taught me. It's like I'm living in some kind of bizarre Rocky movie. He circles around me, lips curled in a smile. He mimics my position as best he can in his animal state.

Jabbing out with a clawed hand, I twist away from him, but just barely. My adrenaline spikes as the fine hairs on his hand brush against my face. Breathing heavy, I take a step back. Prometheus comes even closer.

"We're not supposed to be defensive, remember? Come at me. That's what will surprise her the most."

I scowl but step into range anyway.

Distracted by my thoughts, I miss his next move and his fist makes contact with my side. My breath wheezes in my chest and I swing back without a target. Prometheus chuckles at my decidedly weak attempt.

"You're going to have to try harder than that."

"Don't you have a magic shield you can give me or something." I sigh as he blocks another weak punch.

"You seem to forget that despite being touched by the curse, I'm not actually magical. I didn't even believe in magic before I was cursed. There's nothing magic can give you that will help."

I lower my hands. "I wish you could come with me."

"I wish I could too," he says as his smile turns into a grimace. "I've tried many times to leave the grounds of this castle, but it's something I cannot do."

"What if we could lure her here?"

There must be a way to get her to come to us on our own turf in a way that I wouldn't have to do this alone.

"If I thought it were possible, I would have tried that already."

Prometheus steps forward to attack again, but I hold my hands up to ward him off. "Hear me out. What if I left to get her and managed to bring her here?"

"So now you're not going to simply defeat her, you're going to take her captive and then bring her down through the caves to face me? Do you have any idea how insane that sounds?"

"I know it's crazy, but I'm not saying I'd bring her back physically myself. I'm saying I could somehow goad her into facing you."

He takes a step back, his brow wrinkling as he thinks. "And what would that accomplish? I've been beaten by her before."

"You didn't have my help then."

He sighs and presses forward. "How would you get her here?"

"I have no idea—" I confess and rush to continue as he waves my idea away. "But that's just because I don't know anything about her. With your help I'm sure we could come up with something that would spark a reaction out of her. There has to be something that would make her want to see you. A woman doesn't hold onto a grudge this long without some sort of emotion behind it."

"Unless she's forgotten about me."

"Don't forget, she brought me here. I doubt that means she's forgotten about you." I kick up a cloud of dirt. "You give yourself far too little credit."

"And you give me too much."

Sighing, I glance up at the massive pine trees surrounding our fighting ring, their branches rustling in a magical wind. It's beautiful here. At least he got that. She could have made him a monster and put him in a prison cell. Instead she gave him his home and acres of woodland around it. This isn't the work of someone who would forget about him.

"Think about it, okay? At the very least, wouldn't it make you feel better about me going after her?"

"I don't know if the idea of you provoking her makes me feel any better than the idea of you attacking her."

"Then what *would* make you feel better?"

He hesitates, clawed hands wringing together. When he looks at me, eyes filled with sorrow, my heart nearly breaks.

"Say it."

"Stay with me."

Despite knowing that this is what he wants, hearing him actually say it almost brings me to my knees. He wants me to give up everything and everyone I've ever known to dwell with him in his fantasy prison. Doesn't he know how impossible that would be? What about my future? What about college and my family? I guess I thought I'd break the curse and get back to regular life. I thought he would be coming with *me*.

My pause says it all for me and the vulnerability in his eyes vanishes. Closing himself off from me, he grabs his shirt from the ground and thrusts it on, leaving it unbuttoned.

"I'll do what I can for you, but there's nothing you can do about it that will make me feel better."

He stomps away, sending up small clouds of dirt with every heavy step. I clench and unclench my fists.

Looks like I'll be missing practice today.

Despite looking for him in the castle, I don't see Prometheus again until dinner. He gets there before me and when I enter the room the tension is palpable. Breathing becomes harder to do but I try to ignore it as a servant pulls a chair out for me.

"I looked for you," I manage to cough out as I'm given a heaping plate of something resembling a roast.

"I didn't want to be found."

He doesn't even look at me. I watch him unblinking as he shovels mouthfuls of food past his looming canines. With him acting like this, there's no way I'm going to be able to eat. I push my plate away.

Without waiting for someone to pull my chair out, I strain to move it myself. The heavy chair budges slowly and weighs a million pounds, of course none of the furniture could be the light balsa wood junk we get from IKEA. Prometheus still hasn't looked up and my blood feels close to boiling. With a huff, I grab the high back of the chair and step onto the seat cushion. Jumping off the seat, my foot hooks in the arm rest and I slam into the ground. The glasses on the table rattle and I pull myself up with as much dignity as I can manage and march from the room without a backward glance.

The thrill of my dramatic exit dims as I stand in the dark hallway alone. I really thought he'd say something. I don't know why he's so upset about my suggestion. For all its flaws, I really feel like it has the chance of being brilliant. But only if he'll work with me.

Pressure builds in my chest and I lean against the wall to catch my breath.

I can do this, I know I can. Why can't he at least pretend to believe in me the same way?

Sarah's form is outlined by the gas lamps as she strides toward me down the hallway. I miss having her as an ally. The coldness the staff has given me since my return hasn't let up, but I thought she and I would be able to work things out.

"Wren?" Sarah stands in front of me, arms crossed over her chest. "What are you doing out here?"

"What do you mean?" I push off the wall and puff up my chest.

"Aren't you supposed to be at dinner?"

"I guess I wasn't hungry."

Her eyes narrow as she eyes me over her nose. "What happened?"

"Nothing." It's not even a lie. Nothing technically happened in that room.

"I don't believe you."

I shrug.

"Do you want to talk about it?" she asks with a sigh, her body softening a little for the first time since I've been back. "Why don't we go up to your room?"

I don't trust myself to speak, so I nod and let her hook her arm through mine and lead me up the stairs. Eyes burning with unshed tears, it takes everything in me not to cry. Having her with me when I feel the most alone is almost too much.

Getting to my room, I throw myself on the bed and wrap myself in a protective layer of blankets. With only my face showing, I watch Sarah settle herself into a wingback chair by the fireplace.

"What's happening between you two?"

No easy answer comes to my lips from her direct question. I don't know what I expected her to say, but it wasn't that.

She sighs and runs a hand over her temple. "I can't help you if you won't talk to me."

"Why are you only talking to me now? Where have you been the last week?" She opens her mouth to answer and I bluster on. "Why is everyone so mad at me for being here? Why isn't anyone happy or even just grateful that I'm willing to take on the sorceress to end your curse?"

Sarah is quiet for a second. "There's a lot you still don't know."

"And whose fault is that?"

"Not everyone feels like breaking the curse would be such a good thing."

I give a disbelieving laugh. "How can that even be? Why wouldn't you want to be free?"

"Some think the master shouldn't be free. There are some who feel he is deserving of the punishment he got."

"How could anyone believe a person should have to live like him? What could he possibly have done that would make him equal to the curse? How could anyone be so heartless?"

Sarah takes a deep breath. "There's a reason why the sorceress gave him this curse. The master did something that caused her to act. Some of the servants feel that she did the right thing and they're willing to live like this to ensure he suffers."

"Are you not going to tell me what he did?"

"That seems like a question to ask him."

I throw the blankets off my shoulders, my anger making me hot. "Then what are we even talking about? What was the purpose of bringing me here and acting like my friend?"

"I do want to be your friend, I—"

"No, you don't! If you did you would've been there for me when I came back. But instead you and all of your buddies have given me the cold shoulder like I'm diseased. I don't care what he's done, no one should have to live like this! And you shouldn't have to either. Didn't you ever think that part of the reason I came back might have been to rescue you too?"

She gapes at me like a goldfish, mouth opening and closing in shocked silence.

"Just leave please."

Her black skirts rustle as she stands, and my mouth fills with the taste of blood as I keep myself from taking it all back.

She gives me a long look, shoulders slumping. "I'm sorry, Wren."

The door clicks softly behind her and I'm alone. Completely alone.

No one wanted me here, just like I thought. They didn't want me to come back and save them. Living with their curse was better than having to deal with my pathetic attempts to change it. Why did I ever think I could make a difference?

Tears burn in long tracks down my cheeks and I rub them away with the back of my hand. I shouldn't be crying about this. Why am I giving so much emotion to people that don't care? If I'm going to do that, I might as well stay with my mom.

I just thought they were different. I thought I could be different.

I was wrong.

Pulling the blankets back up around my shoulders, I sink into the bed. The tears stop coming but my shoulders shake with the barely spent emotion. I take a shuddering gasp and let the blankets bury me completely.

A light knock taps at the door. It's barely loud enough to be heard above the crackling flames of the fire. I push myself deeper into the bed. The knock comes again, harder this time.

"Wren?"

I don't bother to move.

"Wren? I need to talk to you."

Seems to be a theme. Everyone wants to talk on their own time and no one is willing to talk when I need it.

"Please, Wren, I'm . . . I'm sorry about how I acted," Prometheus's voice breaks and he knocks on the door again. "Please let me in."

I don't think I could physically manage getting up even if I wanted to. So instead of opening the door as my heart is begging me to, I let his pleas go unanswered.

There's a muffled thump from the other side of the door like something heavy landed on the carpet. I keep my eyes open as long as I can, but in the heavy silence I finally find sleep.

Heavy knocking raps at the door and I wake with the distinct feeling of déjà vu.

"Wren? I've got some food for you."

I don't answer, but Sarah doesn't seem to expect me to because the door flings open and she trounces into the room, her arms heavy with an over-filled tray. She sets it on the small table in front of my bed and drags the whole thing closer so that all I have to do is reach over and I'll find my hands filled with pastries.

"I expect this to get eaten." Sarah's brow creases as she watches me pull myself out of the deep recesses of my blanket sanctuary, my clothes from yesterday a wrinkled mess. "Everything on this tray has been picked out especially for you."

"By who?" I manage to croak as I rub sleep out of my eyes.

"Your presence here is appreciated. Everyone wanted to make sure you were going to be okay."

I glance at the tray with new eyes. What does she mean "everyone"? The tray is covered with all different kinds of food, from sweet pastries and juices to savory egg tarts and omelets. It probably wasn't put together by one person, unless that person was trying to clean out the fridge.

Sarah watches my eyes glisten as I pick a tart off the tray. "We wanted you to know we appreciated your sacrifice. You were right, it's not just about the master."

My mouth fills with the taste of onions and chives as I chew. The food is delicious, so much better than my first week here. I don't know what changed, but I sure appreciate it.

"Thank you."

She waves away my words with an open hand. "I should have been there for you when you came back."

"Do you really think he deserves his curse so much?"

A frown mars her face and her arms move to cross before she relaxes them again. "There are many kinds of evil in this world. I feel that there are crimes he has committed to which forgiveness may not be an option."

"And you still won't tell me what he did?"

"It is still his secret to tell."

Her words don't give me the same rage as they did last night. Maybe she's right. She shouldn't have to tell me what Prometheus did. *He* should have told me what he did.

Sarah shifts on her feet. "The master wants to speak with you."

"I know, he came last night."

"And you refused him?"

I put the rest of the tart down. "I'm not subject to him. He can't decide when we talk and when we don't. I have a say in that too. After his behavior last night, I didn't feel like I wanted to talk to him."

"I can't say that I blame you."

She opens her mouth to say more as a knock pounds on the door. Immediately her mouth closes and she glances around as though looking for a place to hide.

"Wren? Are you awake?"

I cross my arms over my chest. "Yes, why?"

"I'd like to talk to you."

"Maybe I don't want to talk to you."

He rumbles a sigh deep in his chest. "I was wrong."

My heartbeat quickens and Sarah's jaw drops. "What did you say?"

"I was wrong. I'm wrong. I should've thought about what you were asking instead of saying no right away. There might be something we can do with that idea."

Sarah's brows raise in disbelief. I lose the ability to speak and the room grows silent.

"Please let me in. I'm so, so sorry."

I glance at Sarah and she raises her arms as though to say, "I don't know." Would he be mad to find her here? Would it be worse to make him wait?

"I'm not alone."

There's a long pause from the other side of the door. "Who's with you?"

"Sarah."

In the silence, I can almost picture the sadness my words would wreak across his face, that I let Sarah in the room instead of him. How his eyes would narrow, brows falling. I straighten myself up to steel my emotions. There are things I need to know.

"Would you still like to come in?"

His answer is quiet, "Yes."

The door squeaks on its hinges as he swings it open. He looks terrible, clothes wrinkled and eyes sunk in more than normal.

Sarah takes him in and bobs a curtsey. "I'll be back later for your tray."

Her skirts rustle as she moves past him, closing the door behind her.

Prometheus stands in the middle of the room, shoulders low and hands open at his side. I wait for him to break the silence. As he turns his gaze on me, I wish I'd stayed in my protective cocoon of blankets.

"I'm sorry, Wren."

"You said that."

"I shouldn't have gotten so upset right away," he sighs. "I got worried about you. I don't like the idea of you going against her at all, let alone with the idea of making her mad on purpose."

"I think trying to kill her will make her a little mad, don't you think?"

"But provoking her could give her a reason to kill you right away."

"And trying to kill her doesn't give her that reason?"

He clenches his hands into fists. "You're making this harder than it has to be."

"I'm trying to help everyone, the least all of you could do is be a little nicer. You think I'm not scared? You think the idea of taking on a sorceress doesn't make me worried? You're crazy if you think I'm doing this on some sort of bizarre impulse. There are things in this life that are more important than fear and this is one of them."

"And what is this then."

My chest heaves under his gaze. He steps closer as my mouth gets drier.

"Freedom, love."

A smile pulls at the corner of his mouth. "And which one do you want for me?"

"Do I have to choose?"

I've never felt more bared and vulnerable before. Even this slight confession opens me up to him far more than I would like.

He slinks closer, body moving like a hunting panther. Butterflies spread through my stomach with every step as I remain rooted to the spot.

"What would you like from me, Wren?"

He knows. I know he knows. But it doesn't keep the red-hot blush from spreading across my face like wildfire. Prometheus leans against the side of the bed and I don't know whether to move closer or farther away.

"Wren." He trails the pad of his fingers along my jaw line and I shiver at his touch.

Arching toward him, his fingers travel down my neck.

"Wren," he whispers, leaning closer to me. His eyes linger on my lips.

I don't know where this is going, where it could be going. Despite how I feel, he has questions to answer and I have work to do.

His breath caresses my cheek and I turn my head away.

Like I've broken a spell cast over us, he immediately steps back. His hands curl into fists at his sides and the hints of wonder in his face fade away.

"I'm sorry."

He doesn't respond, but I really am sorry. I don't know what's happening with us. I don't know what to do.

"I shouldn't have . . . I don't know what I was thinking."

Backing up, he runs a hand through his hair. I slip out of bed. The urge to follow him is overwhelming and my feet travel quickly across the soft area rug.

"Stop." He holds a hand up. "Just stop."

"You don't understand, I—"

"No, I think I do understand. I'm sorry I ever thought anything different and made you uncomfortable."

"Please, I didn't—"

"Stop."

I grab his arm, my fingers digging into the material of his shirt to make him stop. "Prometheus. It's not what you think."

He doesn't pull out of my grip and I hold him even tighter. Looking over his shoulder, he hides his face from me.

"Please don't go."

"I'm nothing but a monster."

"No." I shake my head. "That's not it at all. I haven't thought of you as a monster in a long time."

I bite my lip as he turns his head to face me, his brown gaze searing through me. "Is that true?"

"I wouldn't say it if it wasn't."

His lips quirk into a smile.

"There are some things we need to talk about." I release his arm and take a step back. "People have been talking since I've been here and I don't think I can wait any longer for you to bring it up yourself."

He folds his arms over his chest. "What do you mean?"

"I know you did something, something that must have been pretty terrible. Your servants won't talk about it, but they're pretty determined that I not break the curse binding you here. What did you do?"

Prometheus shuffles on his feet, clawed toes digging into the rug. "I'm not sure I know what you're talking about."

"I think you do. It's time for you to tell me."

He takes another step back, leaning against the wall as he focuses his dark gaze on me. "The curse started as something specific. She wanted the monster within to be seen by all. The sorceress turned me into this beast so that everyone would see me as I truly was. She thought that if I looked this way, the town would take care of me for her. What she didn't expect was for my father to step in and close me off from the world. This castle has been my prison for far longer than it's been hidden."

I sit on the bed as he pauses, drawing my legs under me as my body grows tense.

"When she came to check on me and discovered me still alive, she flew into a rage. She used her magic to kill my father, sending a bolt of lightning into his heart. Then she brought the flood. I don't know what it did to the town, but it buried us. I thought for sure that it would sweep away the castle, I thought I'd drown under layers of water and mud. But then it stopped and we were in this cave. She visited only once after that. That's when she told me how I could break the curse. And now I can say it to you because you were able to break it yourself. She made it so that someone would have to love me enough to be able to leave but choose to fight for me instead. I attacked her and she's never deigned to visit since. The girls started arriving shortly after that. All different kinds every few years. None could see past the vision of the beast the sorceress created. No one until you."

"But why did she do it?" the words shoot out of my throat like bullets from a gun.

He runs a hand through his thick hair. "I did something I shouldn't have."

"That's usually how it goes."

"I . . . took something."

Well, that's not as bad as I thought it was going to be. I mean it's not like he killed anyone. Sarah thinks he should be a monster forever because he stole something? That's a pretty harsh judicial system.

He sighs and doesn't meet my eyes. "I took something important to a group of people who'd been living here. I was young and stupid and didn't think much about how my actions might affect anyone else."

"What did you take?"

"The fire stone."

That thing Ruby said she used to look for?

"It was something their tribe said brought them life. It sounded like myth, I didn't take it seriously. But one time I visited their village with my father and happened to see the fire stone in passing. It was beautiful, like a living flame enclosed in a clear crystal.

"I told my friends about it later and together we made a plan to take it. You have to understand, my family was pretty important to our town. I hadn't really had a lot of consequences in my youth. My father was a stern man but he worked hard and saw little of me. My mother spent her time taking care of my sister. I was pretty much left to my own devices."

"So you were just another spoiled rich kid is what you're trying to say."

He groans. "I guess so. But I didn't know it. I don't want you to think poorly of me, but that's inevitable with this story."

I fold my arms across my chest and wait for him to finish.

"The fire stone wasn't well protected. They left it in a wood base in the middle of the village. Not exactly the most secure place for your most valuable possession, you know? So it wasn't hard to sneak in later that night and steal it. I wrapped it in my coat and rode hard for home. That night as I laid in bed, I held it and watched the flames wink within the crystal. I didn't think much about the natives at all.

"Catastrophe struck their village the same night the stone was taken. When they woke in the morning, they discovered their entire crop had withered into ash. I didn't hear about their poor fate right away though. It took days before word reached town and by then, the damage had spread.

"Each night a new tragedy struck. The second night it was their horses. Not a single horse was spared, they all lay rotting like a warning of what would come next. It was the third night that finally drew the town's attention. On the third night, the lack of the stone's presence spread a disease. Their illness threatened to wipe out the whole town."

His shoulders shake and he takes a few deep breaths. I mimic his motions, pushing away the feelings of pain that come with his words.

"The sorceress hadn't been in the village when I stole the stone. She'd been visiting a neighboring town. She came home and learned her only sister had died and the stone was gone. The survivors told her what I had done. She came at me like an avenging angel."

"I don't blame her." I hold my hands against my chest to push the burning feeling in my heart away.

"She placed her curse on me and took the fire stone back with her, but it was too late. The village didn't make it. They had to move elsewhere, their homes standing as a ghostly reminder of what I had done." He pushes harder into the wall as though hoping to be consumed by it. "If I could go back, I would. I wish I had never even heard of the stone. Being responsible for those people's deaths is something that weighs on me every day."

He sighs. "Now you know why I deserve the curse."

Chapter Eleven

Despite everything Prometheus said, I do my best to keep moving forward. I don't want to think differently of him. He's not the same man he was when he stole the stone. He's had over a century to think over what he did. Nothing I say now will change what happened, it will only add to his burden. And I'm not sure I want to do that. What happened to that village was terrible, but I'm not altogether sure it was completely his fault. He didn't know what taking the stone would do. If he could take it back, he would. This burden is his to carry.

As I walk onto the training field, Prometheus steps back in surprise. "What are you doing here?"

"I have training to do, don't I?"

His brows slam down over his dark eyes. "We'd finished talking about that."

"That doesn't change what I think is right. You're a different man now. The Prometheus I know would never do something so stupid."

He nods, but his face is hesitant. "How can you forgive me for this? So many others have never been willing to, but you're here ready to fight to free me again without a second thought."

"I don't know. Maybe it's because I never knew them. I didn't know any of the people who died. But I know you. I know that the penance you've already served has made you a better person. And that's a person I want to fight for."

He closes his eyes. "I want to believe you. I want to believe that I'm better now. If I could go back . . ."

"If you could go back?"

"I would take it all back. I'd never take that stone. I'd never be so selfish."

Nodding, I wait for him to meet my gaze. He has to be able to forgive himself. I hope that saying those words will help.

Moving past this, I brace my hands against my hips. "Now, are you going to teach me how to use that or what?"

He's holding a long sword and it looks practically dainty in his hands. Prometheus glances at the weapon and back at me. "You want to learn how to use this?"

"Why not? Any weapon is a good weapon when you're out-matched right?"

He sighs. "Not really. Why don't we focus on one? The better you can get at one weapon the better. There's no need to be mediocre at a dozen weapons when you could be proficient at one."

"Then what are you going to teach me?"

Prometheus stalks over to the weapons shed sitting against the castle wall. He goes inside and there's the jangle of metal smacking against itself and then he walks out with a wooden short sword.

"Seriously? Is that it?"

"You're too small to do well with anything else here."

I straighten out to my full height. "I'm not that small."

Prometheus chuckles, standing almost two feet taller than me, he makes the short sword look more like a dagger.

"Stop arguing and take it."

I grab hold of the proffered weapon, the wood smooth in my hand. It's less than two feet long and tapers into a wicked point. It could do some serious damage if I really learn how to use it.

"Hold it in your right hand," he instructs, moving behind me to assist. "This sword is one you can use one handed, so tell me if the weight becomes too much. Now grip it with your thumb and first two fingers, the other two should curl loosely around the hilt."

I shift my grip.

"Good. Spread your feet so they're shoulder width apart with your right foot just a little forward and bend your knees a little."

"I feel like a duck."

"It might feel a little awkward, but you'll get it. Now hold it up, lining your wrist with your forearm. You should be using your shoulder and your triceps to hold it up. These muscles take longer to tire."

Adjusting my stance, I notice what he's saying. The weight of the sword doesn't seem to be as much, even though my arm is already thinking about aching.

"Not bad. Okay, now all you need is a small movement from your elbow or shoulder to change the center of gravity of the sword. Try it, you should be able to cut down in a nice, straight line."

I jerk my arm and the sword swings in a weak arc.

"Well, not exactly," Prometheus says with a chuckle. "Pull your left shoulder back just a bit. It should feel like you're ready to attack in this position."

I hold the sword up and shift my shoulders.

"Do you feel it?"

"I feel a little ridiculous."

"Keep working through that motion."

I raise and lower the sword. Up and down and up and down. After the twentieth time my shoulder starts to burn. Hissing through my teeth as I raise it again, Prometheus steps in to stop me.

"Ready to add some more?"

The exhaustion in my muscles says no, but I nod my head anyway. He's not going to stop me from doing this.

"Hold it out and cut forward."

"Cut forward?"

"It's a little like a lunge. You can step forward while you do it. Just jab forward."

So I'm not a lumberjack anymore, I'm some weird ballerina. I jab forward and the awkward motion pulls at my body in places I've never felt before.

Sweat beads on my brow as he gestures for me to repeat the motion.

"Are you sure this is the right weapon for me?"

"There's no weapon that doesn't hurt to learn," he says with a half-smile. "Pain is part of the process."

My shoulder feels like I'm about to pull it out of joint with each movement, but I grind my teeth together and keep going. As much as

I hate to admit it, he's probably right. There's no fighting style I can learn that won't push me to my limits.

"Ready for a break?"

I drop the sword in the dirt with a vigorous, "Yes!"

"Good," he pauses and gives me a devious grin. "Now run five laps."

"Are you kidding me?" My jaw practically touches the dirt in my disbelief.

Prometheus nods. "I don't want your legs to think I've forgotten about them."

Heaven forbid I go to bed tonight with any part of my body not hurting.

"Are you going to do any of these exercises or are you just going to stand there all day?" If I have to work so hard, I shouldn't be the only one.

He shrugs. "Sure, I don't mind a little exercise."

I stick my tongue out at his back as he turns to pull his shirt off. Glancing away before my eyes can linger too long on muscled contours of his back, I take a deep breath and start my first lap.

My legs move without too much prompting. He's right, they haven't been working too hard. It's my shoulder that groans with every swing of my arm as I set a steady pace.

There's a heavy thumping behind me, then Prometheus practically sprints ahead of me. He glances back with an easy grin before continuing even faster forward.

I curse under my breath. Of course. Why should five laps be anything to him? I'm the only weak mortal around here.

My breath comes in short gasps, chest pricking with pain as I pick up the pace. I can't let him show me up that easily. Legs pumping, I start closing the distance between us. He's set a comfortable pace for himself, not thinking I could possibly catch up. He's underestimated me.

Shoulder aching with every swing of my arm, my feet pound the dirt path. I try to focus my breathing. In, in, out. In, in, out. Catching a second wind, my body flies across the ground. My hair comes loose from its ponytail and streams behind me like a black ribbon.

Prometheus keeps his pace as we whip around lap after lap. As we curve around the final bend, I strain forward, feeling the veins in my neck pop with the exertion. He glances back at me with a big grin, his breathing even. The jerk.

My shoulder knocks into his side as I meet up with him. It catches him off guard and he veers off course for a moment. Sweat drips down my face as I smile wildly with my small victory. He swerves back on track and matches pace with me, which smarts because I know he could pass me if he wanted.

Dust billows behind us as we sprint even faster. There's no set finish line, but I've marked the place where we started and I focus in on it. It's the only thing I can see, the bare patch of dirt where my wooden sword lays discarded.

Prometheus gives me a little shove on the shoulder, his hand hot on my skin. My foot catches against itself and I stumble. My knee slams into the ground and my body jolts forward still carried by the momentum of my sprinting, and my face hits the dirt. Prometheus slows ahead of me as I cough out puffs of dust.

Sitting up, I brush dirt off of my face and, in the silence left behind, Prometheus begins laughing. Small at first, then building until he's laughing so hard he has to rest his hands on his knees as he bends double. I sneeze and a cloud of dust spreads over the ground. Prometheus howls at this, falling to the earth beside me as tears streak down his face.

"Ha, ha, ha," I comment dryly.

He doesn't respond, his laughing dissolving into silent shaking. I brush dirt off my hands and pull myself into sitting. With raised brows, I wait for Prometheus to calm down.

Letting out a last wheeze, he looks at me with a wide grin and wipes his tears away.

"You finished?"

"Careful or I might start up again."

He climbs to his feet and holds a hand out for me. Begrudgingly, I take up his offer and he lifts me off the ground without waiting. When I'm safe on the ground, we start back to the castle.

"Not even a thank you?"

"Not even."

Prometheus chuckles again. "You did good today."

"Sure."

"No really. You might be able to get some proficiency after all."

I halt in my steps.

The idea of not getting pummeled when I go up against the sorceress is an appealing concept.

He nods. "If you keep working at it like you did today. It was good to see some passion in your training."

I know he's talking about our run and my cheeks get warm. "I have plenty of passion."

"I believe that."

"Do you?" I give him a sidelong glance.

He smiles. "There've been a few moments when you've let your emotions out a little more. You don't have to be so guarded with me."

"What do you mean?" Butterflies work their way up my stomach and lodge in my throat.

"You hold back a lot. Don't. I like seeing you be so real."

"I don't hold back."

He runs a hand down my arm. "What are you so afraid of?"

That's a stupid question. Anyone who's ever lived knows what there is to be afraid of when dealing with people. Do I need to remind him about the rejection I faced when I came back to the castle? How much courage did that take that wasn't reciprocated or received well for a while? Even from him?

Silence extends between us and Prometheus sighs. "I'm not trying to stir things up. All I wanted was to let you know that I'm here for you. Let me be here for you."

He reaches out to caress my face, his palm almost dwarfing me. I lean into his touch, even as a part of me whispers to pull away. It's not safe to let someone in like this. Relying on someone always leads to pain. If there's one thing life has taught me, it's that. Still, I stay safe in his touch.

Pulling back, he reaches for my hand and leads me into the castle. The air inside is chilly, my sweat freezing down my spine as we enter the foyer. This feels more like the cave we're actually in rather than the warm summer day it is out in the enchanted forest.

"Why don't you take a bath and we'll meet up for dinner?"

"Are you saying I smell?"

He wrinkles his nose. "Are you going to make me say it?"

I give him a punch on the arm. "You're not much of a gentleman, are you?"

"I guess I've been the beast too long."

His self-deprecating joke takes me off guard and a chuckle escapes my throat. "Maybe so."

"Go, clean up. I'll see you later."

He stalks down the polished hall, servants scattering in his wake. Shaking my head, I climb the stairs with straining limbs. A warm bath will feel pretty good no matter that it was Prometheus's idea. I only hope Sarah will have thought of it so I don't have to wait. That's my level of spoiled now. It's not enough to have a maid, I need her to anticipate my every need as well.

At the top of the stairs, I slip off my shoes and hold them in my hand, feet sinking into the plush rug. The door to my room stands open, a trail of steam trickling through the doorway. Sarah waits in my room holding a thick towel and a polite smile.

"Oh, thank goodness. You are an angel."

Her smile grows a little larger. "I thought after a day outside you'd need a little wash."

"You thought right."

I peel off layers of sweaty clothes and sink into the steaming copper tub set up in the middle of the room.

As I sink further into the water, I release a satisfied groan. This is heaven.

"Thank you, Sarah," I say with eyes closed in contentment.

"Of course."

I peek an eye at her as she rubs her hands together. "Are you still planning on going after the sorceress?"

"That is the whole reason I'm here."

"I'm sure it's not the entire reason for your return."

I pause. "No, you're right."

"You truly care for him?"

Sinking lower in the water, I cover half my face while Sarah stares at me, head tilted. She waits for me to answer while the pressure in my chest increases.

"I do," I finally say, lifting my head just enough for the words before lowering myself back into my watery shield.

"And he's told you everything?"

I nod.

"How can you still care so much for him? He is directly responsible for the losses of so many people. Doesn't that bother you?"

"Haven't you ever made a choice that had consequences you didn't expect?"

She opens her mouth to answer before closing it. "Yes."

"Did that make you a bad person?"

"No one has ever suffered so much from the choices I've made."

"But couldn't that happen fairly easily? Am I a good person just because the worst case scenario didn't happen? Is he a bad person just because it did?"

Sarah's lips form a tight line. "Maybe you'd feel differently if you had known the people."

"I'm sure I would." I shrug. "But I know that at some point forgiveness is the only way forward."

Maybe this is something I should be working more on for my Mom. Maybe I should have let her have her second chance to be a family.

"Do you want to be trapped here forever?"

She shakes her head.

"Do you see any way for you to escape this curse without offering Prometheus some forgiveness?"

Sarah sighs.

"Can't you accept his penance and let him be better?"

She runs a hand along her left arm, smoothing out the starched material of her sleeves. "I've carried this anger for a long time."

"But you don't have to carry it forever."

Her brows wrinkle and she sinks into the wingback chair. "I don't know if I can do it."

"If you can try a little harder to forgive him, it could make so much difference in how our fight for your freedom goes."

"I do want to be free," she says in a small voice.

I hold a hand out for her and she takes it even as I drip water onto the rug. "Then choose to be free."

She nods, jaw tight.

"It will get better."

As I walk down the stairs to dinner, I can't help but wonder if I over-simplified things for Sarah. Will things really get better? Did I make a promise I can't made good on? If I can't defeat the sorceress, I don't think anything will get better for them. If anything, it could get worse.

But at least we'll all go down fighting.

Prometheus stands as I enter the dining room, the rich smell of stew and fresh bread filling the room as a fire crackles in the massive fireplace.

"I like your hair," he comments as I settle into my chair.

"Thanks."

I run my hand over the top, smoothing it out without messing it up. Sarah braided and twisted it into some sort of bun. I have to admit that it's beautiful, but definitely not something from my time. At least I kept my own clothes.

"Are you feeling better after your bath?"

"A rest was just what I needed."

Our words feels stiff, too formal after everything that's happened between us. But I don't know how to talk to him without disclosing how much his staff has grown to hate him. Maybe he already knows. I'd imagine after so long it would be hard to miss. But then again, if he doesn't know, then I don't want to be the one to tell him.

The server heaps my china bowl full of stew and places two slices of crusty bread on a small plate set beside it.

"Do you think you'll be able to keep up this pace?" he asks before ladling in a large mouthful of stew.

"What do you mean?"

I tear off a piece of bread while I wait for him to chew.

"It's a lot of hard work. It was hard for me when I was first learn-ing, and I'm . . . well, I'm a man."

"Are you implying this work is harder for me because I'm a woman? You really have been down here a long time."

He clears his throat. "Well, you see, in my time—"

"Your time was a long time ago. Believe me, if a woman wants to learn how to use a sword in the current time, the only thing that would stop her is herself."

"So, this hasn't been too much for you then?"

"I won't say I'm not sore." My shoulder aches even after the bath. I can only imagine how great it will feel after tomorrow. "But I'm more than capable of keeping up with your training."

"I'm glad to hear it." He gives me a smile and shovels in more stew.

I follow his example, the meat practically melting against my tongue. We continue to eat in silence, and I use my bread to mop up the last of the stew juices when my bowl sits empty. My stomach is so full it forms a round lump under my tank top and the combination of being so full and so worn out has my eyelids drooping as Prometheus finishes his meal.

"Wren, you don't have to wait for me," he says when my head droops and bounces back up as I catch myself falling asleep. "I'll see you in the morning."

I don't need to be told twice. On aching feet, I stumble out of my seat and up the stairs, collapsing onto the bed and falling asleep before I can even think of getting undressed.

⊷🞊⊶

My days develop a rhythm. Breakfast in the dining room, training on the practice field, a bath, and dinner back in the dining room. Sometimes the bath is hot and other times I have Sarah make it as cold as possible without any freezers full of ice. I miss ice.

Weeks pass this way and Prometheus is right, my skills improve. Focusing on one weapon makes all the difference, despite the fact that I'd still like to work with something a little more intimidating. Is it so much to ask to use a weapon that would really make people pause? Maybe even something just a little bit bigger? Every time I bring it up Prometheus shakes his head. It's not happening.

But I feel like it's time. How much longer will he keep me down here working on the same weapon when we could be developing a plan to take down the sorceress? Probably forever if he's not pushed into it. It's much easier for both of us to hide behind what we're in control of instead of bringing in the sorceress. But the time has come. All this training is pointless if we don't have any plan of what to do with it.

I wait through breakfast to bring it up, preferring the open field to vet his anger in. He marches out of the weapons shed with our usual wooden swords to spar with and I cough to clear my throat. Glancing up at me, he stops dead in his tracks. What I'm wanting must look pretty obvious then.

"No," he says, shaking his head and folding his arms over his chest. "You're not ready."

"Maybe I would be if you let us use real swords."

"If we use real swords, you'll find some way to kill yourself."

"My life expectancy was never very long anyway."

He groans. "Why can't you wait until I give you the go ahead. Must you always be pushing?"

"I don't want to grow old here until you're ready. Let me help you already."

"Every day you're here helps me. Every day you remind me more of my humanity. Can't you be satisfied with that for now?"

I mimic his pose. "And what about Sarah and the others? Should they be grateful of your growing humanity while nothing changes for them?"

I'm so tired of having this same fight over and over again. I don't know what he thinks will change. That one day I'll casually tell him over breakfast that I'm not interested in going after the sorceress anymore? He's crazy.

"Fine," he says with a tight jaw. "We'll use real swords today."

His body is stiff as he heads into the weapons shed again. There's a lot of banging around inside it before he emerges with two shining short swords. I meet him in the field and he hands me one, the metal of the hilt cold in my grip.

Prometheus's lips are thin, his shoulders tight as he meets me in the painted ring he's created. He holds his sword casually, but I'm not fooled. Every day we've been out here he's shown me how much of a master he is.

We assume starting position, despite the fact that I'm still adjusting to the subtle differences of the real sword compared to the wooden one, and one of the problems is weight. This one is far heavier than what I've been using. He starts slow and I follow him through the motions of attacking and defending. I watch him with intensity, but he never looks at my face. His eyes remain on my feet, a scowl permanently etched across his face.

Slowly the speed increases, my arms moving quicker to block his thrusts. Our swords clang as they knock into each other as we fight within the ring of dust. Still he doesn't so much as glance up at me. I'm fighting for my life while he could be sleepwalking.

There's no time to think, no time to strategize as he keeps swinging faster and faster. I barely manage to get my sword up to block him every time and the possibility of taking a hit becomes very real. Sweat trickles down my face, both from the exhaustion and the cold fear of pain.

All the finesse has left my fight and I'm down to survival mode. Prometheus hasn't even broken a sweat despite how quickly he's moving. Frustration turns to anger. Is this his way of teaching me a lesson?

In my last real burst of speed, I duck under his guard and jab for all I'm worth. My sword almost looks like it glances across his chest, but I'm not entirely sure until small beads of blood bubble along the line. Red courses down his chest like a veil and he jerks back in surprise.

I throw my sword in the ground, something I'm sure I'm not supposed to do but seems like it would be cool. "What now?"

"You drew first blood," he says with open shock. "You win."

"Are you okay?"

The wound doesn't look that bad, but who knows?

"You barely scraped me. This is nothing."

With that taken care of, I focus on what I've accomplished and victory punch the air a few times, a second wave of adrenaline coursing through my body and making me jump around.

"So what do we do now?" I ask after I've been able to stand still for a little longer than ten seconds.

"Maybe you're right."

"I'm sorry, what did you say?"

"Maybe you're right. Maybe we should be focusing on the sorceress now," he repeats with a growl.

"You agree I'm ready?"

"No, but that doesn't mean I get to hold you back anymore."

His open lack of confidence pops the small bubble of joy growing within my chest. "If I'm not ready, then why are we talking about this?"

"You drew first blood."

My victory becomes shallow. Perhaps he let me win in more ways than one. Did he let me draw first blood? Was it all a ruse? I hate that I'm leaving this fight more confused than I started it.

"I think we should start working on that plan now."

"The one to lure her back to you?" I could be blown over with a feather.

He nods. "That one. It seems the most reasonable way to attack this."

"Yeah, sure."

Prometheus grabs my sword out of the ground and takes our weapons to the shed. I don't move, I have no idea what to do with all of this. My body is frozen to the ground even as he comes out and walks around me into the castle.

"Aren't you coming?"

"I—yeah."

Like he's spoken the magic words, the shock drains out of me and I scamper up the stairs after him. He strides toward his office without looking back at me. It's like I'm a little kid following my mom around again and the sensation isn't pleasant.

Situating himself behind his desk, I take one of the curved armchairs facing it. He digs through its drawers and pulls out a tube of paper. With a gruff shake, he smooths it out, revealing a map of town. I haven't spent enough time in town to know the layout, but even so I can see dissimilarities between the town I know and the one he knew. For starters, his doesn't have a library but it does have a saloon.

"Do you know where you come out when you leave this place?" Prometheus asks, keeping his gaze carefully away from mine.

Getting up and moving closer to him, I peer over his shoulder, I don't recognize much, but I do see the blue lines of a river.

"Right here." I point to a spot of blue that looks vaguely like it could be the dried-up hole I've gone down more times than sanity should permit.

He scratches the back of his neck. "You come out of a river like some sort of nymph?"

"The river isn't there anymore."

159

He stares at me for a moment and shakes his head. "Okay. So you come out of where the river used to be and then?"

"What does it matter what I do? What does any of that have to do with finding the sorceress?"

"I'd like to have a clear idea of what you're doing while you're gone, every step of the way."

"You'll already have the mirror. Don't tell me you won't be watching regardless of what we decide right now. You're very odd."

He laughs. "You're not the first one to tell me that."

"Well, I won't know what I'm doing when I get out until we make a plan."

"I suppose that makes sense." He rolls his shoulders back. "So let's make a plan."

I glance over his map but the markings don't mean much to me. "Do you have any idea where she might be?"

He shakes his head. "Even if I did, it sounds like things are different enough up above that my knowledge wouldn't be helpful."

So much for the map being a good sign. "What can you tell me about her that would help find where she's been hiding?"

"She most likely hasn't been hiding. Why would she? It's not like anyone is after her but us."

His statement chaffs against my skin. "I think you're simplifying things too far. It's not like witches or sorceresses or whatever are just openly accepted in my time. There'd have to be some element of hiding going on or she'd have been burned at the stake a long time ago."

"You realize that's not how people really handled witches right?"

"What does it matter how they did it? The point is that she wouldn't have been able to be open about who she is." I sigh and count to ten. "Can you at least tell me what she looks like?"

He shrugs. "Couldn't she have changed that too by your logic?"

"So what now? We keep talking in circles until we give up? What do you want me to do with this information?"

Prometheus reaches over and grabs my hand that's been clinging to the desk with a white-knuckle grip. "I'm trying to be relatively realistic. I think she's not someone you can find, but someone who'll find you."

"Do I make a sign then in the middle of town, 'Dear sorceress who cursed Prometheus, I've defeated your curse and am ready to defeat you'?"

He starts, eyes wide. "Oh, for heaven sakes, don't do anything that crazy please. I'll try to remember something for you."

Sinking into his chair, he kneads his forehead with a clawed hand. I take the seat opposite him and steady myself to wait. Silence stretches out between us, each little noise from the hallway becoming louder. I have to focus hard to keep from grinding my teeth together. Patience has never been my strong suit.

I pick at a chip of varnish coming off the chair arm rest. Scraping at it, it flecks off like old nail polish and seems a suitable distraction from Prometheus's "thinking."

"Would you stop that?" he snaps, looking up at me with a frown.

"I'll stop when you've thought of something useful."

He leans against the seat back. "I think she had blonde hair."

"You think she had blonde hair?"

"Hey! I told you I would try, if you can't work with what I'm giving you then that's your problem."

His tone stills my picking fingers. I haven't seen him this worked up since the first day I was here.

"These are memories I blocked for good reason and now you're trying to get me to remember them for a cause I don't even believe in. I'd stay cursed down here forever if it meant you were safe."

"As lovely as that sounds, you already know where I stand on that."

"Hence why I wasn't going to bring it up. You're the one that asked."

He's got me there. Why ask a question I didn't want the answer to? I chew at the side of my bottom lip.

"Sorry."

Prometheus sighs and leans across the desk. "I know. Everyone is sorry. There's no real solution to anything we want. Probably why it's called a 'curse.'"

"Yeah, I'm sure it'd be called something more friendly if there was a solution that could make everyone happy."

He ignores my sarcasm. "Could the blonde hair be helpful?"

"I don't know." I shrug. "Lots of people have blonde hair."

"Lots of people in town?"

I think over my time at school. "No."

Prometheus smiles. "We have a lead then."

"One more thing," Prometheus says, voice serious. "She'll be very deceptive in how she looks. She's not going to look like a sorceress or any kind of threat."

"Well, that sounds obvious."

"Just hear me out. She won't be what she seems."

I go back to picking at the chair. "That sounds wonderfully cryptic."

He sighs. "We're not going to get anywhere this way. Why don't we discuss what we'll do when you find her. You're still planning on bringing her back here, right? For me to take care of her?"

"Of course."

His shoulders relax. "Good. Now, if things haven't changed too much since I've seen her, I think it's safe to say that she's a prideful woman."

My mouth quirks into a smile and I raise a brow at him.

"I'm trying to find a way to get her here if you could stop judging me for a second." He pauses and I wave at him to continue. "Right, so you'll need to work at her pride, really give her a reason to want to see me again, even if it's just to give me a good punch in the face."

"Who hasn't wanted to do that?" I tease with a grin.

Prometheus frowns. "Be that as it may, it really seems like the best option for getting her to come back and face us together. If everything goes well, you won't ever have to use the swordsmanship you've been learning."

"That sounds like a waste."

"I'd gladly waste any burgeoning talent if it meant you were going to escape from this experience unscathed," he admonishes.

I cross my arms over my chest. "Fine. So I'll just find the sorceress, poke her where it hurts, then hurry back through the caves?"

Prometheus nods, his face a blank mask hiding the emotions he's already discussed with me.

"And you have nothing else to give me that could help with identifying her or provoking her?"

His jaw tenses as he thinks, a million memories floating through his mind. "There was a ring I think."

"A ring?" That could be good.

"A little silver one that she wore. It had a snake on it I think."

I stand and make my way for the door. "So all I need to do is find a woman with blonde hair and a snake ring and figure out a way to provoke her to visit the scene of her crime. Should be a piece of cake."

Prometheus lets out a dry laugh as the door to his office closes behind me.

Chapter Twelve

The fire burns low in the grate as I lay buried beneath a mountain of blankets. My muscles are relaxed and my body is tired, but I still can't sleep.

There's too much I don't know, and no matter how much I push Prometheus to accept me as ready, I know I'm not. I have nothing useful that could defeat a sorceress and no way of finding her. Who's to say she even stayed in Greendale? I couldn't imagine a more boring town to spend centuries in.

And what will I do when I climb out of the hole? Do I go home and hunker down to wait and look? Do I bother dealing with Mom again? I'd rather die than face the wrath of my mother's tarnished image. Because we all know she hasn't been crying over me.

So what? I'll sleep on the streets and live in the library and hope no one tells Mom I've shown up? Yeah, I can't see *that* blowing up in my face at all.

Home it is then.

The boiling pit of anxiety only grows as the fire burns to its last ember. When I'm left alone in darkness, a cold chill creeps over my heart.

What am I doing?

Will I really be able to save Sarah and the other servants and allow Prometheus to finally be a man again? What am I thinking? That I live in some kind of fairy tale where all that matters is that I'm doing my best?

I flop over in the bed, wrapping myself further into the sheets as a desperate cry releases from my throat.

This is impossible.

But after everything I've been through, I can't give up now. Can I?

Despite feeling like I was awake all night, I must have fallen asleep at some point because I wake to the sounds of Sarah wheeling a breakfast tray into the room. She gives me a bright smile that doesn't meet her eyes as I sit up in the bed. Sheets and blankets have been pulled up and more than a few pillows landed on the floor during my stress filled sleep last night.

"You might want more time to collect yourself today before leaving," Sarah explains before sweeping from the room.

So this is it then. They've all decided today is the day. I know I should be happy, maybe even a bit grateful that Prometheus has decided to let me go, but after the solitude of the night, the only thing I have left is fear.

My stomach ties itself into a tight knot, despite the steaming cup of cocoa and several chocolate filled croissants lining the wooden tray. I know I should eat something, but everything in me says no.

I choke down the food without tasting it, a shame really, and take a swig of cocoa when a lump of flaky croissant lodges itself in my throat. If they'd done this for me yesterday, I would have been overjoyed. Why does today have to feel so different?

Clapping my hands together to release the flakes of pastry and sugar, I try not to start as the bedroom door swings open.

"I couldn't wait any longer to see you." Prometheus steps through the door.

He hesitates by the wall, and I reach out a hand to him. "I'm glad you're here. I don't think I could stand any more time alone."

His presence soothes the ruffled feathers of my soul and I lean toward where he stands at the end of the bed.

"You don't have to do this you know." He leans against the bed frame. "You can always change your mind and none of us would think less of you for it."

I tear off another piece of croissant, my appetite returning. "You're crazy. Have you forgotten everything I've done to get to this point?"

He nods while I conveniently forget my hesitation from the night before.

"Sit with me." It's more of a demand than an offer, but he complies without arguing and I pull my legs in to give him more room at the end of the bed.

"You'll be safe right? You won't make any foolhardy decisions?"

"Foolhardy? Are you kidding me?"

He shrugs. "I can't help what I am."

"And what you are must be an old man."

He chuckles and it brings a bright grin to my face.

"Take care of yourself," he sighs.

"Stop acting like we're never going to see each other again. This isn't a funeral."

His mouth twitches into a weak smile. "You're right."

But I can see the lie in his eyes. He doesn't think I can do it, and I've been questioning it too. That's not a good combination when combined with a "foolhardy" mission.

"I'll come back to you, sorceress in tow," I promise with a watery smile.

He reaches over and takes my hand, neither of us feeling the need to fill the silence. I clench his hand tighter, memorizing the feel of the pads of his skin. Despite what we say to each other, this could all be the end. I could walk through that door and never see him again. Walking through that door could give me an expiration date.

Prometheus runs his free hand across my face leaving feather light touches against my jaw. Tears build in my eyes and I have to blink quickly to clear them away before he notices.

"Your presence here has brought me joy I didn't know was possible," he whispers, his impossibly dark eyes staring into mine. "No matter what happens next, know that I'm beyond grateful for what you have already done, what you've already taught me."

"What have I taught you?"

He smiles. "That even a beast like me can be worthy of love."

My cheeks heat and he leans in closer. Breath catching in my throat, I freeze. But he doesn't go in for the kiss I anticipate. Instead he brings his head parallel to mine and rests his cheek against the side of my face.

"I wish you didn't have to go," he says so quietly I can barely hear his words despite the fact that his lips are so close to my ear.

"I'll come back." Remaining stoic is a lost cause. Tears flood down my cheeks, pooling where his face meets mine.

Prometheus releases my hand and takes me into his arms, pressing me close to his chest. My shoulders shake with all the repressed emotions I have for him being released in the hot tracks of tears. He doesn't say anything, instead he rubs a hand up and down my back. I glance up at his face but its twisted into a mask of agony.

I pull away from his hold, he trails his hands down my arms. "I need you to believe in me."

"I know." He squeezes his eyes closed.

"Can you do that for me?"

He nods.

"I need you to say it."

"I believe you can do this."

His words sound like a lie to both of us.

The door looms over me as I stand before it, hand frozen on the handle. It's one thing to talk about leaving and talk about taking on the sorceress, but it feels completely different to actually be going.

Prometheus stands in the kitchen doorway. I wanted him to come with me to say goodbye, but actually seeing me go is proving too much. For both of us.

"I'll be back, probably in a couple of weeks."

"Stay safe." His voice is a low rumble that goes straight to my heart.

Turning the doorknob, a blast of cold air shoots from the cave and blasts my loose dark hair over my shoulders. I don't look back to see Prometheus one last time. If I do, I know I'll never leave.

My shoes slap against the stone steps as I descend into the darkness. Grabbing the flashlight out of my bag, I straighten my shoulders for a fake vote of confidence. I'm doing the right thing. I have to be.

The faint dripping of water on the cave walls echoes my footsteps with eerie precision. The dank dark walls around me feel more open than ever before, reminding me I'm doing this alone.

There's a part of me that still can't believe I'm doing this for Prometheus. I don't know if I've ever put myself in harm's way for any interests other than my own. Coming to Greendale definitely doesn't count as selfless. Is he the first person I've ever wanted to really do something for? Figures I'd need a beast to show me how to be a better human being.

With so far still to go, I have a lot of time to consider what my next move should be. I never did figure out where I was going to stay. I should let Mom know I'm alive. Ruby might want to know where I've been. I do kind of owe it to her to let her know.

So, I'm going home then?

The word feels hollow when I use it for the building where my mother lives. The use of "home" feels more appropriate when talking about Prometheus' castle, as bizarre as that sounds. A castle shouldn't be homey, but that's what it became as I grew to know Prometheus. The older I've gotten, the less Mom feels like home.

If only she'd listen when I told her that when she told me to leave New York.

I have a lot of "if onlys" when it comes to Mom. If only she'd listened to me when I told her I didn't want to move. If only she'd stayed with me when I was little instead of leaving me with Aunt Cara. If only I'd been enough for her and she hadn't had to go off searching for a better life without me.

If I were a healthier person, one truly invested in getting better, I'd have years of therapy ahead of me. Yeah, I don't think so. I'll forgive what I can and keep squashing down what I can't until the pain doesn't hurt anymore. Sounds normal.

I sidle between the two thick walls of rock, amazed at how much quicker this journey gets every time.

When the tight space becomes too much, I turn off the light and close my eyes, using the closeness of the walls to guide me. This method has been the best way of keeping my panic to a minimum, which is good. I don't have time to have a panic attack all alone in a dark cave. That sounds like a sure way to have rolling panic attacks and a mock heart attack feeling which isn't high on my "most wanted experiences" list.

But kissing Prometheus might be.

Even alone in the darkness, my cheeks heat up to magma levels. It's a stupid thing to want. It's a stupid thing to think. But I really did think he would. How he would is beyond me. His beast face wasn't exactly made for kissing. Would he even have been able to pucker? I'm still willing to find out.

After all of this is over, curse broken or not, that's what I want to do.

Marching through the darkness, the idea of finding my courage propels me even faster along my path. I can do it. What's the worst that can happen? He decides he'd rather not kiss me? I've seen the shadow of that desire in his eyes several times. So many times, I thought he'd kiss me. He wouldn't refuse it. Would he?

It doesn't matter. I'm going to try anyway. If I can risk my life for him, the least he could do is let me kiss him.

Blinking back surprise at the beam of light spreading from the hole in the ceiling, I can't believe how quickly I've made it back. Decisions have to be made regardless of whether or not I feel ready for them. Am I really ready to go home to Mom? I don't want to say I'm afraid of her, but that's the sour taste in the back of my mouth when I think about marching up to her front door. That's a little growth, right? Being able to almost admit I'm afraid of Mom.

I drag a hand down my face. This is going to be a disaster.

Looking toward the darkness of the cave with a heart full of longing, I jump for the dangling rung of Bill's ladder. I wrap my fingers around the cool metal and heave myself up the rungs. Going up is definitely harder than coming down. Although, training with Prometheus has grown my muscles and they don't cry out half as much as I think they should. Compared how weak I was coming down here, I practically shimmy up the ladder.

Hot desert air brushes against my face as I level myself out of the hole. Keeping my feet light, I skirt around the hole and trip over the bags of concrete still waiting to fill the hole. I adjust the strap of my bag against my shoulder.

My heart beats a rapid rhythm in my chest and I climb onto the rock I'd originally tied Bill's rope to on my first journey. I'm not ready to face Mom yet. I cross my legs and dig around in my bag for one of the snacks I packed so many weeks ago.

Instead of feeling the plastic packages I expect, my hand brushes against rough cloth. Brows creased in confusion, I pull the bundle out. Unwrapping it, my chest gets tight as I repress the overwhelming emotion it creates. Inside the cloth are several pastries and the flaky crumbs they've left behind. Sarah must have packed this for me.

I grab a croissant and savor its buttery layers in my mouth. This is a great way to kill time at the very least, and at most maybe I won't have to sit with the family during an awkward dinner. They wouldn't make me if I've already eaten, right?

Finishing up the treat, I fold the cloth back over the remaining treats. As I set it in my bag, I notice something else in the bottom that shouldn't be there. A small square of folded paper sits bright against the dark interior of my bag.

My fingers shake as I pull out the paper. There's only one other person I can think of that would've left something for me. I rub my sweaty palms against my pants and unfold the note.

Wren,

We both know why you had to leave, and I won't deny the honor that your sacrifice brings. You have undertaken a task of great courage that I'm still not sure I deserve, but as is the way of things, I am unable to make that decision. Only you can decide who is worth sacrificing for. Still, I am grateful for such overwhelming evidence that I have found my way into your heart the same way you have become part of mine.

Having this time together has changed me in more ways that I should be willing to admit. After so many years as a beast, I had forgotten what it was like to be a man. Thank you for reminding me I could still be more than a monster. Thank you for reminding me life is worth fighting for. I didn't always give you the curtesy you deserved in this process, but know that my hesitation was completely on your behalf. You are too precious a woman to be lost to the kind of evil the sorceress is. I feared she would take one look at your goodness and decide to destroy you. That wasn't fair of me for either you or her. I am deserving of the punishment she gave me.

Fear keeps all of us from becoming the best we could possibly be. I've definitely let it affect me thus. Courage is a skill and one you have in abundance. If I had been as brave as you, I never would have become the beast I've been forced to be. Thank you for awakening my courage. When the sorceress comes to me, I promise to fight with everything I have and to use the strength she has given me with the courage you have reminded me to have.

If things go bad and we don't see each other again, please don't succumb to fear. Don't follow my example, Wren. It's not worth following. The path I chose only brings pain. Life is already full of pain, don't add more to it by having fear.

Know that no matter what happens, I have loved you, Wren. I loved you from the first time you fought with me. You never let me bully you and that was the most endearing thing you could have done. When you broke the curse and left, it almost broke my heart. To know that you could find love for me and be willing to leave it behind confirmed every negative thought I've ever had about myself. And yet I wanted you to be free. You coming back was the most delicious pain I've ever felt. It both killed me and brought me back to life.

Thank you for loving me, Wren. Know that I will always love you, beast or not, cursed or not.

Prometheus

Silent tears burn agonizing trails down my face. Why couldn't he have said anything like this when we were together?

I wrap my arms around my legs, curling them into my chest. His words are beautiful, a wonderful reminder that no matter what happens with Mom, Prometheus will care for me. Will love me. Despite being a beast, he is beautiful.

Pressing my lips to the thick paper, I fold it back up and place it carefully in my bag. Something tells me I'm going to need his words as I try to accomplish this task.

I stand with hesitation. There's no reason for me to stay here any longer, but I'm having a hard time finding the will to turn toward

Mom's house. Sleeping on a park bench is starting to look a lot more appealing. Why did I think I needed to be the bigger person?

My feet drag along the ground as I walk through the long dead grass. It rustles under my feet in the long stretch between the hole and the edge of town. The caution tape the police put up after my first fall has long since blown away leaving the whole area with a feeling of death and desolation. The same way I feel the farther I get from Prometheus.

My shoe smacks against the concrete sidewalk and my body jolts. Town looked so far away when I first started walking.

The sun sinks low behind the mountains leaving the road awash in shadowy light. The streetlights haven't come on yet so the world looks more mysterious than it usually does under the light of day. Newspaper flutters against the gate of the high school in the weak breath of wind as I walk by and all around me is silence. It's like the whole town went to bed early. Maybe I'll get lucky and Mom will be asleep already too.

Dragging my feet, the feeling of dread builds in my stomach the closer I get to Mom's house. What will she do to me this time? I can't imagine how much her wrath will have grown with a second disappearance. Yeah, she's going to kill me.

The streetlights flicker on one by one as I walk under them. Houses watch me with the blank eyes of their windows in the faint light. Their outdated fronts and modest lawns a perfect representation of the people who live in this town. Why would Mom want to be that? Compared to New York, this place is nothing.

At least something good has come out of being here though. To think these people have lived here for over a hundred years without knowing what lay below the sleepy structures of their town. What would they have done if they had known a beast lingered beneath the ground? Would Greendale have become another ghost town, long forgotten in the aging memories of the West?

Mom's house looms to the left of me and as I turn toward it, my sneaker catches on a lip of broken concrete. I tumble to the ground, landing in the logic defying plush front lawn. No one's told Bill we live in a desert, apparently.

My fingers thread through the grass and I rip out large handfuls and toss them onto the sidewalk. A light blinks on in the front room and I squint to make out the figures walking around. A woman in a pink dress comes from the kitchen carrying a platter of something. *Mom*, my heart whispers.

As much as I hate it, there's a part of me that's happy to see her. The same part that has always been willing to forgive her most selfish moments. It's like I'm four years old again, hoping she'll come home and hold me like the moms on TV. It was a stupid dream.

I move like a ghost to the door, my feet leaving damp footprints from the grass on the front walk. My hand lingers in the air, halfway between knocking and opening the door. I'm supposed to live here, it shouldn't be such a big question of how to announce my presence. And yet, I can't get myself to move and make a decision either way.

Laughter echoes from the kitchen upstairs. I recognize Mom's voice and suddenly her being mad at me doesn't seem like the worst-case scenario.

What if she didn't care I left again?

That thought had never entered my mind before. I knew she'd be mad. And I guess I hoped that somewhere deep inside her, the parts untouched by her many fake layers of makeup and the self-loathing that made her change so much, she would remember what it meant to be a mother and worry about me. But my disappearance the second time could have been a relief.

The porch light flickers on and before I can recover from my series of self-destructive thoughts, the front door swings open. My heart bubbles into my chest and my hand stays poised to knock on the door as Ruby steps out and almost into me.

"Oh!" she gasps, a full garbage bag held between us. "Wren?"

"Surprise."

"You're back? You're really here?" Her blue eyes go so wide they look like orbs.

"In the flesh."

"Oh wow. Oh gosh. Mom is going to be so happy to see you!"

I ignore the way her use of "mom" pinches my heart as Ruby throws the trash bag onto the pristine lawn and leads me inside. She grabs my hand and pulls me up the stairs so fast I almost trip.

"Guess who I found?" she trills as we stand in the hallway between the kitchen and the family room.

"Did Pumpkin come back?" Bill asks from the kitchen and Ruby scowls.

"No, I'm not talking about a cat from five years ago. Think, much more important and much more recent." A grin grows across her porcelain face.

"What are you talking about, Ruby?"

Mom rounds the corner of the kitchen, wiping her hands off on an apron tied around her waist. She catches sight of me as she looks up and freezes. Her mouth falls open in a small *o*, apron still clenched in her hands.

"Surprise?" I repeat.

"Wren?"

Her question is both shocked and devoid of real emotion. What else could I have expected?

Mom's face is a frozen mask while her gaze travels up and down my body. "You decided to come back? You've been gone for weeks but now you want to come back?"

"Something like that."

"Care to explain where you were?"

"I left a note."

Her forehead wrinkles almost imperceptibly as her mouth turns into a small frown. "This is not a hotel, Wren. You can't just come and go whenever you feel like it. It's rude to all of us that you find our family so disposable. We asked you to come and be with us. If there was a problem, I would have helped you with it."

"I'm sorry. I shouldn't have left that way."

She blinks, tears filling her eyes. "You are?"

"I should have been willing to give you another chance."

"I'm sorry too." She reaches out for me and buries me in a hug while she breathes in the dry desert sand from my hair.

Releasing me with all the grace of a southern lady, Mom moves to the side and lets me pass. I breeze past her and down the stairs, closing the door to my room behind me.

This place really doesn't feel like home still, but I'm willing to try.

But at least I did the right thing, right? At least I get some sense of accomplishment from that.

I throw my backpack to the floor and bury myself in the blanket. If everything goes well, I won't be here very long. I never asked Prometheus what he wanted after all of this is over, but I should have. What is my grand plan? To commute to school from his castle under the ground? Thinking about it now makes me feel dumb. Of course I wouldn't do that. And after all my hard work, am I not going to finish high school? That wouldn't make sense. I'm not giving up the rest of my life because of this curse. Am I?

The darkness grows inside my room and upstairs the hum of conversation continues.

I half expect Ruby to knock on my door. I can't imagine she's too happy with me right now. But as my lids grow heavy and the trip takes its toll on me, no one ever comes.

The sun hasn't even come up by the time I'm washed, dressed in clean clothes, and stealing a granola bar and water bottles from the kitchen. My messenger bag is securely slung across my shoulder, its weight a comfort I can't explain.

I don't know where I'm going, but I know I won't find answers if I stay here. Good thing my well-meaning Mom isn't trying to get me to go to school. There's no time for those distractions.

My feet lead me out the door and on my way. I consider going to the library, but that hasn't seemed to have helped much if I'm being honest with myself. I don't know enough about where to look for it to be a worthwhile trip.

So I wander. I march past the library and the school and head toward main street. I've only driven past it once when Mom first brought me here, so it seems worth checking out.

A long row of two-story brick buildings highlights that I've made it to main street. The signs highlighting each store are faded, the 1950's type proclaiming their age. Despite being the only hub for shopping, there's no one out. Is it a weekday? I don't even know anymore. Maybe I should have paid more attention before leaving the school behind.

The first store I pass has a bright red "closed" sign in the window, and the level of dust on the windowsill says it's been closed for a while. Each store I walk by looks similar until I get to a small convenience store. It has a modern neon "open" sign flashing over and over in a rotating loop. At least there's signs of life somewhere.

A bell hung over the door jingles as I push the door open. A pleasant flush of air conditioning pushes past me into the street and I move faster to get inside before too much rushes out. A girl in her mid-twenties snaps her gum as she watches me.

"Can I help you?" she drawls, tone very much suggesting she has no interest in providing help.

"Just looking."

I step down the aisles, the shelves offering nothing exciting. Lots of road trip snacks, beef jerky and chips, and Band-Aids and deodorant. Convenience stores are weird places.

"Shouldn't you be in school?"

I glance up at the check girl. "Playing hooky today. You know any good places to go?"

"Will you leave if I tell you?"

"Of course."

She closes the magazine, a polished nail holding her place as she leans across the counter. "There's a place where you can see the old town. People don't really go there much anymore. It used to be a little tourist spot, but it's dried up. It's a great spot for hanging out when you don't want to be found."

"Want to point me in the right direction?"

"Head right when you get out and keep going straight. There's an old sign for it at the end of main street."

"Thanks."

Heading for the door, I pause before opening it. The wall next to the exit is plastered with local advertisements and missing posters. It's mostly cats and dogs, but there's one picture of me with Mom's phone number on it.

Pushing the door harder than necessary, I try to leave my faded image behind.

Chapter Thirteen

Sweat coats my spine as I speed walk past a few open businesses and a lot of long closed storefronts. My feet fly across the sidewalk. One mention of the old town and I'm gone.

Main street peters out with a green sign proclaiming "Authentic Old Greendale." The arrow points to the right and I take it despite the heavy layers of graffiti covering the majority of information. What more could it really say though? Hours for a gift shop that's no longer running? Geeze, this whole place feels like a ghost town despite people living in it.

The distance to "Authentic Greendale" was covered up by a particularly foul word so I don't know how long I have to walk, but I'm getting used to these long trips. When all of this is over, I should get a job and buy a car. No more walking again. Ever.

Heat from the sidewalk leeches into the rubber of my shoes, making a small oven to cook my toes. With all the abuse my shoes are getting, I doubt they'll make it another month. At least my legs don't hurt. I should thank Prometheus for all the laps he made me run. They've come in handy after all. I'm sure he'd give me that side smile of his, a hint of canine showing as he shakes his head.

I miss that.

I miss his steady presence despite everything happening around him. I don't think anyone could ever describe me as steady. I'm not reliable, let alone steady. I guess he's had a lot more time to smooth out those rough edges than I have. But that's okay. I'll keep working at it. I just have to be better than I was yesterday.

Swerving at the last second, I just barely miss getting taken out by a hanging welcome sign. The hinges on one side pulled out of the wood, making it hang lopsided and perpendicular to the ground. I don't know whether or not to take that as a good sign.

I don't really want to run into anyone, so I guess that should be good.

Grit grinds under my shoes as the sand of the desert has made good headway in burying this part of Greendale. Splashes of bright colors mar the browns and blacks of the flaking buildings. The graffiti artists have been here too. The simple structures look like any other 1800s town with their straight-forward architecture and wood slat sidewalks. It's ordinary in how generic it looks, and yet as I step through time, it tugs at my heart. This is what life looked like when Prometheus was on top, before he made a stupid mistake that would ruin his future.

The glass in the windows is wavy with age, and I brush off a layer of grime to peek through into the first worn wood building. An antique black barber chair sits in the middle of the room with tarnished silver mirrors hanging on the wall. Cute.

I move to walk away, but before I can, my mind invents for me an image of Prometheus walking into this room in his usual button-down shirt and some tall black boots. The barber greets him with a smile and another man in the room says something that gets all of them laughing. The Prometheus of my imagined memory looks so young, so carefree. He'd never have expected the life he got, cursed to live in a castle under the ground.

Tears prick at the corner of my eyes and I pick up the pace. The building next to the barbershop is set up like a little country store, each building being preserved like a museum. Little plaques screwed into the frames of the doors tell a story about what life in Greendale would have looked like.

Clenching and unclenching my fists, I try to focus on finding something, anything useful. These buildings hold nothing but ghosts.

At the end of the "original" town, a cement building that looks like it was built in the 70s sits with a squat roof and a cement porch complete with a few rotting picnic tables. There's no way they're considering this an authentic building. It has to be a museum to complete the historic experience.

Ignoring everything else, I run across the wood slats to the museum at the end. My hip knocks into one of the tables and it collapses in a creaking puff of dust. I wrap my hands around the doorknob and pull, putting my full weight into it. It doesn't budge.

Dusting my hands off, I try again. Not even a creak to say I'm trying. Why'd they bother locking the door? No one comes here anyway.

Jaw clenched, I breathe a sigh through my nose. There has to be a way in. I'm just going to pretend that any past partiers didn't find the way in first.

Running my hand along the sandpaper-like surface of the wall, I walk around the building looking for another door, a window, anything. Along the back wall is another door, probably the workers entrance or an emergency exit, if they even believed in those when this crap hole was built. I give the handle a tug, but am far less surprised this time when the door doesn't swing open.

There's also a couple of windows on the back wall, their smooth glass confirming this isn't an original structure if the cement wasn't enough of a clue. There are a couple half windows, but to the right of the door is a standard size that I could definitely fit through.

My fingernails dig into the dry wood of the windowsill, white paint flaking off as I tug at the frame. The window budges a little, but the wood of the frame has swollen in the sill after so many years of abuse. I try again and the wood frame squeals as it slides.

"Just a little further," I groan as my arms shake.

It moves a couple more inches and I back away from the window, shaking my arms out as I inspect the narrow space. It's going to be tight, but unless I'm willing to break the window, this might be as good as it gets. And I'd really rather not break the window.

Willing strength into my body, I lift myself up onto the sill. Twisting sideways, I force my head and shoulders into the dark room. I try not to think about how vulnerable I am, halfway in and halfway out, but a touch of anxiety makes my chest tighten. Maybe that will make getting through a little easier. I'm a little smaller, right?

Turns out my chest isn't the problem, it's my hips. My chest falls through like it's been buttered, but my hips keep me firmly in place, stuck between the window and the frame. Bracing my hands on either side, I push, willing myself through. Nothing happens. I try pushing and wiggling. Still stuck. Great. After all that worry about facing a sorceress, I'm going to die trapped in an abandoned museum.

Hanging, I let my arms fall toward the floor. I wiggle a few times in my limp position, but unsurprisingly I stay firmly hooked. I should've brought some spray oil.

Deciding I've had enough recovery time, I push against the wall and the window, swinging my legs and wiggling my hips. I slide forward only a quarter of an inch. But that's all the encouragement I need. I try again and get similar results. Then I'm falling, sliding through as the bulk of my hips come free.

I thump onto the ground face first, tumbling as the rest of my body falls after it. My nose rubs along the carpet and I flip over in an attempt to keep from growing a giant rug-burn across my face. Breathing heavily, I wipe my sweaty hands on my pants and clamber to my feet. I'm in.

My eyes have time to adjust to the light as I blink away dust. It's just an old office. I've fallen behind the desk, just missing the heavy chair pushed underneath it. A typewriter sits on the desk and a large filing cabinet rests against the wall. Good grief this place is ancient.

Stomping around the desk, I throw open the only door, half expecting that to be locked too. The hallway beyond is darker than the office room. Working here must have felt like working in a cave, and not nearly as nice a one as Prometheus's.

I grab the flashlight out of my bag and flick it on. White walls and brown carpet, yuck. Following the hallway as it twists away from the office, I hope to get out of the workers area and into the actual museum.

It's so quiet in here. Not surprising since I'm the only one inside, but still. Goose bumps prickle across my arms. I don't like it.

The beam of the flashlight lands on metal double doors. Seems promising. My increased pace makes soft thuds across the carpet.

The door is surprisingly light as I push the metal bar for it to open. It clangs against the wall, the noise echoing in what must be a large open space. I swing the flashlight toward the ceiling but the beam isn't strong enough to reach it. I think I've found the museum space.

I adjust the light and sure enough, it finds a half wall covered in pictures and plaques. Stepping forward, my breath catches in my chest. This could be it. I might actually find what I'm looking for.

Ignoring the exhibits closest to me, I weave through them toward what must be the front. I'm fairly positive I'll need to go all the way back to the beginning for what I'm looking for. When the light finds a sign for the gift shop, I'm confident I've found the front of the museum. I swing the flashlight toward the first exhibit and sigh. It's a painting. And not a very exciting one at that. The little sign next to it says, "An artist's depiction of what Greendale looked like before being settled." It's just a painting of a desert with a few mountains in the background and the faint outline of what might have been the river that's long since dried up.

I follow the trail of exhibits. The one next to the painting talks about what made Greendale so appealing to settlers. Honestly, no matter what this fancy historian says, I think the allure of free land would get people to come, even though this whole town is a crap hole.

Glancing at the next wall, I pause. "People of the Fire Stone" is highlighted in big letters above artifacts and a few black and white pictures. These people are what set the stage for Prometheus's curse. I scan over the small info blurb. It doesn't really say anything I didn't know before. A people that worshiped the fire stone and lived in the area. But I gasp out loud when I read the last sentence. "Instead of having a shaman or healing woman, these people looked to a woman they only called 'sorceress' for guidance." Surely Prometheus must have known that before he went after the stone. How stupid could he have been?

I peer at the small black and white photo, the flashlight making a bright glare against the glass. I'm surprised by how different they all look. Fair and dark, light hair and black hair, all standing together in the same animal pelt clothes. Scanning their faces, I try to commit each one to memory. One of these women could be walking around town right now and I would never know it. They're nothing like what I expected despite how Prometheus described the sorceress.

The temptation to break the glass and steal the picture over-whelms me and I have to clench my fists to keep myself in check. The Wren of only a few months ago wouldn't have hesitated to take it. It's not like anyone's going to come and make sure it's still here. At least that's what I would have convinced myself. I flinch at the memory of stealing the guidance counselor's picture. He definitely would notice that. In my desire to feel something, I did my best to hurt anyone unfortunate enough to be around me. The only person who should have been on the receiving end of that wrath was my mother. And I never did anything like that to her. What would she have done if I had taken her red lipstick? Would she have ever talked to me about it or just shrugged it off?

Whatever. No matter what I did, it wouldn't have changed the decisions she made. She had chosen her path long before I came on the scene.

Sweeping over the group one last time, a woman with a sweep of dark hair catches my eye. I press my face closer to the glass, not believing what I'm seeing. It's not possible.

It's my Mom. Preserved behind the glass of this ancient museum is my mother.

I stop breathing as I stare at her all too familiar face, complete with a dark lipped grin. What could she possibly be doing in this picture? Is this a gag?

Even as I think it, I know it's not possible. No one besides the checkout girl knew I was coming here and the checkout girl never would have known why I was coming, or even that I'd break into this building.

I step away from the glass, breath coming in shallow pants. There's no way. There's just no possible way. How could she be? And yet all the evidence points in that direction.

Mom is the sorceress.

I don't remember how I got out of the museum. One minute I'm stumbling away from the evidence I can't accept, and the next I'm panting on the dirt road of the restored town.

My mind is a mess, whirling with thoughts that still don't make sense. I lurch forward, dust clouding my feet. My mouth is dry but I can't find the mental focus to even grab one of the water bottles.

Mom is the sorceress.

How is it even possible that she could be a sorceress and I never knew? A witch I'd believe, she has the temperament for it, but sorceress? Sure we weren't close but that seems like kind of a big deal to hide from someone you live with. And what does that make me? Do I have some magic too?

It seems unbelievable and yet the biggest problem I have with this discovery is that she could have hurt Prometheus like that. My clueless mother doesn't seem to have the strength for grudges and yet she cursed him for over a century? How?

My foot slams against the sidewalk, and blinking I realize I've left the original town behind. Where do I go now? What do I do? Do I try to bring her back so Prometheus can destroy her? We've never been close, but I have a hard time with the idea of being instrumental in her death.

Skin cold, I keep walking. But my purpose is gone. I don't know what to do now. I want to run back to Prometheus and tell him what I've discovered. I need him to tell me what to do next. He never wanted me to go after the sorceress in the first place, so what would he say if he knew my mom was the one we were after? How could he possibly feel the same way about me if he knew my family was responsible for his endless torment?

No, I can't go back to him. At least not until I've made a plan.

But I can't focus. I can't make a plan with my thoughts in shambles like this. I don't know what to do. I have no one I can talk to, and definitely no one around here who would believe me.

Could I ask her? Could I ask Mom what happened? Why she did it and if she'd be willing to face Prometheus to break the curse? Just imagining her cruel smile as I explained the situation is enough to keep me from traveling any farther along that thought train. Just because I've forgiven him obviously doesn't mean she has. I'm stuck. There's no simple solution for me. Not that facing the sorceress ever felt like a simple solution. At least it wasn't going against blood at that point. Geez.

My feet retrace the steps I took this morning, leading me down main street and past the library. The late afternoon light sends long shadows along the ground, the temperature changing drastically every time I walk through the shadows and back into the sun.

I guess I'm going home then. Really what else would I do? Switch back to my original idea of sleeping on park benches?

Mom's house grows in front of me and I hold in the heavy sigh that just seeing her house elicits. This is going to be anything but fun.

Ruby sits on the front step, throwing small pebbles across the front walk.

"Hey."

She glances up at me with a smile that doesn't reach her eyes. "Mom told me not to bother waiting out here for you. She said you'd probably just disappeared again."

"Not this time. Disappointed?" I ask with a laugh.

"I don't know." She runs a hand through her hair. "I thought your prickliness would be the biggest problem with getting to know you. I never imagined it would be hard because you'd disappear so often."

"There's a reason for that—"

She holds up a hand to stop me. "I know you think there's a reason for all of this, and maybe there is, but there was no reason not to tell me you were leaving. Did I not tell you how upset I was the first time? Common courtesy would dictate—"

"I've never been big on common courtesy. It's not exactly something I was taught at home."

She raises a brow. "I don't believe that. Mom is very courteous."

"Only because you fit what she's looking for." I scowl. "Listen, I don't want to talk about her. I'm sorry I didn't tell you."

My apology sits in the air between us. Ruby itches behind her ear, silver ring gleaming in the late afternoon light.

"I don't know if I believe you." She looks up at me, blue eyes wide.

I can't say that I blame her. I sling my hands in my front pockets. "Well I am sorry. I really am. Out of all the craziness in this backcountry town, you're one of my favorite parts. I know that might sound unbelievable but it's true. You're the best part of the family my mom has tried to make here."

"Tried?" Ruby asks with a small smile.

"I'm not sure how I feel about Bill." A grin spreads across my face as Ruby laughs. "It could happen though. We might just become a family yet."

"We will if Mom has anything to say about it."

"But we're not going to let her know she has that much power." I give her a wink.

Ruby stands and brushes off her jeans. "You joining us for family dinner tonight?"

"It's not like I have any better plans."

Maybe if I pay attention I'll figure out something about Mom's magic. There's no way she can hide that from all of us so easily.

She opens the door and we climb the stairs to where the smell of lasagna has permeated the floor. Standing at the stove, Mom's wearing a frilly pink apron, singing to herself as she sautés green beans.

"Hey, Ruby. Can you set the table for me?"

"Of course."

"And could you—" Mom halts as she notices me standing behind Ruby. "Oh, Wren. I didn't realize you'd be joining us tonight."

I don't have the emotional capacity to deal with her discussion of me like I'm a neighborhood kid and not her own daughter. She's a sorceress. We kind of have bigger problems than where I'm eating dinner. "Well, you're in luck. It'll be a full family affair."

"Is that so?"

"Yep. So I'll just get to helping Ruby, unless there was something else you wanted me to do."

Ruby hands me a stack of plates and I follow her into the dining room.

This could all come together so easily. The sorceress is my own mother. If I could betray her, this could all be over quickly. I should have no problem getting her to come to the cave with me. But could I?

And what then? I'll have to ask Prometheus what he thinks about my grand plans of graduating early and going back to New York. If the curse is broken, will he follow me? Would I want him to if it was at the cost of my mother?

I set the plates down and massage the tension headache growing in my forehead. I move the plates to their appropriate places in front of the four chairs. Ruby watches me, forehead wrinkled.

"I've just got a lot on my mind."

"Would it help to talk about it?"

I'm going to go with no. "Not really. This isn't something that you would really understand."

"I'm here if you need me."

"Thanks."

It's sweet, but I really think she'd be one of the ones trying to get me committed. I can't imagine any of what I'd have to say fitting in her perfect world. I wonder what Ruby was like before Mom met Bill. Maybe someday I'll have enough time to get to know her better and find out.

Table set, I slump into my spot. Ruby takes her place opposite me and as if on cue, Mom swoops in with her tray of lasagna.

"Dad is pulling in right now," she announces, and I do my best not to flinch. I wanted to try, but he's not my dad.

"Where are my girls?" Bill announces sing-songily up the stairs.

"Waiting for you at the table!"

Bill sweeps into the room, slinging his suit jacket on the back of his chair and giving Mom a peck on the cheek. "How are my favorite people?"

"Perfect," Mom says breathlessly. "And look who decided to join us for dinner."

Bill glances at me as he puts his napkin in his lap. "Welcome home, Wren. We've been so worried about you."

"Sorry to worry you, Bill. I've been in the middle of a few adventures is all."

Bill laughs. "I know how that goes."

"How was work, darling?"

I tune out their mundane conversation to keep from throwing up.

Digging into the food, I have to admit she's become a much better cook than when I lived with her.

"Is it good to be home?" Bill turns his attention to me, a smear of red sauce next to his thin lips.

"Sure." I shovel food in my mouth to keep from having to talk.

"With all the adventures you've been having, I imagine it's going to be hard to finish the school year with any great success."

Mom's smile turns up at the corners.

"I'm sure I'll be able to handle it. Make up work is usually more like busy work anyway," I say through a mouthful.

Mom flinches as a spray of red sauce shoots from my mouth to her white tablecloth. But I know what she is now. I don't know how we could fix the relationship between us now. I don't even know if we'll have the time to.

Using the crust of the garlic bread Mom put in the middle of the table, I wipe any remaining sauce off my face. The grotesque move is instantly rewarded when Mom's lips pinch into a thin line.

"I know I've taught you better manners than that."

"Too bad you never stuck around to reinforce them."

Her jaw goes slack and my heart twinges. I didn't need to be so mean. Maybe if I had a regular mom, like the one Ruby thinks she has, I wouldn't have so much pent up. I need someone to talk to, but I know the last person I can really talk to is Mom. I need to stop messing around and get down to business. I have to find a way to bring her to Prometheus.

No one's said a word, although I half expected Bill to say something in defense of my mother. Forks scrap across plates, and the red blush on Mom's cheeks has become a permanent feature. I look at Ruby but she keeps her eyes on her plate. I'm alone in fixing this. I guess that makes sense. No one asked me to crap on my mom at the dinner table.

"Sorry, Mom. I shouldn't have said that." She doesn't even glance up. It's true though. No matter what she's done, I don't need to be rude to her. But even as I think about making it up to her, a plan starts to form in the back of my mind. "Do you want to see the place I've been heading off to?"

Mom grabs Bill's empty plate and stacks it on top of hers, taking them into the kitchen. "What do you mean?"

"Do you want to see where I've been going? I think that's the only way for you to really understand what I've been up to."

Mom steps back into the dining room and glances at Bill. He gives her a shrug, eyes big.

"I just thought . . . you didn't want me to shut you out of my life, right? I wanted to share this experience with you. We wouldn't have to stay a long time, just poke around and see what's captured my attention. That'd be cool right?" I play the bonding card hard even as guilt prickles at the back of my mind. But it's the only way I can see her climbing into that hole with me. Even at that, I don't know that she'd risk her safety by trusting that ladder.

"I . . ."

"Please?" I put my hands together like I'm praying. Praying she'll give in and come so this doesn't have to be any harder.

She throws her arms wide. "Fine. But not tonight. Tonight you're doing the dishes and going right to bed. Tomorrow is Saturday, so I'll have time to join you in your little adventure. Maybe if you have some supervision you won't get into so much trouble."

"Thanks."

I grab Ruby's plate and take it to the sink. I don't even care that she's given me a chore for this. Getting her to leave Bill and come with me was so much easier than I thought it would be, I'd do a million chores for that. Not that I'd tell her that.

"Can I come too?" Ruby asks Mom as she sinks into her chair.

I glance up as Mom opens her mouth to respond, but Bill cuts her off before she can even begin. "Why don't you let them have some quality time together, Ruby? You and I can do something fun, just the two of us."

Ruby stomps down the stairs as I load the last of the plates into the dishwasher. I feel bad for her, but there's no way I'm asking her to come with us.

Mom covers the lasagna pan with tinfoil and puts it in the fridge. I start for the stairs and she stops me, grabbing my arm. Her smile is so much warmer than I've seen it in a long time, the hint of tears glistening in her eyes.

"Thanks for letting me in, Wren."

I nod and she kisses my cheek before letting me go.

Each step I take down the stairs feels heavier than the last. Each movement is a betrayal to my family, but what else can I do?

I didn't ask her to curse Prometheus.

Chapter Fourteen

Sleep eludes me. My chest is tight as I roll back and forth, searching for a comfortable position in bed as the streetlight casts shadows across the wall. But there is no comfort for me.

I've gotten Mom in position. She's going with me to the cave tomorrow. I'll be betraying her and readying her for Prometheus's sword, and no amount of sweet talk can change that simple fact. And I haven't even told her what's happening. Would that make it better? To tell her I'm taking her to Prometheus so she can face a part of her past and make it better? Or should I fight her myself as Prometheus trained me to do.

Knowing she's the sorceress changes things. How did she ever defeat Prometheus in the first place? The mom I know doesn't seem strong enough to curse someone, or even hateful enough to do it. Has time made her weaker? Made her more willing to succumb to an average life? Somehow I'm not buying it.

There's a piece to this that I'm missing. I'm completely sure of it. And that fear combined with the ache of betrayal in my chest turns me into a bundle of nerves ready to explode.

When the first rays of dawn drift across my bed, I leap from my room and into the shower. I'm not waiting a second longer.

The hot water cascades down my back, but even that does nothing to smooth the rippled lines of tension running through my body. I scrub at my head with aggressive fingers, and by the time I get out, my body is more mangled than when I got in. Still, it feels better to be moving.

French braiding my hair into two long braids, I apply a thick line of black eyeliner and mascara before calling it good enough. I look like I've put on war paint, and I have to step away from the mirror before the panic in my chest grows. It's too close to the truth.

Mom's going to know something's going on, I can't help but think as I drift up the stairs. I've replaced my usual black gear with spandex pants and a workout top. I don't know what I should prepare for and this seemed like a good catch all. Maybe she'll just think we're going to be working out. I guess getting to Prometheus is a bit of a workout. So it's not really a lie, right?

Looking around the room, I debate if I should bring anything else. My gaze rests on my suitcase where I know I've packed my pocketknife. Sweat beads along my temple as I wonder if I should take it. Will Mom turn on me when she finds out what I've done? Ignoring the shaking in my hand, I grab the smooth case and shove it in the waistband of my pants before heading upstairs.

"Morning, sweetheart."

I practically jolt out of my skin, eyes wide and heart pumping fast. "You're awake?"

"Oh yes," she hums to herself as she flips French toast in a pan. "I was too excited about our day together to sleep."

She reaches out for me and runs a finger along a pink stripe in my top. "This is cute."

"I didn't want to wreck my school clothes."

"You don't need to worry about that," Mom says with a laugh as I back up into the counter. "I'm still hoping you'll let me shop for you."

"I don't think I'll ever be ready to look like Ruby."

Mom ignores my tone as she hands me a plate piled with French toast. "We'll see."

I stumble to the table that's already been set with a small vase of bright pink flowers, powdered sugar, and maple syrup. Even knowing everything I do about my mom, this takes me back. How could a sorceress be so concerned with such mundane things?

Numb, I sink into my chair and grab the syrup. Mom breezes in with a plate of her own and a jug of orange juice that she pours into a glass and hands to me.

"Are you excited about our big day?" Mom asks, her bright red mouth split in a wide smile.

"Not as excited as you, I guess."

The need to tell her what's happening grows with each passing moment. How can I not tell my own mother that I'm leading her to her doom? Or is she playing me for a fool so that I change my mind. Would I be willing to choose her over Prometheus? I don't think so.

"I'm very interested to see what you've been up to. Not that I've been pleased by your behavior, mind you. You were just so adamant about disliking it here, I'm surprised you found something that absorbed your attention so soon. Maybe it's something you can continue enjoying while living at home and going to school." She points her fork at me and her face gets serious.

"I'll see what I can do."

"You do that. And eat your breakfast. I didn't slave over a hot stove so you could skip the most important meal of the day."

I take a bite and it sinks like a brick in my stomach. I take another and I'm afraid it will lodge in my throat and choke me. Afraid of it happening, but also almost hoping it will happen. It'd be nice to have something stop me from the course I've chosen. It doesn't matter that I could change it myself. I'd never turn my back on Prometheus like that. He's counting on me and there's no way I'm letting him down.

Mom continues humming to herself as we eat. I clear my plate under her watchful eye and take it to the sink to rinse off and shove into the dishwasher. Mom follows behind me and wraps me in a big hug as I turn around.

"Thank you for letting me into your life. You have no idea how much this means to me."

Taking a deep breath, I swallow down the lump that threatens to leap out of my throat. My stomach churns and hot tears prick at the corner of my eyes.

"You might want some water or something." I grab my black messenger bag and sling it over my shoulder.

"Way ahead of you," she says with a smile as she puts on a backpack of her own.

"Well, there's no use in waiting. We might as well get going."

I lead her down the stairs like a lamb to the slaughter. She chatters away behind me, slipping on a pair of hiking shoes.

My shoulders are tense, my stomach sitting like a rock as we walk down the walkway to the sidewalk. Mom links her arm through mine as we set off toward the cave.

"I can't wait to see what has so completely consumed your attention since you've been here. You haven't been able to spare a single day to be with me. I thought you might be busy with schoolwork and I'd have to wait until summer for us to be together, so imagine my surprise when you just disappeared for weeks. That's so unlike you, Wren. You never did things like this in New York."

"I never felt like running away in New York."

The smile slips from Mom's face and I instantly regret my outburst. I'd decided I wasn't going to talk to her like that, not now that we're at the end. I don't know why I thought it would make a difference in our relationship though. One day of niceties doesn't change a lifetime of resentment.

"I'm sorry that coming here made you feel like you had to run away," Mom says, her voice quiet as she stares out at the rising sun. The light hits her face in shades of brilliant orange, and for a moment she looks so young. If I didn't know she was the sorceress . . . it doesn't matter. I do know.

"It would've been nice if you'd asked my opinion before dragging me out here. Or at least listened to me when I explained all my reasons for not wanting to go."

"I felt like us being together was more important than your reasons for staying."

I cross my arms over my chest, trying to hide the growing ache. "Then why didn't you say that? And why did you leave me in the first place? Even before you moved here, we weren't together. You'd left me with Aunt Cara long before Bill."

"Someday when you're grown you'll understand the sacrifices I've had to make," she says with a sigh.

"That's just an adult's way of avoiding the question."

"Excuse me?"

"Whenever adults don't want to answer a question they say, 'you'll understand someday.'..Don't you think I might be old enough, or worth the effort enough to tell me why you've made a choice that directly affects me?"

Mom hesitates, stopping in the same place where we'll leave the comfort of civilization behind. "I'm sorry I never thought about it that way."

"Me too."

I unlink our arms and stomp through the long dry grass. It wraps around my ankles like claws, begging me to reconsider what I'm about to do. But I can't not bring her back. I can't do that to Prometheus or Sarah or any of the others forced to live forever in their enchanted castle.

Mom notices the broken caution tape flapping in the light morning breeze. "Is that where we're going?"

I nod, continuing forward. If I stop, I might not be able to start again.

"How did you even find this?" Mom's heavy footsteps follow along behind me.

"Trying to get away."

She's silent until we get to the big rock. Her gaze roves over my emergency ladder descending into the dark hole.

"Is this safe?"

"I didn't have any problems last time."

Without showing the hesitation beating at my heart, I grab the ladder and work my way down. Mom stands at the mouth, bits of earth falling through the hole from her feet.

"It's not really safe to stand there. Either come down the ladder or stay back by the rock."

She backs up and I don't see her through the mouth of the hole anymore. The tight knot in my chest eases. At least I know who the sorceress is. I can tell Prometheus and we can work something out together. Maybe we can work something out and Mom will remove the curse willingly.

Then the ladder jiggles, and I look up to see Mom as she climbs down the ladder after me.

"You don't want to stay up there?" There's an embarrassing amount of hopefulness in my voice.

"If I talk, I won't be able to do this," Mom says through clenched teeth. "But I told you I was coming, so I'm coming."

Reaching the end of the ladder, I jump down. My feet slam into the cool earth, sending rocks skittering and I breathe in the chill air. Everything could still be okay. It's possible.

Mom jumps after me and pulls a flashlight out of her backpack, shining it up at the ceiling and all around us. "Holy cow, Wren. Weren't you at least a little bit scared to be down here? What could possibly make you want to come back?"

"You'll see."

I pull out my flashlight and start down the path that's quickly becoming more familiar than the streets I grew up on. Mom stumbles behind me, eyes big and mouth open.

"This is incredible!"

Nodding, I pick up the pace. I don't think I can take much more of Mom's amazement over the place that could quickly become her tomb. Will I have time to talk to Prometheus about her, or will he attack first in the hopes to catch her off guard? How did my choice to save him spiral out of control so quickly?

But there's something eating at me that I can't ignore.

"Mom, why did you soften up so much after I came out?"

She'd never been a warm fuzzy in New York, not after Grandma died. So why now? Why now when her cold exterior could have saved me so much pain?

She sighs. "I know I'm going to lose you. These adventures of yours are just the beginning. It's going to be next to impossible to keep you here and I want to cherish that time together. You reciprocating those wishes made me unbelievably happy."

"If you wanted to keep me with you, shoving me away so hard in the first place probably wasn't the smartest thing to do."

"You just make me so crazy sometimes. Why can't you do what I've asked you to do? Why do you make everything feel like a fight between us?"

"Why is it your way or no way? I have opinions too."

She runs her hand down the side of her face. "I've done everything to make our lives better."

"Better for you."

Mom's footsteps stop. I turn to face her and am startled by the tears glistening in her eyes.

"Is that really how you feel?"

I sigh and wrap my fingers around my bag strap. "I shouldn't have said anything. This really isn't the time for this conversation."

"Then when is the right time?"

Maybe when I don't feel like I'm constantly betraying you. The thought sparks against my brain and I turn away from her. "I don't know."

Mom waves her flashlight in front of us. "I can't believe you ever came down here, let alone kept going. If it were me, I would've shimmied right back up that ladder."

"We're a little different I guess," I say with a dry chuckle.

"That's an understatement."

I glance at Mom and she gives me a small smile.

"I'm sorry things have been so tough between us," Mom says, flashlight clutched to her narrow chest. "I'll try to work harder okay? I'll listen to you this time."

"Promise?"

I don't know why I even bother asking. She might never get a chance to make good on that promise anyway. And that's my fault. No one's making me drag her down here. This was always my decision.

"Promise."

A crack worms its way through my heart and I walk faster through the cave, arms swinging to propel me forward. As if getting to the castle will change everything that's happened and bring back my cold heartless mother who cares nothing for me. I could really use a dose of her right about now.

Mom keeps pace with me, not commenting on the fact that we're almost jogging. She lets me lag into silence, and I'm grateful. Everything she's said has only made this worse. And the worst thing about it is that it hasn't changed my opinion on what I have to do.

When we reach the narrow passage of wall, I don't even hesitate before throwing myself inside it. The pressure I've been traveling with makes the tightness of the walls feel like nothing. For the first time, I'm able to walk with my eyes wide open and it doesn't cause my chest to constrict. Mom hesitates at the opening, but when I don't slow down she climbs in after me.

She coughs as a cloud of dust rains down, dulling her bright blonde hair. I hide a smile behind my hand as she glares at me with a dirt mustache. She opens her mouth to say something then thinks better of it and closes it while shaking her head. I don't think I can remember a time when Mom let herself get dirty like this, ever.

A dirt mustache is a good look for her.

I have to admit, I'm almost proud of her as she wrenches herself through a particularly tight spot. Her backpack catches and she takes it off and pulls it through in a cloud of dust. But she doesn't complain. She really is like a lamb being led to the slaughter, all meekness and timid smiles. And at some point watching her be so benign makes me want to hit her. This isn't her. This isn't how she's ever been. So why now? I feel like it's on purpose. She knows exactly where we're going and is playing this card to keep me from completing my task. Except, if she knows where we're going, wouldn't she just not come?

If I think about this too long, I'm sure to get a headache. But what else is there to think about?

Easing myself out of the earthen hallway, I pause long enough for Mom to work her way out. She dusts off her pants and shakes her head, still watching me with a smile.

"This is so insane, Wren. What made you do this the first time?"

I shrug. She already knows what made me do it. It was her light. Her little magic ball of temptation leading me right to the castle. I never would've made it there without that little push. I'd probably still be wandering through the caves, completely lost and maybe even dead by now. Not that I'll thank her for the directions. If not for the twinkle of magic in the bottom of the cave, I never would have come back and tried to discover a hidden cache of gold. It all comes back to her.

The steady drip of moisture from the cave ceiling fills the silence between us. We're close.

The scent of mildew grows, reminding me of my first night in Prometheus's prison.

Will Mom experience the same welcome I did? Will she stay in that prison cell and wait for her fate to be decided while I try to force Prometheus into leniency?

Mom's flashlight glances off the stone steps leading into the castle and her breath catches. "What is that?"

My heart feels cold. "That's what we've come to see."

Feet moving like lead, I trudge up the steps, Mom following nimbly behind me. There's a light on in the kitchen, gleaming under the door as we get closer.

Mom grabs my arm and stops me. "Wren, where are we going? What is this?"

Instead of answering, I reach for the doorknob and turn it open, giving her a glimpse of the kitchen. Sarah stands behind the counter holding a tray of muffins.

"Wren?" The tray falls to the counter with a clatter. "You're really back?"

"Everyone should stop being so surprised that I follow through." I smile. "I told you I'd bring her, and I have."

Sarah looks behind me to where Mom stands slack jawed. "That's her?"

Her brows raise almost all the way to her hairline as I grab Mom's arm and push us into the room. Sarah chews her top lip and stares at me.

"What?"

She shakes her head. "The master will be able to tell you."

"Where is he?"

"Training of course."

At least someone believed in me.

I march for the training field, Mom trailing behind me with wide eyes and a mouth that keeps gaping like a goldfish. Doubt dances across my mind. She's not that good of an actress. And her expression feels too similar to mine when I first got here, there's just too much truth in her eyes.

The double front doors to the castle stand wide open, giving a great view of the enchanted forest. Goose bumps trail across my arm as I stare at the trees that were almost my grave. Does Mom know that? Did she watch me while I was here like Prometheus watched me when I left?

Taking a sharp left out the doors, the training field looms into view. Prometheus has his back to us, the sharp planes of his shoulders tight as he swings his sword. The tightness around my heart eases. I clench my hands into fists to keep from running to him, leaving my mom and my problems far behind.

"What is that?" Mom whispers as she grabs my arms and holds me back.

I try to shake her off, but she only grips me tighter, her red nails digging into my skin. "What is what?"

"Is that a monster?"

Eyes narrowed, I shake my head. "What are you talking about?"

"That thing over there!"

Mom pulls me toward the castle, her grip so tight I begin to worry she's going to break the skin. I fight against her, moving toward Prometheus and wishing I'd ran to him when I had the chance. We kick up a cloud of dust in our scuffle. With a groan, I pull free from her grip and fall over. Scrambling to my feet, I run toward where Prometheus slowly turns.

Seeing me coming at him, he steps forward and throws his arms open. I leap into the open space and he closes his arms around me, pulling me into a tight hug.

"I missed you," he breathes into my hair.

I let myself relax for as long as I dare before pulling away. The issue of my mother will have to be addressed.

"I didn't think you'd be back so soon."

"Neither did I," I confess to his shoulder. I can't look him in the face yet. "But I found her."

His head jerks up and he looks over me to find the sorceress. I follow his gaze as it lands upon my mom. He takes a step forward and Mom screams. It's so high pitched and shrill, I half expect it to break the glass windows of the castle walls closest to us. Prometheus sets me down, taking slow steps toward where Mom is curling into a ball. Her fight or flight response is definitely broken.

Prometheus picks up his pace and Mom's scream reaches an octave I've never heard a human make before. I follow after him, words dying on my lips. Words that would confess her relation to me. Words that would absolve me of some of my guilt. But they freeze in my throat.

He reaches out a large hand and grips her around the throat. Hauling Mom into the air, her fingers scrabble for purchase on his arm. Her face turns as red as her nails as he holds her level with his angry glare. He looks over her face and glances back at me, brow furrowed.

"What makes you think this is her?"

Any hopes I had of Prometheus being able to recognize her shrivel in my chest. He sets her down and she draws a huge gaping breath, her hands covering the spreading red marks from his grip.

"Don't you recognize her?" My voice sounds small in the empty clearing.

"This is not the woman I fought."

I fall to my knees. My chest feels hollow as Mom meets my gaze, her face red and blotchy and her expression completely betrayed. What have I done?

"Why did you think this woman was the sorceress?"

"That woman." Mom rises unsteadily to her feet. "Is her mother. Who are you?"

Whatever budding trust and friendship that was growing between us this morning has shriveled and died. Mom doesn't even look at me as she braces her hands against her hips, waiting for Prometheus's answer.

"I am the master of this castle," he says simply, hands open at his sides. "You are Wren's mother?"

"Unfortunately, yes."

He turns a stern expression on me. "You brought your mother here with the thought that she was the sorceress?"

"I . . ." Once again the words die on my tongue. "I . . ."

"Why did you think your mother was the sorceress?"

I close my eyes. If I see them, I won't be able to talk. "I saw her in a picture taken in the 1800s. How would that be possible if she weren't the sorceress?"

"Wren, what are you talking about?" Mom turns narrowed eyes toward me. "What picture?"

"I broke into the museum in the old section of town—"

"You broke into a building!" Mom squeals.

Prometheus says nothing, watching me with his dark gaze. I take strength from his calm. He will listen to me, no matter what my reasoning is. We'll work this out.

"In the section of the museum that chronicled Greendale's founding, there was a picture of the original people who lived here. The people you stole from." I look at Prometheus and he nods for me to continue. "So I looked over their faces, hoping to find some clue as to who I was looking for. And there she was, standing surrounded by the rest of the tribe. I'd recognize her face anywhere."

"As flattering as it is that you think it was me—"

"There was a woman in the picture that looked like your mother?" Prometheus asks, staring at Mom closer than he did before. "I suppose she looks a little like the sorceress. She has the right hair."

"You thought that of me too once," I remind him with a small smile. "Plus, only having hair color to go off of is incredibly weak."

Prometheus laughs. "You're right. Did you ask your mom if this was her natural color?"

Mom puffs up her chest and opens her mouth to say something, but I cut her off. "I didn't need to ask, she's always had this hair color."

"Actually." Mom's cheeks turn even more red. "I'm not a natural blonde."

I take a step back. "What?"

"I'm a little more of a brunette. I've gotten really good at coloring it myself." She presses her hands against her burning cheeks. "So maybe you should have asked before lying about what you wanted from me and dragging me down here to visit with your monster."

"He's not my monster." I snap and Prometheus smiles. "He's not even a monster. You're looking at a curse."

Mom laughs. "Right, a curse."

"You're looking at a person you've already called a monster, but I'm the crazy one for suggesting it's the result of a curse?"

Prometheus runs a clawed hand through his hair. "I can't believe you brought her here."

"What do you mean?" I turned to him open mouthed. "You can't believe I brought someone I thought could break the curse?"

"Did you think this through at all? What it would mean if you brought someone who wasn't actually the sorceress?"

My mouth turns to a pout. "Of course I thought it through."

"So you realized that bringing someone who wasn't the sorceress would put the same curse on them you had. Now your mother can't leave."

"I'm sorry, what did you say?" Mom steps forward, pointing a finger at his chest. "Why can't I leave?"

My mouth hangs open, but I shut it quickly. "No. But in fairness to me, she was in the picture! What else was I supposed to think?"

"How long did you think about this before deciding she had to be the sorceress? Did you have anything else to go off of besides her picture?"

"I . . ." I close my eyes and take a breath. "No, I didn't."

Prometheus blows out an exasperated sigh.

"I thought about it."

I honestly can't remember if I thought about it or not, but I'm not going down this way. "But then I got such a great opening to bring her down here, it seemed stupid not to take it. You don't think I had my own misgivings about this? I brought you my mother! My actual mother! Knowing full well that you were planning on destroying the sorceress to regain your freedom. That should count for something."

Mom gasps behind me and I turn to her, mouth jagged.

"Mom, there's so much to this, you need to not judge it based on this one moment."

"You want me to reserve my judgment when you confessed that you tricked me and brought me here so that your monster friend could kill me. Do you realize how that sounds?"

I glance at Prometheus, but he folds his arm across his chest. He's not going to be back up today.

"He's not just my monster friend . . . I . . ." The words stick, but despite everything, I force them out. "I love him."

Chapter Fifteen

Silence greets my statement, which I don't understand since Prometheus would have had to already know this. How else was I able to leave so many times?

Mom gapes at me. "You can't be serious."

A small side smile grows across Prometheus's face, but he says nothing.

"I'm completely serious."

"You don't know what you're saying. This isn't possible. Is it like Stockholm Syndrome or something? You haven't known him long enough to love him, and you're too young to really know what love is. And that's just the basic issues. What about the fact that he's a monster?"

"You don't know what you're talking about." The words are bitter in my mouth and I know I sound like a child.

Mom folds her arms across her chest as an enchanted wind whips through the trees around us, rustling their leaves and sending them spiraling to the ground. "Unfortunately, I'm very aware of what I'm talking about. You think I don't understand love? This is not it."

"You don't think I'm in love because we're not talking about you."

Prometheus reaches over and places a heavy hand on my shoulder. "This doesn't need to be an argument."

I know this isn't the place, but I want him to reciprocate. I want to forget Mom is here at all and hear him tell me he loves me. I said it out loud. Is he laughing at me now? Has this all been a joke to him? To see how far he could push me and what I would do for him?

Shrugging out of his grip, I blink back embarrassed tears. "What do we do now?"

His hand clenches into a fist as he lowers it and looks over my mother. Her shoulders grow tighter the longer he looks, but she's lost my sympathy.

"She's not the woman I remember. She might as well get cozy because we're going to be here together for a long time."

And just like that it hits me that I've trapped Mom in my sanctuary. This is where I have hidden from her. What will I do now? Go home? Try again? Leave her with Prometheus?

Mom holds a hand to her chest as it heaves up and down.

Prometheus reaches out a hand to her. "Come with me. We'll find a nice place for you to lay down for a while."

"I don't—I don't need . . ." Mom looks at his hand as words desert her. She looks up at me, eyes as helpless as a new baby.

"He's not going to hurt you, Mom."

She takes his hand with the least amount of physical touch she can manage, and he leads her back to the castle. Mom glances back at me once, wide eyed, as he takes her up the stairs, but seeing me so close behind them seems to calm her. Prometheus guides her along a hallway to the left of the staircase, in an area I've never been before. He opens the first door we come to, revealing a room covered in cream wallpaper with a modest bed in the middle.

"Will you be comfortable here for a while?"

Mom looks around him to meet my gaze and I give her a curt nod. As long as she doesn't try to leave the castle, she'll be fine. Which is more that I can say for myself.

Prometheus closes the door behind her and gestures for me to follow him. He's silent until we reach my room.

Door closed, he leans against the frame and watches me with dark eyes. "What are we supposed to do now?"

My moth feels dry and words would fail me if I tried. But I'm past the point of trying.

What I said means nothing despite the fact that it's always been an unspoken understanding between us. I need him to say something.

I need some sort of reciprocation so I don't feel like dying every time he looks at me.

"Did you really think she was the sorceress?"

"Yes."

And then I spent the whole time from my discovery to coming here wracked with guilt about it, thank you very much.

"I should have given you more to go off of."

"You think?"

Not talking about what I said feels more and more like a rejection with every minute that passes, making my words sharper than they've been with him for a long time. Matching his sigh, I sink onto the bed. There's no need for me to be standing during this interrogation.

Prometheus steps closer, resting his forearms against the footboard. "I'm sorry if I've made you upset."

"You don't see any reason why I'd be upset?"

"Should I?"

Men seem to be completely oblivious in movies, but I never thought they could be this dense in real life. How does he not see? I know he heard me.

I take a deep breath to steady myself. It's time to just say it. "Didn't you hear what I said back there?"

The little smile grows across his lips. "Of course."

"Don't you think you should say something about it?"

"What would you have me do?"

An incredulous gasp bursts from me. "What do you mean 'what would you have me do'? If you have to ask then that answers my question completely." I bury myself in the heavy blankets. "You can leave now."

"Wren, if you want to talk about what happened, I can do that."

"I don't want to talk anymore."

"You don't have to shut me out."

I don't have to, but I want to. This final rejection is my complete undoing. My breathing is too fast, the stale air in the blankets making me woozy.

"Just leave."

He hesitates by the bed before following my instructions. As the door clicks shut behind him, a river of tears floods my cheeks.

Completely covered by blankets, I let all my pent-up emotions out. My chest heaves as I gasp for air. But there is none under here and I drown in moist layers of sorrow.

I'm such an idiot. I can't believe I let myself believe he might actually . . . no, it's stupid. And I was stupid. I was about to give my mom up to him, believing he felt the same way about me that I so foolishly let myself feel about him. What was I thinking? That just because he'd been trapped in another form and forced to live in relative solitude that I would look more appealing to him?

Have I been throwing myself at him this whole time while he never had any interest in reciprocating? I don't know that I believe that. If I calmed down just a little, I could find all the instances I held onto where it felt like he cared about me. But I don't want to calm down.

If things were different, I might have made my way to Mom's room and laid down on the bed beside her. She'd stroke my hair while I cried about how stupid men are and she'd try to tell me that someday I'd find someone to love again.

But things aren't different, and I'm alone.

A soft rap knocks at the door and my head feels like it weights a million pounds as I sit up in bed. The door swings open, and Sarah barges in, her lips looking more pinched than ever.

"The Master was hoping you would come to breakfast and discuss the matter of your mother."

Breakfast already? Did I really just pass out? I guess crying will do that, but I never thought I was that weak. I'll have to reevaluate myself.

"I don't feel like coming to breakfast."

Sarah frowns. "Your mother is already at breakfast waiting for you."

Hence Prometheus's panic about whether or not I'm coming. Typical man. Only needs me when he's being inconvenienced.

I don't know who I'd rather not face more, Prometheus or my mother.

Sarah stands by the door with her hands braced against her hips. "I'm not supposed to take no for an answer."

"You can't make me," I mumble into my blankets as I sink back into the bed.

"I won't leave until you get up."

"Good. Take a break. Pull up a chair. You're going to be here for a while."

"Wren, you can't hide in here all day. You're going to have to help decide what to do about your mom," Sarah says, tone becoming harder.

I dig deeper into the blanket shell of protection I've created. "I don't care what happens. And why should I have to make any decisions anyway? Isn't she stuck here no matter what? I can't make her love Prometheus. I'm the only one foolish enough to do that."

The bed shifts as Sarah sits down. "Surely you don't believe that."

"I did the one thing Prometheus wanted and it still wasn't enough."

Sarah rests her hand on my back. "I don't think you fully understand what Prometheus wants."

"You don't think he wanted to have the curse broken?"

"But you didn't break his curse, only your own."

"So he doesn't love me because I haven't broken his curse yet?"

"Breaking the curse has nothing to do with how he feels about you."

"What would you know about it," I grumble.

"You'd be surprised how much the help sees. We have eyes almost everywhere."

I poke my head out of the blankets. "What do you know then?"

"Nothing I'd be willing to share with you," Sarah says with a smile. "You'll have to talk to the master if you want to know how he feels."

"What was the point of this then?"

I fling myself back into the blankets, hiding my tear-stained face from Sarah's all-too-observant gaze.

"It seems to me like you need to have a talk with him, one where you don't send him away just because he doesn't say the right thing."

Peeking out, Sarah raises a brow at me.

"He wanted me to tell him what to say. Doesn't he have his own feelings to tell me? I can't tell him how he feels."

"There was a lot going on yesterday. I think you should give him a break and let him try again."

"I don't want to let him try again."

"Then you don't truly love him."

"I . . ." I don't know what to say.

Is she right? If I don't give him another chance, have I killed the love that had been growing for him? Am I acting to rashly?

"Love involves a lot of patience and forgiveness. We're all just people, Wren. We're going to make mistakes." Sarah stands and extends a hand. "Will you come down with me?"

I nod, made completely mute by her revelation. There are things I need to work on. I hope Prometheus can forgive me. I don't know how I'll fix things. How do I let go of his lack of reciprocation? This is a level of growing up that I'm not sure I'm ready for.

Sliding out of bed, I tug at my wrinkled shirt but it's past the point of recovery.

Sarah glides down the hallway, my steps heavy behind her. The echoes of voices drift up the stairs. What could they be talking about? *They're talking about you*, the whispers in my head push the idea forward. I'm sure they both have a lot to say about me. A lot of it not the best. But I need to not care, right? There's no reason for it.

"Wren, so good of you to join us."

Mom sits at the table on Prometheus's right, her face picture perfect. Did she pack makeup in that bag?

I slump into my usual spot and Mom takes my plate, loading it up without waiting for my input. Making a face at the sausage and onion she loads up, I push it around on my plate and grab a muffin off a tray. Mom's careful eyes miss nothing, but she doesn't comment on my choice.

"So what did you have planned for today?" Prometheus asks me as he carefully butters an English muffin in his massive hands.

I shrug. "I didn't plan anything. Was I supposed to?"

"This is your mess to clean up," Mom says as she takes a delicate bite. "I would assume you had something planned to fix all of this."

"This isn't something I can just 'fix.' I can't change the curse that's on you now, only you can do that."

"Or you could find the actual sorceress or whatever and do what you were supposed to in the first place and it would break the curse on all of us."

My fingernails dig crescent holes in my palms as I clench my hands tight. So they were talking about me. I guess my name is inevitably going to come up when the curse is mentioned. Still, to have Mom throw my failures at me feels like more than I can bear.

Slamming the muffin on my plate, I push my chair back and stand. Prometheus watches me with a dark gaze but says nothing as I stalk out the room.

The hallway feels wide and cool after the pressure of the dining room. I trail my hand along the embellished wallpaper as I head to the front doors. I sit on the top stone step and stare out over the enchanted forest. The heavy scent of pine floats through the air, mingling with the dust coming off the training grounds.

What am I going to do? I haven't solved anything. Not even the glaring issue in my pseudo-relationship with Prometheus. I couldn't keep it together long enough to show him I forgave him. Because I have forgiven him, right? What's wrong with me?

And now what? Do I leave Mom here with Prometheus and go to find the sorceress again? I'm tapped out. This problem was bigger than me from the beginning. What was I thinking? That I could swoop in and take care of issues Prometheus hadn't been able to figure out? He's had more than a hundred and fifty years, but that didn't mean anything. I thought I was smarter.

The pulse in my temples pounds a warning of an impending headache if I stay on this track. I need to calm down.

How did everything get so messed up?

I sit thinking for what seems like hours before Prometheus comes to sit next to me. His immense body blocks my view of the house and brings a sense of calm.

He takes a deep breath, turning to me with a little smile. "I'm guessing you and your mother don't get along very well."

"The best we've ever gotten along was when I asked her to come with me to see you."

"So, when you lied?"

"Yes."

I can see where he's going with this and I don't appreciate it. So what if our best moments were based on a lie? I had to lie to her to get her down here to save him. At least that's what I thought I needed to do.

"I don't know how you can fix whatever's been going on there, but I think it would behoove you to try."

"Behoove? Are you serious?"

He smiles. "Sometimes I think you forget how old I actually am."

I flinch at the sting that comes with that statement. Am I just a child to him? "Did you come out here to talk about her?"

"No." He shifts his body on the step. "I wanted to thank you. I never did that yesterday and it wasn't fair of me. It must have taken great courage to think your mom was the sorceress and still bring her here. It means a lot to me that you'd be willing to do that."

My heart flutters in my chest. "I made a promise to you."

"A promise I would have understood if you broke."

"I'm not leaving you here."

"I appreciate that since now you've brought me a long-term guest," he says with a grimace that makes me laugh.

"I am sorry about that."

"I know. I just don't know what to do next."

"Neither do I."

Prometheus doesn't say anything, but moves his hand close to where mine rests on the step. Our fingers touch and I ignore the way it makes my breath catch.

"Is there really no way she could be the sorceress? I swear it was her in the picture."

His brow wrinkles. "Is there anyone you know who would have changed the picture to make you think she was the sorceress?"

"I don't know why anyone would want to do that. It's not like Mom was hurting anyone in Greendale. She was just living her dream. A dumb dream, but her dream. I don't even know anyone. I haven't actually spent much time at Mom's house. I've been here a lot if you recall."

"So, who do you know?"

I chew my bottom lip as I think it over. "Bill, Ruby, the guidance counselor, a few teachers, a checkout girl. No one really."

"Ruby?"

"Bill's daughter."

"So, we're back at the beginning."

"I guess so."

He sighs. "I'm sorry there's so little to go off of."

"Me too."

He moves his hand closer, letting his long fingers entwine with mine. "I heard what you said yesterday."

"You did?"

I feel like I'm about to jump out of my skin. I know I wanted him to do something, but now that it's happening I can't handle it. Leaning closer to him, my breath catches in my chest.

What he says now could change everything. My heart hammers so loud I'm sure he can hear it, but there's nothing I can do about it. My heart hasn't listened to me since I got off that airplane.

"I'm sorry I didn't say anything then. I needed to process it and I didn't want to do that in front of your mother."

Makes sense. That makes sense, right?

"You're incredible, Wren. I've never met anyone with as much determination as you. You're beautiful and exacerbating and make me crazy." He pauses, his hand tightening on mine. "What I'm trying to say is that I love you too."

My lips curl in a smile I can't control. "You do?"

Prometheus leans closer and I mimic the action, eyes closed. It's really going to happen this time. And I find I don't care what he looks like or what his fangs will feel like. I just want to be close to him.

"What a touching sentiment."

With a huff of irritation, I look up, expecting Mom to be coming around the corner, but all my blood freezes in my chest as I see Ruby. She claps a couple times, her long hair pulled into a tight ponytail. She's wearing leather pants, and for a moment that's all I can process.

"It's you," Prometheus whispers, his hand pulling from mine.

Ruby folds in a mock bow. "It's me. What did you think of me, Wren? Boring, predictable? Not so boring anymore, am I?"

"How did you get here?"

Probably not the most pressing concern here, but it's the first thing I think of. Ruby stalks up to the first step but doesn't come any closer.

"Hey Prometheus, miss me?" Her lips curl into a feline smile as he stands.

"It's been a long time."

"Wait a second." I stand and Prometheus pushes me behind him. "Are you telling me she's the sorceress?"

He gives me a tight nod, keeping his gaze focused on Ruby. I push around him. He's not keeping me out of this.

"There's no freaking way! How?"

Ruby braces her hands against her hips, looking for all the world like she owns the place. "Poor, sad Wren, so gullible. You never once questioned me. Didn't you wonder why I was so willing to help you? Why I had all the information you needed? Why I didn't follow you into the cave tunnels?"

"But . . . but I fell, I was hurt. Following me would have been risking your safety. It made sense for you to get help."

Ruby cleans nonexistent dirt out from under her fingernails. "Who said I went for help?"

"You did." But even as I say it, I know how ridiculous that sounds. It never crossed my mind that anything she said could have been a lie. I took her at face value and never questioned anything. How could I have been so stupid? If people had been looking for me, there's no way I would have been lost alone in those caves for so long.

"Who is she to you?" Prometheus asks, using his large hand to shove me behind his body again.

"This is Ruby."

"Ruby?" he asks, processing everything much slower than usual. "This is the girl who wants to be your sister?"

She laughs. "I can't believe how completely you believed that ruse. How unbelievably easy was it to convince you that I was following through on your mother's wishes to be the perfect daughter? Honestly, based on everything I knew about you, I expected you to be much harder to crack. Not that I'm complaining."

I jerk my chin high, my pulse rushing through me like a racecar. "Congratulations. You fooled a seventeen-year-old. How proud you must be."

Ruby's smile fades and she turns her attention to Prometheus. "I'm glad I finally found one you liked. I was beginning to worry that my initial thought was correct: no one could love a spoiled rich boy who only thinks of himself."

"A lot has changed since you last saw me." His voice is calm, but his shoulders tense, betraying his concealed anger. "I'm not sure that you could consider yourself an expert on me anymore."

Ruby shakes her head, resting it in her hand as her silver ring glints in the enchanted light. Blonde hair, silver ring. I've seen that ring before. Every day in fact. She never takes it off. How could I have been so stupid? She has everything Prometheus described and I went for my mother instead.

"I think you overestimate yourself. Surely there's not much room for growth in a place like this. I've watched you a lot. I hope you didn't think I'd forgotten about you." She smiles as his fists clench. "Oh yes, I've kept my eyes on you, Prometheus. I had to make sure you remembered why you were here. To make sure you remembered my sister."

"I don't think it'll ever be possible to forget her. You've engrained her into my memory with every girl you sent down here."

With every girl?

Ruby smiles. "Wren, you didn't think my curse was so basic to only be a simple transformation and imprisonment, did you? Oh no, every girl I sent to Prometheus was hand-picked. Each one I knew would be someone Prometheus could love but would never love him back. When I met your mother, I saw an opportunity and pounced on it. I guess in hindsight I shouldn't have been so surprised that you were so gullible. You get it from your mom."

My jaw grinds together, and I take a step forward. Prometheus moves his arm out to stop me. But I'm not sure I'm ready to hear what Ruby has to say. I'd much rather punch her in the teeth.

"I don't think your mother ever really understood what she was doing. I created Bill to act as my father while hanging around Greendale. He met your mother online and she talked so much about her daughter. With everything Bill told me, you sounded like the perfect payback for everything Prometheus had done. I didn't want to send him any more simpleton girls. He needed someone who was going to make him really feel his transformation every day. You were supposed to behave toward him the way you do to your mother, not fall in love with him!"

"Bill's not real?" I don't care what she said about what I was supposed to do. I love Prometheus and nothing she can say will change that.

"Of course not. No, he was specially made. The perfect man your mom was looking for. A man she would do anything to keep, including bringing you here. All it took was a few weeks of nudging from Bill and she made the phone call. Your aunt was so angry." Ruby pauses to laugh. "Honestly, there were times when I wasn't sure if everything was going to work out. Everyone was so worried about keeping you safe, keeping you happy. Could it be that they were just afraid of your wrath?"

"Aunt Cara loves me."

Ruby raises a brow. "But not your mom?"

"Probably not as much."

I know I'm not being completely honest with myself. Mom came all the way down here for me. She loves me, at least in her own way.

"So, what now, Prometheus?" She takes a step closer. "Are you going to fight me? Do you really think you can end the curse now?"

He hesitates. "I will do what has to be done."

"Spoken so gallantly." Ruby comes up another step. "Have you told her, Prometheus? Have you told her the truth?"

"I know why he's here. And between the two of you, you're the real monster." I haven't finished my sentence before Prometheus has shoved me toward the front door, using his body to shield me from Ruby.

"So she doesn't know how you killed my sister?"

"It was an accident," I yell around Prometheus's back.

Ruby laughs but there's no joy in it. "If that's what you call being stabbed."

"Stabbed? What are you talking about? She died because he took the fire stone."

"I'm sure that's easier to believe than the truth. If he'd told you the truth, there's no way you would have been able to forgive him."

"You don't have to—"

"Oh, but I do. Wren deserves to know the truth. Don't you, Wren?"

My body feels like a helium balloon. My thoughts can't focus and everything feels tight and loose at the same time.

"He killed her." Ruby's mouth turns ugly. "Before the curse took its true hold and sunk him underground, it turned him into the monster. He came to the village and thought she was the sorceress. Then stabbed her through the heart. Didn't you?"

"I . . ." His shoulders fall. "Yes."

I know this revelation is supposed to make me shocked, make me feel like Prometheus went too far and reject him. But what do I know about what happened? How can I let his past actions influence how I feel about the man he currently is? I chose to forgive him once. I can do it again. This wasn't right. I know it wasn't. But I know he's sorry. It doesn't change what happened, but it's changed who he is. I have to keep believing that.

Stepping forward, I take his hand in mine. He glances away from where we're connected and I grip him tighter.

"How cute. Look at her pretend she doesn't care that you're a murderer," Ruby sneers.

"Leave her alone. Your problem is with me." Prometheus shakes my hand out of his and stalks toward Ruby, separating himself from me.

"He took the fire stone and when everything started going wrong, he decided the to blame the sorceress. Instead of taking responsibility for his actions and returning the stone, he came after my sister." Ruby ignores Prometheus's approach. "She was completely alone, undefended and unthreatening. And he came into our home and stabbed her."

"I'm sure he was scared." But my resolve has weakened. That seems particularly violent. Why didn't he bring the stone back?

"Yes, poor scared Prometheus. I guess killing someone is okay as long as you were scared when you did it."

"That's not what I meant!" I cross my arms over my chest, standing five steps above her.

Ruby smiles. "Oh, poor baby Wren. It's hard to learn Prometheus isn't the man you thought he was, isn't it?"

"You're not the girl I thought *you* were."

"Like I could ever be that weak." The smile fades from her face. "Since you've won the biggest fool award this time, how about I give you a little prize?"

I'm not stupid enough to think the prize will be Prometheus's freedom, but I can tell that's what she's hoping for. I won't be the fool again.

She waits for me to answer before sighing. "If you're not going to be any fun, then I don't know if I can give you the prize. I don't reward bad behavior, Wren."

I feel pretty certain whatever her prize is, it won't hurt me, right? She wants to hurt Prometheus, not me. Unfolding my arms, I concentrate on not allowing my hands to form fists again. I know how to play along.

"What kind of prize?"

"Good girl." Ruby smiles. "How would you like to go home? Leave all this behind and go back to your regular life. I bet you could even go to New York if you wanted."

I'd never leave Prometheus like that, but I know that's not the answer Ruby is looking for. "My mom is here."

"Ah yes. How could I forget?" Ruby curls her finger, as though motioning me closer. "Come out come out wherever you are!"

The door opens behind me, and my stomach sinks as I turn around. In mentioning Mom, I didn't expect Ruby to bring her out here.

Mom glides through the door, her feet hovering off the ground and her middle pushed out like there's a rope around her waist pulling her forward. She looks at me with wide eyes but doesn't scream.

"Nice of you to join us." Ruby grins, showing almost all her teeth.

"Ruby?" Mom gasps. I feel bad for her, she has a lot to catch up on.

"Welcome to the party! You know, I almost feel bad for you. I never thought Wren would actually believe you were me. I figured she'd hem and haw and stew about it for a while before running back to Prometheus with the problem. But your girl wastes no time. She took you back to him the day after she saw your picture. I can say one thing for her though, when she picks a cause, she sticks to it. No matter what." Ruby turns her gaze to me as she finishes, silent tears running down Mom's face.

"I'm sorry, Mom," I murmur.

She doesn't move to acknowledge me.

"Leave them alone," Prometheus growls.

"Feeling left out? Don't worry. I have a lot planned for you."

He roars, the sound shaking the windows in their frames as he lunges down the rest of the steps toward Ruby with his claws outstretched. Mom screams as Ruby moves a hand casually to the left and sends Prometheus flying. He hits the ground with a heavy smack but gets back on his feet.

I move to follow him, but Ruby turns her hands to me.

"Can't have you getting in the way. This really isn't your fight, is it?" She raises her hands and my feet leave the ground. With a flick of her wrist, she brings us to the tree line. Mom keeps screaming, her voice shrill in my ear as we hit the trunk of a large tree. Vines twist around us, tying us to the trunk.

Prometheus stalks closer to Ruby, his hand clenching something I didn't notice him holding before. He twists as he gets closer, and the morning light reflects off a long length of metal. A sword. A real sword. How did he know to have it here? Where did it come from?

He hefts it up and Ruby uses her magic to flick him to the side again. "Has nothing really changed in the last hundred years? I thought you might come up with a new tactic."

Prometheus turns his dark gaze to me for only a moment before standing again, sword ready in his hand. Me. I'm the new tactic. Not that he would tell Ruby that.

I wiggle my hands around where they're trapped to my side. If I can reach my pocketknife, I might be able to get through the vines and help him.

"What are you doing?" Mom whispers, her gaze still glued to Ruby as she tosses Prometheus again without even being close to breaking a sweat.

I shake my head at her. There's no way I'm going to voice my plan out loud.

The vine digs into my wrist as I move, creating rope burns on my arm. I hiss through my teeth. Mom cries silently next to me, tears dribbling down her face. Wiggling against my restraints, the vine pushes my pocketknife against my hip bone. At least now I know exactly where it is.

Twisting my arm until I'm sure it's about to pop out of its socket, my fingers graze the top of the knife. A heavy thud distracts me, the knife falling back into place as Prometheus hits the ground. I close my eyes, willing myself not to look, not to let myself pay attention to him. I can't help him if I don't get free.

"I guess all that training was for nothing. Did you really think you would be able to take me down? You're nothing, nothing but the beast I created." A crazy gleam has come to Ruby's eye as she wipes the floor figuratively and literally with Prometheus's body.

He leans on his forearm as he struggles to his feet. "I'd rather be this beast than a monster like you."

I wrench my eyes closed tight as Ruby frowns. I can't look at them.

Twisting back into my earlier position, my fingers slide against the cool metal of my knife. Just a little further and it'll be in my hand. Mom hiccups a sob next to me and I tune her out the same as I've had to tune out the others. Trying to comfort my mother would be a waste of time unless I can get free to help.

With one more strain, I hear a pop in my shoulder, but the knife is in my hand. Everything on my right side hurts as I flick it open. I'm sure I've pulled a muscle. Probably more than one. Opening my eyes, I saw at the vines in haggard strokes.

Prometheus stands, ready to face Ruby, his sword discarded five feet from my tree. And now I have my target.

I cut through the bottom vine and it falls to our feet.

"What are you doing?" Mom cries.

"Be quiet," I hiss as I go for the next one.

"You're going to get us killed!"

"Only if you don't shut up!"

Mom clamps her mouth closed, but I worry the damage has already done as Ruby's gaze flicks over to us.

"Enjoying the show?" she purrs as she takes down Prometheus with a wave of her hand. How much more could he possibly take?

I look down at my feet, hoping she'll take that as my agreement to her eventual success. My hand stills. If I don't move she won't see the knife, right?

My strategy pays off as she turns her back to me, all her concentration focused on humiliating Prometheus as thoroughly as possible. I hack faster, my wrist burning from the prolonged motion. Two more layers of vines fall away. With the sorceress distracted, new ones aren't taking their place. This could really work.

The last vine falls to my feet and I slip the knife back into my pants and lunge for the sword. Ruby's focus is still on Prometheus so she doesn't notice my approach. It's a good thing she's so distracted because I'm not terribly quiet. Panic has made me reckless.

The metal hilt is cool in my hand as I grip the hilt of the sword. I heft it, ready for a killing strike as I keep up my pace toward Ruby. There can be no room for hesitation now.

She's saying something to Prometheus, her back toward me, but I don't pay any attention. I don't care to hear her gloating speeches at the moment. The tip of the sword flashes in the enchanted sun as I reach Ruby. I take a deep breath, ignoring the fact that I've never hurt someone like this before, and swing.

Chapter Sixteen

Eyes wide, I wait for the sword to cleave through Ruby's neck. But as I'm completing the swing, Prometheus's gaze flicks over to me and Ruby's concentration is broken. With a roar she swings around and uses her magic to block my swing. The sword blows to the left and my arms shake as I lift it back into position.

Her smile is cruel as she raises a hand to block me again. It doesn't matter how many times she stops me, I'll just keep coming. Sweat trickles down my temples as I step forward and swing.

Ruby flicks me away like I'm a fly. Prometheus sprints at her, claws extended. She turns to face him, delivering a powerful blow to his head with her magic before he can even get close. He hits the ground hard, but I turn away from him. This might be my last opportunity to get her distracted.

Sword held in sweating hands, I raise it over my head, all the training Prometheus worked into me for weeks dissolving. With a savage lunge, I twist the sword forward, slicing toward her neck.

The slight breeze created by my thrust kisses her neck and she spins, magic whirling.

The sword rips from my hands as her blasts hits me in the chest. My breath wheezes from me as my body continues falling forward.

Hoping for a weapon, my hands close over air. There's no time to respond before Ruby grabs me by the neck and lifts me off my feet. I glance over at Prometheus where he lays on the hard-packed earth, but he doesn't move. His eyes follow me, but he has nothing left to give. She's broken him.

"How dare you," Ruby breathes into my face. "How dare you think to destroy me? You really think you can do anything after I took on Prometheus? What are you compared to him? And even he wasn't enough to defeat me."

My hands dangle at my sides as I resist the urge to grip at the hand holding me up. She's right, there's nothing I can do to counter her strength.

"Well, now you've gone and ruined a great joke by trying to kill me. Granted, it wasn't a very good attempt, but you still tried. I wish I could say it was more pathetic than some other things I've seen you do, but unfortunately, you're a girl bent on making all the wrong choices."

"Let . . . me . . . go," I struggle to make the words come out with the limited air supply moving past her unnatural grip.

Ruby laughs, hot air cascading down my red cheeks. "How much do you think it would hurt Prometheus to watch you die like this? Not of old age or some sort of disaster in the castle, but of my hand around your throat. I think that would be a fitting punishment, don't you?"

My feet and hands tingle as they lose oxygen in the blood supply. There's just not enough to go around anymore. Black spots swim in my vision as Ruby's face fades in and out.

"Poor Wren. You know if you'd followed through on my plans, I might have saved you in the end."

Her red lips pull back in a wide grin that shows all her white teeth. I don't want her face to be the last thing I see. Groaning, my hand reaches for the pocketknife.

"Just relax. This will be over so much sooner if you do."

My fingers shake as they close over the knife. Vision almost completely black, I pull the knife free. I can't see Ruby anymore, but I don't need to see her to do what I need to do.

Ruby laughs. "See, Prometheus? There is no redemption for you now."

Wrenching myself into consciousness, I stare into Ruby's crystal blue eyes as I slam my knife into her chest. Her eyes widen and her hand loosens its grip on my throat. I take gulping breaths of air as thick warm blood courses over my hand. I'm still holding the knife.

But I can't seem to let go. Not even as Ruby releases me completely and we stand eye to eye.

My legs shake as everything moves in slow motion. Prometheus stands behind Ruby, looking at her with eyes full of disbelief.

"H-how?" Ruby gasps, crimson blood bubbling at the side of her mouth.

"Why?" I counter.

Why did she do any of this? Why was it so important to put Prometheus down? If he killed her sister, then there should have been other ways to find justice than this curse. And why did she still feel like it was necessary to punish him after all this time?

Ruby laughs, a drop of red staining her chin. "He knows. He's always known. Where is the stone?"

"What's she talking about?"

Prometheus comes to stand next to me. "She's just babbling."

"Don't believe him," Ruby says with a cough, reaching out to hold onto my arm with a much stronger grip than should be possible. "Find it."

Shaking my head, I back away. My hand is soaked in the blood that's still pumping down her chest from where my pocketknife is embedded.

Mom grabs my hand, finally leaving her perceived safety of the fallen vines "We should go."

"Go?" I pull out of her grasp. Everything is starting to come back into focus, and shock ripples through my body as I stare at Ruby. "What are you talking about?"

"We need to get out of here. You know the way, let's go."

Ruby laughs. "Run away, Wren. Just like Prometheus. How fitting."

Mom tries tugging on me again but Prometheus grabs my other arm, keeping me grounded next to him.

"Please," she pleads. "Let's go!"

"You can go," Ruby says with a grin as she sinks to her knees. "Go home."

Fire dances around her fingers and then Mom is gone. One second she's next to me, and the next there's only empty space. A startled shriek erupts from my throat as Ruby laughs.

"What did you do with her?" Prometheus demands, his clawed hands forming fists.

Ruby falls back, the last of her strength giving way. She laughs, but it's a weak imitation of what it used to be. "I put her back home, just like she wanted. You never wanted her to be here anyway, right Wren? Now I've fixed your mistake."

Prometheus grabs my arm to keep me from shaking her. "Are you sure you just put her home? You didn't do anything else with her?"

Doing something much worse would fit with the new image I have of Ruby. If she could punish Prometheus over and over, again and again for over a hundred years, what could she do to me?

"You're free," Ruby whispers, coughing out blood as she lays against the ground.

Prometheus steps forward, dragging me with him. Together we watch as her eyes glaze over in the opaque, unseeing nature of death.

"You did it. You really did it."

I'm still too shocked to comprehend what's happened. But I did do it. Ruby is dead, her blood staining the earth while I stand over her. I'm the victor. Shouldn't I feel better than this?

Wind whips through the trees, sending leaves and branches flying toward us. The ground under our feet shakes. Pebbles skitter back and forth by my sneakers, and Prometheus yanks me back as a large gouge appears in the earth, cracking as it spreads open.

"We need to get inside," he yells to be heard over the wind as it picks up.

The sky darkens even further as he grabs me by my waist and carries me like a sack of potatoes to the door when I don't automatically follow his instructions. He uses his shoulder to bash through the front doors, my heart hammering in my chest.

"What's happening?"

The wind has become a tornado, ripping through the enchanted forest. The castle remains untouched, but everything outside it pulls from the ground and twists through the air.

"You broke the curse."

I glance up at Prometheus as he puts me down, his voice quiet. He leans against the door frame, watching the ground pull apart farther and Ruby's body tumble into the endless darkness. An entire tree rips out of the ground, roots filled with the rich cave earth as it spins toward the castle. With a grunt, Prometheus slams the door closed. A heavy thud hits the door as the tree hits it on its journey toward the cyclone.

"You really did it." Prometheus grabs my hand and I stare into his dark eyes.

"Can we leave then?"

I don't believe Ruby that she put my mom at home safe and sound. She proved herself to be too vindictive for that. Wouldn't she have felt that I needed to be punished for my involvement? Where's my grand curse?

Prometheus gives me a tight nod and we make our way through the castle, ignoring the sharp cracks outside as Ruby's magic dissolves. The castle shudders, candle lights flickering. The halls are oddly empty. Where did the servants go?

I grip Prometheus's arm as he strides resolutely toward the kitchen. His mouth is a firm line. He acts like the scene going on around us doesn't affect him, but I know there's a part of him that's afraid he'll get to the pantry door and only see rows of food storage. How could the curse really be broken after all this time?

The kitchen door is only six feet away when the castle gives a sickening lurch. I tumble to the floor, Prometheus's shoulder smacking against the wall.

"What the crap?"

The chandelier above us swings riotously. My breath catches in my throat as the sound of splitting earth comes from inside the castle.

Prometheus grabs my arm and pulls me to my feet, moving toward the kitchen door faster than I can keep up. He lifts me off my feet and I dangle in the air as the castle sways back and forth like a suspension bridge.

The kitchen door swings open and closed, clapping against the door frame. Prometheus shoulders it open, pushing me forward into the room. It looks like disaster struck here first. Layers of flour coat the floor with milk splashed across it creating a thick white paste.

Glass jars have fallen from the cabinets, breaking and spreading their contents along counters and walls.

Prometheus's claws crunch into the spreading mess and he holds me up higher. The castle rocks and he slides across the wet mess, hitting the island with a groan. I cling tighter to him, wrapping my fingers in the fur lining his shoulders. Dizziness weakens my grip, but Prometheus holds me tighter, feeling the fear washing off me in waves.

His grabs the pantry doorknob, the house shifting and almost making him wrench it off the door as he tries to regain his balance. Twisting it, even with the tumult all around us, the sound of the door clicking open is easily heard. I lick my lips, reminding myself to breathe as he pulls the door open.

It swings as though waiting for us to run away. Prometheus forges ahead, not waiting to see what awaits us. His feet slip along the tile into the cave. Relief fills my chest for a brief moment before the cracking sound comes again. It's been coming from in here.

Prometheus grabs the wooden railing, his claws sinking into it in an attempt to keep us from falling. Falling into the black darkness of the hole opening at the foot of the stairs. There will be no escaping this way.

"We have to go back," I have to yell over din of loose rocks falling into the pit.

He shakes his head. "There's nowhere to go. We have to go this way."

The claws on his feet rip into the stairs as he goes down one and regains his balance. I shake in his arms. My mouth goes dry as he takes another step.

"Stop! We can't go this way, you have to turn back."

"I can't go back. I won't be trapped in there again," his voice breaks.

I reach up and take his face in my hands. Dirt rains from the cave ceiling as the gap grows bigger.

"You're not trapped here anymore, but going forward will kill us both. Please go back. We'll be safe inside. Together."

I don't know if that's true. The breaking of the curse seems to be pulling the fabric of this world apart. The magic that protected it for so long has dissolved in an instant, leaving us vulnerable to the realities of our underground sanctuary.

Prometheus nods, but some of the light has left his eyes. He's resigning himself to die down here, and I don't know how to change that, or even if I should. Facing reality is better than living in a dream, right?

He grips me tighter around the waist and moves slowly toward the kitchen. The sounds of breaking glass come from behind the door and I'm sure navigating the kitchen would have been impossible for me alone. I cling tighter to Prometheus, glad for the way his curse is saving me. Saving us both.

The kitchen floor is streaked red, there must have been a tomato-based sauce in one of the jars. I shiver as cold sweat trickles down my back. I try not to think about how it will look if I die in here.

"Where are we going to go?" I look up at Prometheus for guidance. I have no idea what to do.

He ignores me, moving at a steady pace back through the hallway.

The floor shudders, falling a foot. Prometheus loses his balance and falls to his knees, dropping me hard onto the hardwood floor.

"I don't think we can walk anymore. It's too dangerous."

Prometheus pushes me against the wall, digging his claws into the wall and floor as he forms a living wall around me. He breathes hard against the side of my face as he rests his head against my shoulder. The castle shifts like a boat on a rough sea and the flames lighting the chandelier above us go out.

Wind like a tornado rips through the room. Cupboards rip from the wall, swirling through the empty space around us as the castle collapses in on itself. Prometheus groans as he digs further into the floor. Like water down a drain, the rest of the castle swirls down the floor and into nothing.

Darkness falls over us, as thick as a blanket. With it comes an impossible silence, like all of my senses have been turned down.

I wrap my arms around Prometheus's waist, feeling his body shudder as he tries to keep us upright. The feeling of being blinded and deaf makes me feel like I need to jump out of my skin. I hum to myself to keep from leaping out of Prometheus's arms. It's not a real tune, just sounds to keep me from growing crazy, but Prometheus begins to hum along. The rich deep sounds soothe me more than my own humming ever could.

Closing my eyes, I ignore the fact that I can't see and focus on what I do have. I have Prometheus, and can feel his body all around me, and I have his comfort, the sound of it coursing through me.

We'll survive this. We have to. I don't think Ruby would make a curse that would kill us for breaking it. I saw good in her, every time she helped me back at home, and she'd been sheltering a heartbreak I still don't understand. But all that matters is that we have to survive.

Breaking glass echoes through the hall. A window must have broken to create a sound that loud. I fight against the feelings that tell me the castle will fall apart and we'll be crushed in the rubble. We're going to be okay. We have to be.

I didn't fight to break this curse only to be killed in the aftermath. This is not my ending.

Curling further into the protective shell of Prometheus's body, I close my eyes and wait. There's really nothing else we can do. His chest shudders around me, his breathing slowing as layers of dust settle over us. And then everything stills.

I take a deep breath, coughing on the dust floating in the air. Prometheus stands, his gaze traveling over the darkness around us.

"Is it over?" My voice sounds small in empty expanse.

"I think so. Should we—"

I glance up sharply as his voice turns into a groan. "Are you okay?"

A growl ripples through his chest, burning out of his throat as his back curves in on itself. His outstretched hands reach out toward nothing. Hazy light surrounds his form, blurring my vision. His head thrusts back, eyes unseeing. A ripple spreads across his body like a drop of water hitting a pond. As the ripples move, layers of fur fall away. Pale flesh reveals itself, spreading across his face and down his shoulders, until even his fingertips lose their characteristic claws.

The light fades away and Prometheus falls to his knees. Slender fingers reach up and thread themselves through his thick wavy brown hair.

Shafts of light filter in from the windows at the end of the hallway, highlighting his position on the floor. He turns his head toward me, time seeming to slow. I'm huddled next to the wall, my body prepared for the next onslaught. A small smile grows across his full lips as he watches me.

"You did it," Prometheus breathes, his voice not as deep as it was before.

I nod, not trusting myself to speak.

"You really did it." He looks down at his hands, turning them over as if the other side is hiding remnants of the curse. "I never thought I'd see this again."

Prometheus rises to his feet, his clothing hanging off him. He's lost over a foot and a half of height. He comes toward me, hand outstretched. I use the wall for support as I stand, my body shaking as adrenaline drains out of me.

I laugh as I place my hand in his, my fingers still dwarfed even without the curse.

"What?"

"Nothing, I—" cutting myself off, I take a deep breath. "I'm glad you're okay."

He grins, revealing a mouth without fangs. "I think things are more than okay."

Bright light fills the hallway as the restored front door swings open. Blinking back tears, I wait for my vision to adjust.

Prometheus threads his fingers through mine as he marches toward the door, his jaw tight. I half expect to see the same forest outside the door, or at least all the deep gashes in the earth left behind by the curse breaking. A small part of me is even worried there won't be anything waiting for us on the other side of the door. Just a house floating through endless nothing.

But Prometheus doesn't wait for my fears to take hold and paralyze me. Instead he moves forward with purpose. The only difference from before is that I can almost keep up with him now.

All around us, the castle has been remade into its former glory, with no hint of the devastation that just happened. I shake my head, the magic giving me a headache.

Even before we get to the door, I can hear voices. Prometheus grins in excitement, his teeth flashing like a beacon. He lets go of my hand, almost running the last few feet. Standing outlined in the doorway, I hesitate.

"Welcome home, master."

It's a voice I recognize. Sarah. A smile growing on my own face, I leap after Prometheus and throw my arms around the woman waiting on the other side of the door.

Her body stiffens under me and I pull back. She looks at me with wide eyes, glancing at Prometheus for help. There's no relief, no hate, nothing but confusion in her gaze.

Stepping back, my gaze catches on the view around us. It's definitely not an enchanted forest. Instead, a sweeping green lawn spreads out from the front walk, looking impossibly vibrant with the pale brown mountains in the distance as its background.

Numbness spreads down my body. Prometheus steps up behind me, placing a hand on my shoulder.

"Thank you for the welcome, Sarah. I'm assuming everyone is ready for work? I fear we might have some damage inside that you'll need to address."

"Of course, sir." Sarah flits inside with one last incredulous look at me.

"That's it? The curse is broken and Sarah needs to clean up?"

"She doesn't know anything even happened." Prometheus leans against the doorway. "Their memories were altered by the curse breaking. My staff were only affected to hurt me, not truly cursed in the same way we were. Now that it's broken, it's just you and me now."

I glance at Prometheus, watching his gaze travel over our surroundings. "Where are we?"

"We're home."

"Home?" I'm going to need a lot more to go on than that.

"My home. She let me come back."

Come back? So that means . . . "Wait a second. Are you saying we're in the *past*?"

"I suppose it's your past, my present. If you recall, I never really got to live in your future."

Suddenly I have a hard time breathing. Sitting down, I clench a hand to my chest, forcing myself to keep air coming in and out.

I'm in the past. What an ironic little twist to the curse. Mom got to go home but I came here.

"What year is it?"

He smiles. "Sometime around 1850, I'm hoping."

The information doesn't help. "18-1850? What am I supposed to do with that?"

"Live I guess."

Live in 1850? I've learned enough from my history classes to know that's not something I want. I've already had enough of chamber pots to last a lifetime.

Prometheus grabs my hand, turning me to face him. "Isn't this wonderful? You broke the curse. Look at me! I'm me again! And we're together. I'm going to make it right this time."

He stands before me, a replica of the man in the picture I saw earlier. I peer into his eyes, hoping for something of the man I've spent so many months with. His dark eyes flicker over my face. His eyes. They're perfect. They're exactly the same as before.

"It really is you."

"It is. I'm the same man as before, just a little better looking," Prometheus says with a laugh. "And you have no idea how long I've wanted to do this."

He leans in closer, his gaze traveling down to my lips. My heart jumps up in my throat, but I don't back away. I've wanted this too.

Closing my eyes, I lean into him, our lips touching. Gently, his lips caress mine. His hand presses against my lower back, pressing me closer to him. I lose myself in the warmth flowing from my middle through my limbs. He pulls away and I feel lightheaded looking at him.

"That was definitely worth the wait."

Face red, I chuckle and run a hand through my hair. The thought of kissing him had helped propel me through the cave with Mom, but I never imagined I'd be kissing a man instead of a monster.

And now we've kissed. On his front step. In 1850. In front of half his staff.

They mill around in the front lawn, waiting to get to work. Prometheus waves them in and my face flushes further at the side glances I get from a few of them as they walk in.

I guess it makes sense that they'd be more than a little shocked. People don't really display affection like that publicly, right? Plus, I'm not exactly dressed for this time period. Rips run across my spandex pants and tank top, items that wouldn't be acceptable at the best of times.

Prometheus notices my glance and smiles. "Are you finally going to let us dress you?"

I can't match his smile. The reminder that I might be stuck here makes my blood run cold. Prometheus places his hand on my lower back and leads me into the castle.

Everything looks brighter than it did before. Real natural light floods through every window, making the foyer feel immense as it spreads up through two stories. The paintings on the wall feel less sinister in the light and colors pop out everywhere.

I half expect Prometheus to take me to my room to change, but his guiding hand doesn't even get me close to the stairs. Instead, he takes me to the kitchen where the pantry door is hanging wide open. My breath catches, but there's only shelves inside filled with preserves that should have been damaged when the curse broke.

Blinking back hot tears, I turn away from the sight. This room means nothing to me now.

"I thought it would still be here," Prometheus says quietly.

But it isn't.

"I guess Ruby is getting the final laugh after all."

I broke the curse but I can never go home. What do I do now? Was it worth it?

Prometheus runs his hand along the door frame, face pinched in concentration. Yeah. It was. Breaking the curse on him is worth being stuck here if it means he gets to really live.

He glances up at me, jaw clenched tight. "I'll find a way for you to go home, I promise." He hesitates. "If that's what you want."

"And what do you want?" I have to concentrate hard to keep myself from biting my lip.

"I want you to be happy."

"Good answer."

He grabs my hand and walks me out of the room, closing the kitchen door behind us. I can safely say I never want to go in there again.

Walking back through the hallway, I wonder what's happening with Mom. Did she really make it home? Or did Ruby lie in another "screw you" moment. Would I be content staying here and never finding out what happened to her? I don't know.

But Prometheus has that mirror.

"Can I use the mirror?"

"I'm not sure it will work anymore."

I shrug. "I just have to know my mom's okay."

He nods and hands me the mirror from his pocket. I think of my mom and she appears in the kitchen at home, humming as she adds something to a large stockpot. The knot in my chest eases. At least I know Ruby was honest about that. I'm grateful. Mom was never a part of this.

Prometheus rubs his thumb along the back of my hand, the muscles in his neck tight. He walks us down the hallway and up the stairs. The building pressure in my chest grows as he ushers me into my room. His room? I don't know what to do with this time period.

He exhales a long breath as the door closes behind him. "What would you have me do?"

I gape at him, the question taking me off guard. "What do you mean?"

"I'm so grateful, so unbelievably grateful for you breaking the curse. I'm under no disillusion that this could have been done without you. You are my savior. And now because of me, it's like you've been cursed instead. I . . ."

"What?"

"I will never be able to repay you for what you've done. Please tell me how to make this better?"

He falls to his knees, staring up at me with sorrowful eyes. I grab his hands and try to make him rise.

"None of this is your fault." Even though part of it is. A lot of it is. But he didn't ask me to do this. I made this choice all on my own.

"Could you be happy here? With me?"

It's a big decision, but one that has mostly been taken from me. I don't know if there's any way to go back, regardless of what I want.

"I had plans in my old life." Maybe they weren't amazing, but I still had them. "I was going to go to school in New York."

He gives me a smile. "I'd never take that away from you, Wren. I'll take you to London with me, have you enrolled in the best school. Just stay with me."

Staring into his dark eyes, I try to block out my feelings of guilt. I've never let guilt guide me before, so why now? Why should it dictate one of the most important decisions in my life?

I chew at my bottom lip. Trying not to think about it doesn't really help.

"Please stay."

The words hang between us. A promise and a plea. And I know. It's a decision I made a long time ago. It shouldn't be so hard to move forward with it now. I want to stay. I want to be with him.

Placing my hands on either side of his face, I lean forward with a small smile.

"I'll stay."

Epilogue

The starched layers of my dress press against my legs, but the weight has become all too familiar. Sarah supplied so many gowns that I haven't had the opportunity to try to slip into my old things. Not that it would matter. I didn't bring them to London with me anyway.

Prometheus whisked me away as soon as he could, making good on the dreams he promised me. I can't say that attending school here was like I thought my experience at NYU would be, but this definitely has its perks.

The hundreds of candles lighting the ballroom flicker as more people than I care to count press into the room. Prometheus glances up from his conversation with someone wearing matching cravats. I catch his gaze, and his lips curl into a side smile, making my legs go weak.

It's still strange to see him this way, completely human without any trace of the beast, but my heart knew him long before my eyes did.

He says something I can't hear over the sounds of music coming from the quartet in the corner and so many people talking in such close proximity. Then he bows and makes his way toward me.

"What a surprise." His gaze travels down the outfit I packed specifically for the dance tonight. "What does it remind me of?"

I can't hide the grin that spreads across my face. The dress is layers on layers of black lace and satin, the whole effect feeling very vampire in London-esque.

"I figured since I was staying here that I might as well merge in bits of my old life."

Prometheus grins as he places his hand in the small of my back to lead me onto the floor. "Ah, yes, the 1800s' version of your black tank top and bracelets?"

"Did I pull it off?"

He presses me close enough that I hear a few gasps behind us, but I tune them out as he leans close to my ear. "It's perfect."

And in that small moment, as I gaze into the same eyes that got me through the curse, it is.

Acknowledgments

There are so many people to thank in helping me get to this point. It has truly been a journey.

Thanks Mom and Dad. You found my secret fanfiction writing, told me it was good, and encouraged me to write my own original pieces. As the many filled notebooks we found in storage prove, I really listened to you. Thank you for always being there for me. Thank you for encouraging me and getting me to go to writing conferences. They really changed everything.

Danny. You encouraged me to write and let me stay home to do it. It's been a huge sacrifice, and I'm so grateful that you never mentioned me giving up to help us get to better our situation. I'm also grateful for the many nights and weekends you've spent watching our boys so that I could write, edit, go to writing groups and conferences. This book is as much your achievement as it is mine.

Thank you Megan for always reading my manuscripts in whatever level of "doneness" they were in. You've always been my first fan.

Thank you Kristina and Jake for always being willing to listen to me as I talked about all my different story ideas and problems.

My boys. You are an incredible joy in my life and often give me new fodder for books. You don't usually give me the time to write them, but I love you all so much!

Big, big thanks go to my writing group. To NaNoWriMo and the League of Utah Writers for helping to pull us together. Seriously readers, if you're trying to write, find your community. They will get you through this process. Thank yous go to Alan, Brandon, Roz, Janelle, Heidi, Tyler, Travis, Andee, Justin, Rachel, and everyone else in our group. I really couldn't have done this without you.

Alan, thank you for reading everything and always being a "fan-girl" for me. Your enthusiasm has gotten me through many rough moments.

Brandon! Without your help with queries I never would have gotten anywhere. Your book, *Query Letters Made Simple*, made all the difference.

Thanks Uncle Mark for going over contracts with me. You gave me the confidence to be able to sign my name and make this happen.

Melanie. Thank you for being my best friend. For listening to my ramblings every step of the way through this book and through life. I couldn't get through this without you.

Carla. We didn't end up being able to work together, but you were the first one in the industry to believe in me, and I'll never forget that feeling. It was all I wanted for so long, and you made that dream come true.

Angie, I still hope that we can someday work together, but for now I am content that this book represents so much of what you've taught me. It's only getting better, and I reflect often on your belief in me.

Ms. Piragis. You told me I was gifted and worked with me so much through eighth grade. Your encouragement is something I've never forgotten. It took me a while, but here it is! A published book! Just like you predicted.

Thank you to the great team at Cedar Fort. You guys took my mess and helped me turn it into something worth reading. Thanks for taking me on and for giving me encouragement every step of the way. You guys are awesome!

About the Author

Elizabeth A. Drysdale won her first writing award at the age of seven and is an active member of the League of Utah Writers. She spent much of her childhood roaming through woods and climbing trees creating adventures to be someone else in. She's kept her nose in a book, either writing or reading, ever since graduating from Excelsior College. Elizabeth has a love of travel that often inspires her heroines to end up places very different from where they started. Originally from the back woods of Massachusetts, she lives in a small town in Northern Utah with her husband, three sons, one dog, and eight chickens.